PRAISE FO
HER HIDDEN G

"Brings to life Franklin's grit and spirit... An important contribution to the historical record."

— *Washington Post*

"Marie Benedict brings human warmth and in-depth science to a novel on the life of Rosalind Franklin... Benedict is terrific at showing how male exclusivity operates and has researched the science in magnificent depth... A humanly, as well as scientifically, engaging read."

— *Financial Times*

"Benedict adeptly brings forward another accomplished, intriguing, and unjustly overlooked or oversimplified real-life woman in a welcoming and involving historical novel."

— *Booklist*

"Benedict again illuminates an overlooked female historical figure, accessibly highlighting Franklin's scientific achievements and also depicting some of her personal life."

— *Library Journal*

"Marie Benedict has a remarkable talent for forcing open the cracks of history to draw extraordinary women into the sunlight. In *Her Hidden Genius*, Benedict weaves together molecular biology and human psychology to bring vivid life to Rosalind Franklin, whose discovery of DNA's exquisite double helix structure takes on the narrative intensity of a thriller. Fans of historical fiction will devour this complex portrait of a brilliant and trailblazing genius and the price she paid to advance the frontiers of science."

— Beatriz Williams, *New York Times* bestselling author of *Our Woman in Moscow*

"Marie Benedict does it again, pulling another brilliant woman out of the shadows of history into an illuminating portrait for posterity. This eye-opening novel deftly explores the life of Rosalind Franklin—the wronged heroine of world-changing discoveries—and her singular pursuit of science. Educational and astounding. Brava!"

— Stephanie Dray, *New York Times* bestselling author of *America's First Daughter*

"What an important book this is. Through Marie Benedict's trademark insight and immersive historical research, Rosalind Franklin and her extraordinary legacy are beautifully restored to public recognition. So brilliantly sketched is this brilliant woman that you will find yourself both infuriated by the misogynistic battles she faces and inspired by the intellectual achievements she manages to secure regardless. A must-read for anyone interested in science or forgotten heroines."

— Kate Moore, *New York Times* bestselling author of *The Radium Girls* and *The Woman They Could Not Silence*

"Impeccably researched and beautifully written, *Her Hidden Genius* is a remarkable story of strength, perseverance, and achievement. Marie Benedict once again shines a light on women in science, vibrantly bringing Rosalind Franklin's genius to life in the pages of her novel."

— Jillian Cantor, *USA Today* bestselling author of *Half Life*

"Marie Benedict has given us an immense gift: a peek into the inner world of Rosalind Franklin, one of the most brilliant—and overlooked—scientists of her time. Her Hidden Genius describes the discovery of DNA in exquisite beauty, weaving the structure of the double helix effortlessly into a poignant and compelling narrative. This is Benedict's best work yet, a book that will break your heart, rattle your expectations, and ultimately leave you stunned by the sacrifices one woman made for science."

— Nathalia Holt, *New York Times* bestselling author of *Rise of the Rocket Girls*

PRAISE FOR
THE MYSTERY OF MRS. CHRISTIE

An Instant *New York Times* Bestseller
A *USA Today* Bestseller

"It's an empowering and wonderful tribute... *The Mystery of Mrs. Christie* reads like a modern domestic thriller in the vein of *Gone Girl* and *The Girl on the Train*. It's also a nod to classic whodunits that channels Christie's talent for writing unsolvable mysteries packed with puzzles, red herrings and, most especially, unreliable narrators. Until the closing chapters, Benedict forces us to ask who is more credible: Agatha or Archie?"

— *The Washington Post*

"[A] gripping historical fiction tale of true mystery."

— *Good Morning America*

"[A] clever reconstruction of Agatha Christie's mysterious 11-day disappearance in 1926."

— *E! News*

"[Marie Benedict] keeps the reader guessing: Which narrator is reliable? Who is the real villain? A compelling portrait of a marriage gone desperately sour."

— *Kirkus Reviews*

"With elements of a classic mystery novel, *The Mystery of Mrs. Christie* is gripping, making it possible to believe that, with her real-life disappearance, Agatha Christie surpassed herself and pulled off the perfect, unsolvable mystery."

— *Foreword Reviews*

"*The Mystery of Mrs. Christie* is part domestic thriller, part Golden Age mystery—and all Marie Benedict! An absorbing and immersive plunge into the disturbed private life of one of the world's most beloved authors, who confounded police, journalists, and generations of biographers when she disappeared from her home, like something out of one of her own novels. But you just might find a solution to the puzzle here... (No Belgian detectives required. Knitting spinsters sold separately.)"

— Lauren Willig, *New York Times* bestselling author

"A winning whodunit from the thrilling life story of the mistress of whodunits, Agatha Christie herself, *The Mystery of Mrs. Christie* is a deft, fascinating page-turner replete with richly drawn characters and plot twists that would stump Hercule Poirot."

— Kate Quinn, *New York Times* bestselling author of *The Alice Network*, *The Huntress*, and *The Rose Code*

"What a read! Agatha Christie is so beautifully drawn, you could easily believe Benedict knew her intimately. Each page uncovers fresh layers of pain, rage, genius and suffering, culminating with a firecracker of an ending. I loved it."

— Stuart Turton, bestselling author of *The Devil and the Dark Water* and *The 7 ½ Deaths of Evelyn Hardcastle*

"With twists, surprises, and an ending that packs a punch in more ways than one, *The Mystery of Mrs. Christie* is a whodunit infinitely worthy of its famous heroine. Benedict's exploration of Agatha Christie's life and mysterious disappearance will have book club discussions running overtime. Quite simply, I loved it!"

— Lisa Wingate, #1 *New York Times* bestselling author of *Before We Were Yours* and *The Book of Lost Friends*

"Brilliantly constructed and richly detailed, *The Mystery of Mrs. Christie* is both a twisty mystery and immersive portrait of the domestic and professional life of the legendary Agatha Christie. This is a must-read for fans of Agatha Christie."

— Chanel Cleeton, *New York Times* & *USA Today* bestselling author of *The Last Train to Key West* and *Next Year in Havana*

PRAISE FOR *LADY CLEMENTINE*

A *Glamour* Best Book of 2020
A PopSugar Best New Book to Read in January 2020

"[A] fascinating fictionalized account of the consummate political wife."

— *People Magazine*

"[A] fascinating historical novel about Clementine, Winston Churchill's wife, keen political partner, and trusted confidant."

— *Christian Science Monitor*

"This outstanding story deserves wide readership. Fans of historical fiction, especially set around World War II; readers who appreciate strong, intelligent female leads; or those who just want to read a compelling page-turner will enjoy this gem of a novel."

— *Library Journal*, Starred Review

"A rousing tale of ambition and love."

— *Kirkus Reviews*

"Winning...the personality of Clementine reverberates in this intimate, first-person account. An intriguing novel, and the focus on the heroic counsel of a woman that has national and international impacts will resonate."

— *Publishers Weekly*

"In her latest novel, *Lady Clementine*, Marie Benedict has gifted us all with another thoughtful and illuminating behind-the-scenes look at one of history's most unusual and extraordinary women. Benedict stuns readers with a glorious assortment of Clementine Churchill's most personal secrets: her scandalous childhood, her unexpected role as a social outsider, her maternal insecurities, and the daily struggles she faces to smooth her husband's political blunders and to keep up with his relent-less demands for guidance and attention. With a historian's eye and a writer's heart, Benedict provides an unforgettable glimpse into the private world of a brilliant woman whose impact and influence on world events deserves to be acknowledged."

— Lynda Cohen Loigman, author of *The Two-Family House* and *The Wartime Sisters*

"The atmospheric prose of Marie Benedict draws me in every single time. *Lady Clementine*'s powerful and spirited story is both compelling and immersive. Benedict fully inhabits the measured and intelligent voice of Clementine Churchill. Entranced throughout, I discovered the secrets behind a familiar story I thought I knew. Deftly moving from the early nineteen hundreds through World War II, Benedict skillfully paints a vivid picture of the times and life of Clementine, the remarkable woman who was the steady force beside Winston Churchill."

— Patti Callahan Henry, *New York Times* bestselling author of *Becoming Mrs. Lewis*

"Benedict is a true master at weaving the threads of the past into a compelling story for today. Here is the fictionalized account of the person who was the unequivocal wind beneath Winston Churchill's wings—a woman whose impact on the world-shaper that was WWII has been begging to be told. A remarkable story of a remarkable woman."

— Susan Meissner, bestselling author of *The Last Year of the War*

PRAISE FOR *THE ONLY WOMAN IN THE ROOM*

An Instant *New York Times* Bestseller
A *USA Today* Bestseller

"A novelist that makes a career out of writing about 'The Only Women in the Room'... In Benedict's telling, that story is a ready-made thriller as well as a feminist parable."

— *New York Times*

"In writing her narratively connected, fictionalized biographies, Benedict is not unlike an archaeologist digging up clues to moments of epiphany."

— *Newsweek*

"Benedict paints a shining portrait of a complicated woman who knows the astonishing power of her beauty but longs to be recognized for her sharp intellect. Readers will be enthralled."

— *Publishers Weekly*

"Once again, Benedict shines a literary spotlight on a historical figure whose talents and achievements have been overlooked, with sparkling results. *The Only Woman in the Room* is a page-turning tapestry of intrigue and glamour about a woman who refuses to be taken for granted. Spellbinding and timely."

— Fiona Davis, national bestselling author of *The Masterpiece*

"Deftly portrays the fascinating life of a Hollywood icon whose scientific accomplishments have long been eclipsed by her sensuous beauty...follows a remarkable path of survival through the dangers of world war—and those at home, behind closed doors. A read as intriguing and captivating as Ms. Lamarr herself."

— Kristina McMorris, *New York Times* bestselling author of *The Edge of Lost* and *Sold on a Monday*

PRAISE FOR *CARNEGIE'S MAID*

A *USA Today* Bestseller

"*Carnegie's Maid* brings to life a particular moment in the ascendancy of Andrew Carnegie while enriching that moment with a sympathetic understanding of what it meant to be an immigrant living in poverty at that time. This would be an accomplishment for any book, but for one that cleverly disguises itself as a historical romance, it's an absolute treasure. The Carnegie legacy may be debatable, but Ms. Benedict's talent for bringing history to life is not."

— *Pittsburgh Post-Gazette*

"[An] excellent historical novel."

— *Publishers Weekly*

"With its well-drawn characters, good pacing, and excellent sense of time and place, this volume should charm lovers of historicals, romance, and the Civil War period. Neither saccharine nor overly dramatized."

— *Library Journal*

"In *Carnegie's Maid*, Marie Benedict skillfully introduces us to Clara, a young woman who immigrates to America in the 1860s and unexpectedly becomes the maid to Andrew Carnegie's mother. Clara becomes close to Andrew Carnegie and helps to make him America's first philanthropist. Downton Abbey fans should flock to this charming tale of fateful turns and unexpected romance, and the often unsung role of women in history."

— Pam Jenoff, *New York Times* bestselling author of *The Orphan's Tale* and *The Lost Girls of Paris*

PRAISE FOR
THE OTHER EINSTEIN

"An engaging and thought-provoking fictional telling of the poignant story of an overshadowed woman scientist."

— *Booklist*

"Intimate and immersive historical novel… Prepare to be moved by this provocative history of a woman whose experiences will resonate with today's readers."

— *Library Journal*, Editors' Pick

"An intriguing…reimagining of one of the strongest intellectual partnerships of the nineteenth century."

— *Kirkus Reviews*

"Superb…haunting story of Einstein's brilliant first wife who was lost in his shadow."

— Sue Monk Kidd, *New York Times* bestselling author of *The Invention of Wings*

"*The Other Einstein* is phenomenal and heartbreaking, and phenomenally heartbreaking."

— Erika Robuck, national bestselling author of *Hemingway's Girl*

ALSO BY MARIE BENEDICT

The Other Einstein

Carnegie's Maid

The Only Woman in the Room

Lady Clementine

The Mystery of Mrs. Christie

HER HIDDEN GENIUS

A NOVEL

MARIE BENEDICT

Published by Sourcebooks Landmark, an imprint of Sourcebooks
P.O. Box 4410, Naperville, Illinois 60567-4410
(630) 961-3900
sourcebooks.com

Library of Congress Cataloging-in-Publication Data

Names: Benedict, Marie, author.
Title: Her hidden genius : a novel / Marie Benedict.
Description: Naperville, Illinois : Sourcebooks Landmark, [2022]
Identifiers: LCCN 2021030453 (print) | LCCN 2021030454 (ebook) | (hardcover) | (epub)
Classification: LCC PS3620.E75 H47 2022 (print) | LCC PS3620.E75 (ebook) | DDC 813/.6--dc23
LC record available at https://lccn.loc.gov/2021030453
LC ebook record available at https://lccn.loc.gov/2021030454

Printed and bound in Canada.
MBP 10 9 8 7 6 5 4 3 2 1

PART ONE

CHAPTER ONE

February 3, 1947
Paris, France

A THIN MIST HOVERS OVER THE SEINE IN THE EARLY MORNING air. *Strange*, I think. *It isn't yellow like the haze that floats over the murky Thames at home in London but a robin's-egg blue.* Could it be that the mist—lighter than fog, with fewer water molecules and less density—is reflecting the clearer Seine? I marvel at the meeting of sky and ground, breathtaking even in winter with the spires of Notre-Dame looming over the thin wisps of cloud. Papa would call it heaven touching earth, but I believe in science, not God.

I shake off thoughts of my family and try to simply enjoy the walk from my flat in the sixth arrondissement to the fourth. With each passing block, the cafés of the Left Bank, their sidewalk tables busy even on an early Monday morning in February, peel away, and by the time I cross over the Seine, I enter the orderly, elegant world of the Right Bank. Even though there are differences in the two arrondissements, they both bear scars of the war in their somewhat damaged buildings and still-wary inhabitants. It's the same at home, although in Paris, the citizens rather than their structures seem to have born more of the brunt; perhaps the specter of the Nazi occupation still looms in their midst.

A rogue, disturbing question enters my mind, one with no measurable scientific foundation, I'm quite certain. When the Nazis shot innocent French citizens and blameless Jews, did molecules from the German soldiers who loaded the bullets pass through their victims? Is Paris not only riddled with physical remains of the war but also permeated with microscopic scientific evidence of its enemies and victims as well, blended together in a way that would have horrified the Nazis? Would the detritus of Germans and Jews be identical under close analysis?

I doubt this is the sort of inquiry French physicist Jean Perrin anticipated when he was awarded the Nobel Prize in 1926 for proving that molecules exist. *Imagine,* I think with a shake of my head, *that until twenty years ago, the very existence of the subuniverse that dominates my work was open to debate.*

I stop short as I approach the Laboratoire Central des Services Chimiques. I am confused. Could this really be the venerable chemistry institution? The building has the patina of age but not necessarily the sort of respectability and stateliness I'd expected from an organization that has produced such excellent and innovative research. It could be any governmental building anywhere. As I climb the steps to the front doors, I can almost hear Papa critique my decision: *The hard work and the commitment to science is commendable*, he had said, *but why must you take a position in Paris, a city still digging out from the weight of occupation and terrible loss? A place where the Nazis*—he said the word with considerable effort—*once governed, leaving traces of their evil behind them?* With effort, I banish Papa from my thoughts.

"*Bonjour*," I greet the receptionist in French. "*Je m'appelle Rosalind Franklin, et j'ai un rendez-vous.*"

To my ears, my voice sounds raspy and my French stilted. But the smartly dressed young woman—her lips a bright slash of red and her tiny waist encircled by a thick leather belt—replies with ease and a welcoming grin. "*Ah, bienvenue! Monsieur Mathieu vous attend.*"

"Monsieur Mathieu himself is waiting for me?" I blurt out to the woman, forgetting to hold my tongue for a moment before speaking, as I know I should. Without that pause and careful consideration of my words, I can be perceived as brusque, even combative in more heated environments. It's a legacy of a childhood with parents who encouraged conversation and debate even with their daughter, I suppose, and a father who was expert at both.

"Monsieur Mathieu indeed!" a voice calls out from across the lobby, and I look over to see a familiar figure stride toward me with hand outstretched. "I couldn't let our newest *chercheur* arrive without a proper greeting, could I? It's a pleasure to welcome you to Paris."

"What an unexpected honor, sir," I reply to the senior scientist at the Ministry of Defense, who has a hand in much of the governmental scientific research in the country, thinking how wonderful my title *chercheur*—which means researcher—sounds coming from a native French speaker. Even though, on paper, it doesn't appear quite as lofty as my former role of assistant research officer at the British Coal Utilisation Research Association (which we called, among ourselves, BCURA), *chercheur* sounds impossibly exotic. "I certainly didn't expect to see you on my first day."

"You are a protégé of my dear friend, Madame Adrienne Weill, and I would not want to be subjected to her wrath if I disappointed her," he says with a wry grin, and I smile at the surprisingly impish gentleman, as well-known for his scientific prowess as his underground wartime service in the Resistance. My friendship with Adrienne, the French scientist who'd befriended me during my years at Cambridge, had yielded many unexpected benefits, not the least of which was the introduction to Monsieur Mathieu. It came at the most urgent and necessary time.

"You and Madame Weill have taken extraordinary care of me," I reply, thinking of the many favors she's done for me over the years. "You secured me this position, and she found me a flat."

"An extraordinary mind deserves extraordinary care," he says, the smile now gone and his face serious. "After seeing you present your paper at the Royal Institution in London in which you handily imposed order on the disordered realm of coal—and then watching you correct that other speaker's measurements of X-ray diagrams so handily—I *had* to offer you a position here. How could we miss the chance to have a *chercheur* with such facile understanding of *trous dans le charbon*?" He pauses, then a smile reemerges, and he says, "Or holes in coal, as I've heard you describe it?"

He laughs heartily at his use of my English phrase "holes in coal" *and* the memory, much to my relief. Because when I stood up at the Royal Institution conference to point out the flaws in the speaker's data, not everyone responded favorably. Two of the scientists in the audience called out for me to sit down—one even yelled "women should know their place"—and I could see the dismay register on several others' faces. Not at the outbursts by the two scientists but at *my* audacity in correcting a male peer.

After we finish laughing, he compliments my research into the microstructure of coal. It's true that I used my own methods of experimentation and an unusual form of measurement—a single molecule of helium—but I wouldn't say the coal field has been completely organized as a result.

"You do know that I can apply my methods to subjects other than coal?" I offer, thinking how surprised my family would be to witness this rather deft management of French banter. Somehow, it is almost easier to exchange light small talk in French than English, where I am awkward—either too shy or too blunt. It's as if the French language itself emboldens me and smooths over my sharp edges.

"We are counting on it," he exclaims. Even though our laughter has subsided, his smile remains, and he adds, "Although you may soon see that a good flat is harder to come by than a good position for a scientist in postwar France, and you may be more effusive in your thanks to Madame Weill than to me."

I know my great fortune that Adrienne was able to secure me a room in an enormous flat on rue Garancière only a few blocks from famous Left Bank haunts like the Café de Flore and Les Deux Magots. The flat's owner, a professor's austere widow who has not relinquished her mourning black attire and prefers to be referred to only as Madame, had only taken me in at the request of Adrienne, who'd worked with her late husband; accommodations in Paris are otherwise almost impossible to find. Never mind the once-weekly use of the bathtub and the after-hours access to the kitchen, the flat's soaring ceilings and the walls of bookshelves in the library-turned-bedroom are a dream.

"Come." He gestures toward a long hallway extending from the lobby. "Monsieur Jacques Mering eagerly awaits his new *chercheur*."

Monsieur Mathieu leads me through a warren of hallways, past three groups of white-coated researchers, including, much to my astonishment, several women. I'd heard that the French value intelligence above all else—whether it comes from a man or woman is of no matter to them—and I'd always dismissed these declarations as just talk, since they usually came from Frenchmen. But the sheer number of women working here is undeniable, a shocking difference from my last position at BCURA.

Finally, we stop. We stand before an open door that reveals a vast, airy space lined with black lab tables and equipment and a beehive of scientists, each so deeply engrossed in their tasks that our presence doesn't even seem to register. This hum of scientific apparatus operating and bright minds engrossed in pioneering research is like a symphony to me. I don't believe in an afterlife, but if I did, it would resemble this room.

A man suddenly glances up. Bright green eyes meet mine, and crinkles appear at the corners as his face lights in a smile. The grin stays firmly fixed on his lips as he approaches us, making the high arches of his cheekbones more pronounced. I cannot help but smile in return; his joy is infectious.

"Ah, Mademoiselle Franklin, we have been most anxious to welcome you to Paris," the man says. "Docteur Franklin, I mean."

"Yes, Docteur Franklin," Monsieur Mathieu says, "I'd like to introduce you to the head of the *labo* in which you'll be working. This is Monsieur Jacques Mering."

"A pleasure," Monsieur Mering says, his hand outstretched in greeting. "We have been waiting for you."

My breath catches at this warm welcome, and I think, *It seems I've finally arrived.*

CHAPTER TWO

February 3, 1947
Paris, France

LET ME INTRODUCE YOU TO THE *LABO*," MONSIEUR MERING says with a smile and a grand sweeping gesture around the room. With Monsieur Mathieu in tow, he steers me from table to table, interrupting the *chercheurs* and assistants midproject with such collegial ease they cannot help but be good-natured in response. *How different is Monsieur Mering's approach to his staff from Professor Norrish at Cambridge or even Dr. Bangham at BCURA*, I think with a slight shudder at the memories.

Guiding me to an empty corner at a long, wide black lab table, my new superior sits down on a stool next to me. While Monsieur Mathieu looks on, Monsieur Mering says, "You have impressed us with your groundbreaking analysis of the atomic structure of coal, as I'm sure Monsieur Mathieu has told you. Your innovative experimentation methods allowed you a unique glimpse into coal's structure and helped us understand the differences among types, and we're hoping that our techniques here will give you the means to go even further in your exploration of minuscule worlds, in this case carbons. Monsieur Mathieu, as you know, is one of the foremost experts in X-ray crystallography, and to my great fortune, he has been my teacher. I hope to become yours."

His words—such a straightforward entreaty—move me. I am not used to being spoken to by a scientific colleague as if he's fortunate to work with *me*. The exchange always seems to go the other way.

Glancing at each gentleman, I answer, "It would be my honor. I'm looking forward to learning the technique and seeing where it leads me." I never dared to hope that Messieurs Mathieu and Mering would have the same aspirations about me.

Ever since my meeting with Monsieur Mathieu three months ago, I'd been dreaming about what molecular worlds I might find using this somewhat new scientific approach. Through it, a narrow X-ray beam is directed onto a crystalline substance that locks the atoms in place and diffracts the X-rays, which make impressions on photographic film. When multiple photographs are taken at different angles and conditions, scientists can calculate the atomic and molecular three-dimensional structure of that substance by studying the pattern and measuring the diffracted beams.

Monsieur Mathieu chimes in, "So are we. Our institution does not have particular industrial goals but instead maintains that if we allow our scientists the latitude to research and explore according to their interests and talents, we will find use in the discoveries. With your skills and our methods, we are very hopeful about the ultimate purposefulness of your work."

As Monsieur Mathieu takes his leave, another *chercheur*

appears at Monsieur Mering's side, pulling him away and leaving me alone at what he has identified as my workstation. Here sits the sort of equipment I'd seen at other *chercheur*'s areas—a powerful microscope, an array of beakers and tubes, materials to prepare slides, and a Bunsen burner—but there is also a stack of papers sitting next to the sink assigned to my station. Flipping through them, I see that they are reports describing the projects of the *labo*'s other *chercheurs* and Monsieur Mering himself. I settle in on my chair and lose myself in the descriptions of Mering's elegant glimpses into clay, silicates, and other fine materials using X-ray diffraction techniques; if he shares only a portion of his crystallography skills with me, he will make a fine teacher. When I glance up, two hours have passed, and more than ever, I want to learn the language that X-ray crystallography can teach me, and then I want to subject any number of substances to its powers. How many minute realms can it give me access to? Worlds that can tell us the very *stuff* of life?

The minutes continue to tick by as I review the materials on the projects underway in the *labo.* I feel a gnawing in my stomach, but I ignore it. If I wish away the usual midday hunger, act as if it is happening to someone other than myself, perhaps such everyday needs and distractions needn't dilute my focus or present obstacles. Besides, where would I even lunch, and with whom? At BCURA, I'd grown used to eating a home-packed lunch alone at a hastily scrubbed lab table while my male colleagues ate at a local pub. While I'd resented the alienation, I knew I was lucky to use my skills as a scientist to help serve in the war, instead of doing agricultural work in the Women's Land Army as my father had advocated.

"Mademoiselle Franklin?" A voice rouses me, and I feel a slight pressure on my shoulder.

I pull my gaze away from the materials reluctantly and stare up into the face of a young woman, a fellow *chercheur* by the look of her lab coat, with bright blue eyes magnified by thick glasses. "*Oui*?" I say.

"We are hoping that you'll join us for lunch." She gestures to the group of lab-coated men and women surrounding me—perhaps a dozen in all—and I wonder how long they've been standing there, trying to get my attention. Mama always said I was impervious to the real world when I was deep in "my science," as she called it.

After the relative lack of collegiality at BCURA—and at Cambridge before that, where I was often the only woman in a laboratory or a classroom full of aloof men—I scarcely know how to respond. Is this a real welcome or some sort of awkward, mandatory invitation? I don't want anyone to feel obliged. I have grown used to working and dining alone, and I'd steeled myself for it before leaving London.

"Lunch?" I blurt out without taking that all-important pause.

"You do eat, don't you?" the young woman asks, not unkindly.

"Oh my. Yes, of course."

One of the men adds, "Most days, we lunch at Chez Solange and—"

The woman interrupts, "And then we engage in a special ritual afterward that we will share with you."

I am swept up in their wave of spirited conversation and gestures as we leave our building and cross the Seine. In comparison to this radiant setting and these animated Parisians, London and its citizens seem gloomy. Why is it that the people who suffered firsthand through the occupation and evils of the Nazis seem more hopeful and positive than those who endured it from afar? Not that I'm discounting the horrible loss of life that the English people have suffered from the Blitz and on the battlefields, but they did not have to stare the Nazis in the face and watch them march down their streets like the Parisians.

While walking toward the restaurant, I listen as two of the *chercheurs*—one man and one woman—debate an essay in the political journal *Les Temps Modernes*, edited by Simone de Beauvoir and Jean-Paul Sartre. While I've heard of the two writers, I'm not terribly familiar with the writings in their journal, and I'm rapt as the two researchers espouse their wildly different reactions to the essay yet somehow laugh amiably at the end of the argument. No mindless twaddle passes the lips of these vivacious scientists.

Over a traditional French *déjeuner* of cassoulet and salad, I stay quiet, absorbing the discussion, which shifts from Sartre and de Beauvoir to the current political situation in France. As men and women alike enter the fray of this good-natured argument, I am struck by the free flow of ideas between the sexes; the eloquent presentation of a position seems valued regardless of who's speaking. The female *chercheurs* see no need for either the false demureness or strident argumentativeness that is pervasive among women in England outside the all-girl secondary school environments like the one I experienced at St. Paul's. How unexpected is this aspect of French society. If anything, this French style of exchange mirrors that of the Franklin family, which most English folks regard as strange.

"What do you think, Mademoiselle Franklin?"

"Please call me Rosalind." I'd noticed that they all refer to one another by their first names—not that I could recite them if quizzed—and I don't want them to think I stand on ceremony. And I would certainly never insist on the formal, more appropriate "Docteur."

"Well, Rosalind," another woman—Geneviève, perhaps—asks, "what do you think? Should France go the way of America or the Soviet Union in its future political structure? What form should our fair country take as it rises up from the ashes of the Nazis' devastation?"

"I don't know if I like either option."

Two men, Alain and Gabriel, I think, each of whom had been the strongest advocate for the opposing position, glance at each other, and Alain asks, "What do you mean?"

Gabriel chimes in, "Yes, tell us what *you* believe."

Can they really be so interested in my views? Outside of my immediate family, I don't find that most men are terribly intrigued by my opinions—on science or anything else.

"Well," I allow myself that extra beat to assemble my thoughts. It's a stratagem instilled in me by my longtime childhood governess Nannie Griffiths, who'd witnessed my propensity for unfiltered comments more times than she could count. Here, however, I decide not to temper my words or my feelings. "Both America and the Soviet Union are already bent on a destructive path with their stockpiling of weapons and building of ever-more deadly machinery. Haven't we had enough of war and bloodshed? Wouldn't we be better off focusing on unity than divisive identities?" My voice escalates as I articulate this position, one I've debated with my father. "It seems a fresh, new path would be better."

The entire table has grown quiet. Even the side conversations that had been bubbling alongside the discussion of the politics of America and the Soviet Union have stopped. Every eye is upon me, and I feel like crawling under the table. Have I erred as badly as I did with Professor Norrish at Cambridge when I bluntly pointed out a crucial error in his research? That particular misstep had yielded an enormous row with Norrish as well as his insistence that I repeat his research, all of which derailed my doctorate by over a year. I don't want to ever make such blunders again.

"This one seems a bit shy, but she has spirit," Alain says to Gabriel in a voice he clearly expects me to hear. "Once she gets riled up, that is."

"She does indeed," Gabriel agrees, then adds, "That fire will be a welcome addition to the *labo*."

I don't know what to say. Am I meant to reply to these remarks, audible but ostensibly for each other? Could it be possible that they actually like my brusquely stated opinions, that they don't find them offensive or unseemly for a woman?

As we begin to rise from the table and slide on our coats, one of the women asks, "On to Les Cafés de PC?"

"*Mais bien sûr,*" Alain answers.

"We're going to another café? Don't we have to return to work?" I ask, a little panicked at this seemingly long absence from the *labo* on my first day.

They laugh, and one of the men cries out, "The *labo* and Les Cafés de PC are very nearly one and the same! Come, we will show you."

During our journey back across the Seine, one of the men points out the École de Physique et de Chimie, the very place where Marie and Pierre Curie made their famous discoveries that yielded the Nobel Prize. It thrills me to think that I'm acting as a physical chemist in the same space as my illustrious idol.

Once inside our building, instead of returning to our *labo*, the group heads to an unused part of the building that houses an empty laboratory. Without a word, the group disperses, and each *chercheur* undertakes a specific job. Three start rinsing laboratory flasks while another secures a bag of ground coffee from a locked cabinet, and another two take the newly cleaned flasks and begin boiling water and coffee in them over Bunsen burners. Within a span of several minutes, we are all sipping *café* from evaporating dishes and continuing the political conversation where it left off over lunch.

As I peer around the room at these scientists drinking coffee out of lab equipment while lounging on the tops of lab tables and desks, I break out in laughter at this incongruous scene. Soon, my colleagues are laughing alongside me. I open the door to a thought I'd previously told myself I could never entertain. Could it be possible that for the first time in my life, I've found a place to belong?

CHAPTER THREE

March 14, 1947
Paris, France

Monsieur Mering keeps his eyes fixed upon me as I mount the crystal sample on the goniometer, precisely as he instructed. I then adjust the goniometer so the crystal is positioned as we'd agreed; we want to secure very specific angles and patterns once the X-ray passes through the crystal so we can take those reflections and—using the Fourier transform method—create a three-dimensional model of its atoms. I return to his side, impatient to unlock the inner realm of this crystal and lay bare its long-held secrets.

"You might be the quickest study of X-ray crystallography I've ever encountered," Monsieur Mering whispers as he guides my hand to the piece of the crystallography equipment—the part's name is still unknown to me after weeks at the *labo*, much to my embarrassment—that launches the X-ray beam. I imagine the beam penetrate the crystal and then diffract into a variety of directions, leaving patterns for us to study on the X-ray film, and then I think about the possibilities of this incredible tool, the world of unimaginable minuteness it allows us to see. Although the process is laborious and the equipment is no wand, it's a bit like scientific magic, albeit a slow-moving one, as the process can take hours or days while we wait for the image to finalize.

"Thank you," I reply, trying to keep my flushed cheeks hidden behind the equipment. It is high praise coming from the man who learned the technique from Monsieur Mathieu, who, in turn, learned it from one of the founders of X-ray crystallography, Nobel Prize winner William Henry Bragg, at the Royal Institution in London. But my face cools quickly because in truth, my primary focus is on the microworlds that will open to me with this technique. I wonder: Could it be used with substances other than crystals? Stated a different way, what substances could we make crystalline so that we might use this method?

"Don't tell the others," he adds with a conspiratorial wink, keeping his tone low and glancing around the busy room, humming with scientists conferring and glass beakers clinking. "Some of them still aren't entirely adept at it."

"Not to worry, sir," I answer. While my sense of duty to Monsieur Mering means that I wouldn't dream of telling my new friends about this slight, I do already feel protective of them and have to restrain myself from openly defending their skills. Even though we've only known each other for six weeks, my sense of camaraderie is so strong that I feel certain they'd do the same for me.

"When did I become a 'sir'?" Our eyes meet, and his flash with merriment. For the first time today, I am fully aware of another person instead of the science at my disposal. "I may be in charge of this *labo*, and we may technically be within the purview of the Ministry of Defense, but I'm not running a military operation. I am not now, nor will I ever be, a 'sir.'"

"Understood, s—" I stop myself from the habit, left over from my unpleasant years studying under Professor Norrish at Cambridge. Even when I got to BCURA, where informality and independence ruled the day under the more avuncular Dr. Bangham, I could not shake the habit. I'll have to work harder on it here, as I don't wish to be labelled an outsider. "Monsieur Mering."

I wonder who he really is behind the affable manner and sharp mind. Over one of our now-regular lunches at Chez Solange, the other *chercheurs* have shared rumors with me that he's actually Jewish, but like many French-Jewish scientists during the Nazi occupation, he moved out of Paris for a less dangerous lab in the countryside and didn't declare his Jewishness. While living without proper identity papers in wartime would have carried risks for Monsieur Mering, the decision would have been, of course, far less risky than the alternative; we all knew Jewish people who'd been taken away by the Nazis and killed in the concentration camps, and in fact, my family took in Jewish refugees lucky enough to escape during the war. In smaller group discussion while walking back to the *labo*, two of the female *chercheurs*—Geneviève and Marie—had whispered that despite his perfect French, Monsieur Mering had actually been born in Russia. They also disclosed that they found him attractive, a confession that made me blush. I share their view but don't want to admit it, even to myself. Beyond this, no one seems to know any details about Monsieur Mering's *current* personal life, which is strange given the breadth of collegiality and socializing that happens within and without the *labo*.

Who is Jacques Mering? Oh yes, I would very much like to know. Why do I feel like a girl when I think about him, even though I'm a woman of twenty-six?

"So," Monsieur Mering says in his best approximation of a professorial manner. "Tell me what you see when you look at this image." He hands me an image that we took earlier in the week; the sample we prepared for the X-ray machine today will be bombarded with X-ray beams for more than a day in order to capture an image like this.

I study the scattered dots on the film and the concentric rings at its center in varying shades of gray, white, and black. Using the strange sort of gift I've had at my disposal my entire life, I allow my gaze to soften, and the patterns make themselves known to me.

"Well, of course, I'd have to make all the proper measurements, but the way these spots change in intensity, meaning that the X-rays have been concentrated in some areas and blocked in others due to the nature of the crystal"—I point to the dots on the film—"can give us a sense of the architecture of the atoms."

"What do you see?"

Reaching for a pencil and piece of paper nearby, I rough out a three-dimensional image. "If I had to guess—which I don't like to do, as I prefer to operate with all the possible data—from this perspective, the structure might look like this." I hesitate for a moment before handing him the sketch. How can I hazard a guess? It goes against my scientific training to share a conclusion without full experimentation or proof; it goes against the perfectionism that's been part of me since childhood, the loathing of abandonment in any form. And yet I cannot say no to him, and I do not want to disappoint him. So I place the drawing in his hand.

His eyes widen almost imperceptibly, and then, without commenting on the sketch, he asks, "Is there anything you'd change as you capture the next image?"

"There are a variety of angles I might use to aim the X-ray to change the diffraction, and I have some notions about how to position the crystal so I'm more likely to capture the full structure." I write down a few calculations and show him my X-ray crystallography plan for this particular sample.

"*Incroyable*," he pronounces as his eyes stay on mine. "And your eye for patterns is astonishing. With your expertise in preparing materials for study and analysis and all your innovative techniques, I cannot wait to see what you'll discover. Imagine what you find about the architecture of these substances might reveal to us about their behavior and function."

"I certainly hope I live up to your expectations, Monsieur Mering."

The laughter usually present in his eyes or at the corners of his mouth disappears, and for a moment, I think I've disappointed him. But then he says, "Rosalind," and my breath catches, hearing my given name on his lips for the first time. "How can you even suggest such a thing? You have already exceeded every one of my hopes about you."

CHAPTER FOUR

March 22, 1947
Paris, France

"I DO BELIEVE YOU'VE FALLEN IN LOVE WITH PARIS, ROSALIND. You've bloomed in a way you never did at Cambridge. Even your clothes have become very French," Adrienne pronounces as she sips from her after-dinner espresso.

I smooth my full, emerald-green skirt into which I've tucked a crisp white blouse in the new style, and I appreciate the compliment. Usually, it is only my mind that Adrienne praises.

She continues, gesturing around her rather sparse but cozy apartment in which she has prominently displayed her family photos, which she managed to abscond with when she left Paris for London just before the Nazis took hold and then brought back with her when it was safe to return. Adrienne suspected that her Jewishness and her science would make her a target for the Nazis, and wisely, luckily, she escaped just in time. "I had expected you'd be at my home every Sunday for dinner, but it's been hard to get—" She pauses, searching for a word. "How do the English say it—on your dance card."

I laugh at the sophisticated Adrienne trying on a colloquial English phrase for size. It doesn't fit, of course, because Adrienne's intellect and worldview are far too broad for the narrowness of English society. "I apologize, Adrienne. It's just that the other *chercheurs* keep me busy on the weekends. We did a bit of skiing when the weather was still cold, and now that it's warmer, we've been hiking in the Chantilly Forest and taken in a few exhibits at the Grand Palais on rainy afternoons."

"Sounds marvelous. And entirely appropriate for your age and interests. And I'm hoping I'll see you more regularly when the weather warms in the spring, and you can join me and some friends in regular tennis matches," she says, reminding me of the sport we enjoyed playing together when we both lived in Cambridge. Her fork is poised above a pudding I brought to the dinner, a concoction I cobbled together with the scant items available in the food markets these days—namely tinned milk, cream cheese, sugar, a bit of chopped chocolate sent from home, and banana. "Anyway, as much as I adore you, I wouldn't want you to spend your weekends with an old woman."

I almost snort aloud at this remark. No one would ever call Adrienne Weill an old woman. True, she is in her late forties and received her scientific training from Marie Curie herself, but the brilliant Jewish physicist and engineer is more engaged in the *life* around her than most men or women twenty years younger. In her position as a metallurgist within a naval research laboratory sponsored by the government, she is intimately involved with not only the emerging science but the politics as well.

"I'm guessing that your family has already visited? And that they've been filling your 'dance card' as well?" she asks with a wry smile. Adrienne and her daughter, Marianne, who'd accompanied her to London, had come to know my family very well during their years in England. We always included them in the Jewish holidays, and my siblings found excuses to visit me at Cambridge, where I stayed in the boardinghouse Adrienne ran for a few of her students in addition to teaching. How different my life would be without this rare friend, an example of the rich sort of life a female scientist could lead. *Imagine*, I think, *if I'd never knocked on her door at Cambridge requesting the French lessons that she'd promised to those of us who donated to the fund for her professorial salary*.

"Only Jenifer and Colin so far." I tell her about the visits by Colin, the older of my two younger brothers, and my sister, Jenifer, who, at nine years younger than me and still at St. Paul's, sometimes feels more like a niece than a sibling. "Although Mama is planning on coming to stay at the flat next week when Madame goes away for a fortnight. I'll fashion a bed for her in the parlor."

"Your mother doesn't wish to stay in a hotel?" Adrienne looks surprised.

"She wants to experience my life, and that means staying where I stay, eating where I eat, and visiting the *labo*. Or at least that's what she says."

Adrienne arches a magnificent brow. "You suspect other motives?"

"You know my parents were hesitant about me coming to Paris. They worried that the city was still struggling after the war and that I might not—"

Adrienne interjects, "Be able to live in the standard in which they'd raised you."

I admit, privately, the Franklin family is part of a rather exclusive Anglo-Jewish community that can trace its lineage not only to the great sixteenth-century Rabbi Loew of Prague but to King David, founder of Jerusalem and king of Israel in 1000 BC. Soon after my ancestors moved from Poland to England in the 1700s, they entered the business and financial world, beginning centuries of affluence and high-ranking government appointments, including a cabinet position. But while the Franklin family has accumulated great wealth, Papa has always been insistent that we live carefully, relatively modestly, without any ostentation. This means that even though our grandfather has a grand town house in London and an estate in Buckinghamshire, my four siblings and I travelled by tube, grew up comfortably but conservatively in our Bayswater house, and devoted a considerable amount of our free time to philanthropy, especially by assisting Jewish refugees fleeing Hitler in securing hundreds of entry permits for them and taking in children from the Kindertransport. This was in addition to our usual efforts for Papa's favorite charity, the Working Men's College, where Papa served as director and taught in the evenings in a program designed to bridge the divide in classes and provide opportunities for the working class.

As I always do when my family's wealth is mentioned, I feel my cheeks grow hot, with a blend of embarrassment and anger. Adrienne knows better than most that my family has never flouted its prosperity; in fact, my father goes to great lengths to minimize it.

Working hard to keep my voice measured, I say, "Not really.

It was more that they didn't like the idea of me being so far away, on the heels of the war."

"I understand perfectly, Rosalind. You're a lovely young woman living on your own in a city very recently occupied by the Nazis. It's only natural that Ellis and Muriel are concerned about your safety." After a sip of her espresso, she says, "So of course you must show your mother that she has nothing to fear and everything to celebrate about you living in Paris."

I smile, thinking how well Adrienne understands the workings of my family. "That is precisely my plan. I've planned the four days of her visit down to the last detail. I will cook her several French meals using the abundant supplies found at the market—"

We laugh at the notorious shortages of the marketplaces.

I continue, "And then, she and I will explore an Impressionist exhibit over the weekend and attend the Comédie-Française. Before she leaves, I will ensure that she receives a full tour of the *labo*, and I will introduce her to my charming *chercheur* friends. That way, she can report that I'm engaged in important work and that I'm not lonely. Two of my father's primary concerns."

"*Parfait*," Adrienne says with a quick nod. "Do I need to enlist Marcel for your mother's visit to the *labo*?"

"I don't think you need to wrangle Monsieur Mathieu away from his important duties. I'm certain that Monsieur Mering can provide the appropriate pomp to the *labo* and praise my work to my mother."

"Ah, Monsieur Mering." Adrienne's eyes linger on my face. "We haven't talked of the *labo* yet. The work and the people."

Thrilled to share the details of my new work in X-ray crystallography with someone who not only understands but is intrigued, I launch into a spirited report of my discoveries and the antics of my fellow *chercheurs*. The only topic I avoid discussing is Monsieur Mering himself. Lately, I've found that my feelings about him are complicated, and I think about him as a man—instead of as a scientist—far more frequently than I'd like.

"It seems as though you've forged a real connection with your fellow scientists." She smiles. "Who knows? Perhaps you'll marry one like I did. And stay in France for good."

"I could never do that. I can't be a scientist and also be a wife and mother," I blurt out, having exhausted my small supply of reserve. Adrienne is used to my outbursts, but this time, with this proclamation, I may have gone too far.

"Why is that, Rosalind?" Her shoulders stiffen, and I immediately want to pluck from the air the words I just spewed into them. How could I have said this to Adrienne of all people? I always stick my foot in it. Even if I believe what I said—and I do—I should not have made such a statement to the woman who's provided me with the example of a successful life as a female scientist and the means to achieve it. "*I* am a scientist and a mother. And before my husband died, I was a wife."

"But I fear you are the extraordinary exception, Adrienne. And you succeeded because your husband was in full support of your career, much like Pierre Curie was with his wife; such men are singular. And it worked when you became a mother because your schedule allowed you time to devote to Marianne. It's not fair to a child to have an absent mother; a professional cannot provide the care and affection a child needs."

"How can you say that? You and your four siblings were raised in large part by Nannie Griffiths while your mother poured her time and attention into your father and her volunteer work—much to the benefit of the poorer people in England and Jewish refugees everywhere—and you don't seem the worse for it."

Her words sting, all the more because they're true. How can I protest against a fact? My very nature and training go against it.

"Oh, Adrienne, I am terribly sorry. I didn't mean—"

She waves me off, a signal that the dispute is over and status quo has been regained in the French manner. "You are young. You are innocent. Time—and perhaps love—will change your mind."

I want to disagree, to tell her that I've long since decided that science and love are not meant to coexist. But Adrienne is not going to give me that opportunity. Instead, like the excellent scientific examiner she is, she senses something amiss in my responses, and she is determined to ferret it out.

"Tell me more about Monsieur Mering. You've hardly mentioned him at all, and yet I'm certain he's ubiquitous in the *labo*."

My cheeks burn again, and I find myself unable to meet her gaze. "He is an excellent scientist. And teacher."

"And I'm certain you are an excellent student." She grows quiet and still. "Be careful, *ma chère*. You're exactly the sort of attractive young girl that would catch his eye."

CHAPTER FIVE

May 21, 1947
London, England

I watch as David and Myrtle exchange vows under the chuppah. Tears well in my eyes watching my older sibling gaze on his bride with tenderness, a soft expression rarely seen from my stoic brother. Or any Franklin really. Sentimentality and open displays of affection are not often in evidence in our family—they are actively discouraged, in fact—and observing them firsthand elicits an unexpected reaction in me. Papa would be horrified, so I glance down to hide my eyes.

By the time the rabbi incants his blessings, my tears have dried, and I know it's safe to look up. The bride and groom begin their walk down the aisle to much applause, and I see a phalanx of Franklins in the aisle across from me, studying the couple. My parents shake hands with the Sebag-Montefiores, Myrtle's mother and father, and I see their pride in this union, a merger with another wealthy, established Jewish family.

I follow the line of guests pouring into the reception room, my younger sister, Jenifer, and my younger brothers, Roland and Colin, ages twenty-one and twenty-four respectively, in tow. We join three of Papa's five brothers and sisters; they've gathered together to watch the wedding guests queue to congratulate the couple, who stand in the receiving line alongside my parents and the Sebag-Montefiores.

"Such excess. Just think what the money spent on this wedding could do for women in the hands of the Fawcett Society or the Townswomen's Guild." Aunt Alice is commenting on the lavish flower arrangements, the glasses of wine passed on silver trays by white-suited waiters, and the kosher hors d'oeuvres containing rationed meats that must have cost the Sebag-Montefiores a small fortune. I'm not surprised by her perspective, even though it hasn't prompted her to abandon her lovely flat or comfortable lifestyle. Although she was presented at court nearly forty years ago, she quickly eschewed that life of high society for one of socialist politics advocating for women, closely shorn hair, and the nebulous, long-term relationship with a female roommate that no one will discuss. That said, I'm a little shocked she'd dare to utter her sentiments here.

Staring at the scene through his thick glasses, Uncle Hugh snorts. "Well said, Alice," he says, then falls silent. Even though he maintains the same beliefs about capitalism and women as Aunt Alice—he was, in fact, jailed for his strident suffragist views when he attacked Winston Churchill with a bullwhip for his failure to support the women's vote—he knows better than to elaborate when so deep in the bosom of the Franklin and Sebag-Montefiore families. His is not the sort of philanthropy the Franklin siblings, of whom Papa is the youngest, were encouraged to practice by our patriarch, my grandfather Arthur Franklin, who passed away nearly a decade ago.

I hear a loud tsking and turn to see Aunt Mamie standing behind us. "That's enough, you two. This is a celebration of David and Myrtle and their new lives together as Franklins. Not a condemnation of the Sebag-Montefiores' generosity." Aunt Mamie, although a member of London County Council as part of the Labour Party, is more moderate in her views, certainly more than Alice. Her years at the side of her husband, my uncle Norman Bentwich, while he served as attorney general of Palestine under the British Mandate, have tempered any extreme perspectives. "Especially when their good works and philanthropy are so extensive. Have you forgotten all they did for Jewish children orphaned by the war?"

My aunts face each other with cheeks flushed in righteous indignation, one of very few emotions tolerated in the Franklin family. Papa would be furious to have any outbursts at David's wedding, so I attempt to defuse the spark I see catching among my aunts and uncle.

"It's the first time I've seen you all since I moved to Paris," I say to them, a plain effort to steer the conversation to more benign ground.

"Ah yes, Rosalind. How *is* Paris?" Aunt Mamie asks, tearing her eyes away from her sister and giving my hand a squeeze.

"Wonderful. The laboratory is engaged in the most scintillating work—finding new ways to peer into the microuniverse. Oh, and my colleagues are brilliant and fun and—"

"Couldn't you have done laboratory work here in London?"

Aunt Alice interrupts me with a wrinkle of her nose, as if I've said something distasteful to her. Is it Paris or my scientific work to which she objects, I wonder. Strange, as she's always presented herself as living outside the norm and supporting those who've made similar choices. "Why do you have to traipse all the way to Paris? Especially when there are so many English people affected by the war who need your help?"

"I hope my scientific discoveries benefit the people of more than just one country, Aunt Alice. One day, anyway."

"No, Rosalind," she says, "you misunderstand me. I mean that if you were here, you could be assisting in any number of English charities in which our family is involved—helping refugees or families of military men—when you aren't working. Or perhaps *instead* of your job."

Franklin women are encouraged to be well-educated and smart and in fact are exposed to the same sort of conversational debate and rigors as the men in the family; for example, Papa always included me in the same activities as my brothers, from Alpine hikes to carpentry. But Franklin women are meant to use their intellectual gifts for the betterment of mankind through charity, governmental positions, good works, and of course, a suitable marriage. Not a salaried position. After all, we needn't undertake paid labor to support ourselves; trusts take care of that, as do our male family members who work in financial firms, bankers all. To the Franklins, I am the outcast and the strange one with my dedication to science. I wonder what path Jenifer will choose as she gets older.

Even though she doesn't always agree with my choices, Aunt Mamie has defended me over the years, and tonight is no exception. As she opens her mouth to intervene on my behalf, I hear a familiar squeal. "Miss Rosalind!"

Relief and glee course through me as I see my favorite family member—my cousin Ursula—come racing toward me. "Miss Ursula!" I call back. The daughter of Papa's eldest brother, Cecil, Ursula was more than a cousin to me; we'd been schoolmates and dear friends at St. Paul's too, which fostered in us a double closeness. In fact, in some ways, since Jenifer is so much younger than me and at an entirely different life stage, Ursula feels more like my sister. Even though we are different in many ways—her path after St. Paul's has been in keeping with the Franklin traditions with her philanthropic work and dating Jewish men—we have an honesty and intimacy that comes from a lifetime together and an appreciation of each other.

We delight in our childhood nicknames, even though they garner glances. Weekends with our grandfather at Chartridge Lodge, his country estate in Buckinghamshire, meant referring to everyone formally, even close family. The ritual of referring to each other as "Miss" has stayed with us, a reminder of our shared heritage.

We embrace briefly, and as we lock arms and slink away from the aunts, uncles, and siblings, I whisper, "You rescued me."

Ursula, known for her humor and vivaciousness, giggles. She understands well the fierce manner and opinions of our aunts and uncles, and we've extricated each other many times over the years.

As we begin perambulating around the crowded reception room, she elbows me. "You look stunning. Paris agrees with you."

I smile. I'd been hoping Ursula would approve of my outfit. "It's an homage to Christian Dior's New Look. It's all the rage in Paris."

"Did you get your dress at Dior?" Her eyes widen. She knows

Papa's views on ostentatious spending. In fact, I have barely recovered from the dressing-down I received upon arrival last night when Papa learned that I'd flown from Paris to London instead of taking the considerably cheaper but infinitely more nauseating and time-consuming ferry ride across the Channel.

"Of course not," I mock-slap her arm. "I made it myself. And I had Mama send me parachute silk to make the crinoline so the skirt flares properly. Silk is in woefully short supply in Paris, as you might imagine."

I extricate my arm from hers and spin for her. Ursula is the only person with whom I can be the tiniest bit frivolous and not feel judged.

"It makes our London fashions look so dowdy and boxy. The cinched waist, the narrow shoulders, and the swingy full skirt of your dress are so flattering. " She runs her hand down the straight skirt of her otherwise very elegant peach dress, which beautifully compliments her peaches-and-cream complexion and dark-brown hair with springy curls. "And your hair? The way you've grown it longer and swept the sides back with combs, is that part of the New Look as well?"

"No, I've just copied some of the hairdos I see on the Parisian ladies. They're very fashionable and free with their styles, Miss Ursula. It's hard to believe they were living under the thumb of the Nazis only two years ago." I shake my head.

"Well, the Parisian life suits you. Better watch out, Miss Rosalind, or you'll catch the eye of one of the French scientists!" she teases good-naturedly. My views on science and marriage are well-known to Ursula. To all my family, in truth. So much so that my aunts and uncles no longer broach the topic of my prospects.

But still, this time, her jibe cuts uncomfortably close to the truth. I feel my cheeks warm. I hope I'm not blushing, because Ursula, of all people, will never let that pass without interrogation or, at the very least, comment. And my feelings are too new and unfamiliar for me to discuss.

I venture a change of subject. "So have you seen—"

She interrupts me. "Don't you dare try to veer me off course, Miss Rosalind. I see your flushed face. What is happening?"

"Don't be silly. Nothing." I wave her off.

"Why the red face?"

"It's stuffy in here." I fan my face with my hand, as if I'm cooling myself down.

She links her arm through mine again, as she's done since childhood. "Dear cousin, you cannot keep secrets from me."

"It's just that—" I hesitate, not wanting to say too much but knowing I must tell Ursula *something*. "The Frenchmen are very different from Englishmen."

"Aha." A gleam sparks in her eyes. "The famous French flirting. Have you fallen victim to it, Miss Rosalind?"

"Of course not, Miss Ursula." I smile to myself, thinking of Monsieur Mering but not daring to speak his name aloud. "But the flirting does warm one's cheeks."

CHAPTER SIX

November 8, 1947
Paris, France

I push my hair out of my eyes, realizing that I've probably smeared sludge from the X-ray crystallography equipment all over my cheek and forehead. *No matter*, I think. *I have the place to myself.* Who else would be in the *labo* on a Saturday besides me?

Returning to all fours, I stare down at the apparatus that I've disassembled for cleaning. The X-ray tube lies to the right and the diffusion pumps to the left. I have several important experiments planned for Monday and Tuesday, and I know that unless I clear the pumps of accumulated debris, not to mention grease from the vacuum, I will not be able to conduct the tests in the time frame I've set out for myself. Not to mention that I don't want to be burdened by the safety precautions the *labo* wants its scientists to follow when we experiment more with the equipment; they slow the process, and in any event, no definitive scientific study has proven a precise harm caused by the radiation and equipment.

The literature to date has focused on the outlying, egregious cases of great harm.

Even though I've become most adept with the apparatus and the sorts of investigations I can conduct with it, coming into the *labo* on the weekends has become necessary. In the past, my attention never wavered, but lately I find my focus riven in two. At any moment during my workdays, I am deeply engaged in my studies, and yet somehow, I am also very aware of the whereabouts and the doings of Monsieur Mering. Whether he's in the *labo* or his office, whether he's alone studying the results of his own projects or busy consulting another *chercheur* about their work, I know precisely where he is and with whom. I wish I could cease this constant tabulation, but I find myself unable. While this distractedness has not affected the quality of my work, it has impacted the speed—hence, weekend work to compensate.

Work is progressing, and I am beginning to see the order in things, I tell myself when I'm alone in my room at the widow's flat and furious with myself for allowing thoughts of a man—never mind that he's brilliant and funny and kind—to overtake my concentration. In fact, my X-ray analysis of carbons and graphites is proving so illuminating I'm planning to draft a paper on my findings, if Monsieur Mering agrees, of course. Perhaps several papers.

As I reach for the benzene to clean the tubes, I hear a door slam. I jump, nearly spilling the clear, highly flammable liquid. Steadying myself on my knees, I put down the bottle and turn to identify the source of the noise.

"Rosalind," I hear a voice call out, and my heart beats a little quicker. Could it be Monsieur Mering? It would be our first time alone in the *labo*. Or anywhere, for that matter.

"Yes?" I answer as I push myself to standing and sweep the sides of my hair back into their combs. I try to brush the stains on my white lab jacket, but I realize that it will require a deep cleaning to remove the black smears from the cleaning. *Should I remove it?* I wonder. *No*, I think. That would draw attention to the fact that I've risked wearing trousers to work. I don't want to disappoint Monsieur Mering in any way.

"What are you doing here, Rosalind?" I hear the voice again, and from the nasal inflection, I realize that it isn't Monsieur Mering. It is Michel, a new recruit to the ranks of *chercheurs*. "Did you see the sign barring entry?" he asks.

I had indeed seen the sign outside the *labo*—the one declaring it closed for the weekend. I'd simply turned it around and entered anyway. He must have found the dangling paper curious and flipped it over to read it.

I laugh at the question. "Didn't you? It looks as though you've entered the *labo* as well."

"*Touché*," he says, and we laugh together. "I guess that neither of us is good at following the rules."

"Not when it comes to work anyway."

Michel studies my face. "You are covered in dirt."

"Not dirt. It's muck from the crystallography equipment. I'm cleaning it."

"Could it not wait until Monday? It sounded like a group of the *chercheurs* were exploring the Chantilly this weekend, and I heard you say that hiking was one of your passions. Didn't you all go on an excursion to Haute-Savoie this summer?"

I cannot hold back a smile, remembering our week-long trek through the Tour des Glaciers de la Vanoise, a stunning and challenging range of glaciers. The sixteen-mile hike along the Péclet-Polset ridges that began in cloud and mist before dawn following guides with torches and ended with sunrise on the glacier was one of the most glorious moments I can recall.

"Yes, we climbed the Péclet-Polset ridges," I say, watching as Michel's eyebrows lift at the mention of this notoriously difficult hike. "I would have loved to climb in Chantilly, but I couldn't hold off on cleaning the instruments if I want to be ready first thing Monday."

He looks sheepish. "Your dedication is admirable. I'm embarrassed that I came to the office only to pick up a coat I forgot. The weather will turn chilly tomorrow," he says, holding up a brown tweed overcoat. "How is Jacques doing, by the way? Any updates?"

For a second, my mind is so full of Monsieur Mering that I think he's asking about our supervisor, also named Jacques. But then I realize he must mean my research student, Jacques Maire, who had processed some X-ray films rather hastily last week and injured his hand. It was an instance in which the protocols around the chemical usage were clear and based on conclusive studies, and Jacques should have followed the conventions. Not that this lessens my sympathy for his injuries.

"He's planning on returning to work tomorrow."

"That's a relief."

"Yes," I answer with a sigh, "although I worry that he's coming back too soon; he always seems to be in a rush. I don't want him to have permanent injury to that one finger in particular."

"Did you tell him how you felt?"

"Yes, but he shrugged and told me that I was being worrisome. He's itching to come back."

"Looks like he's working for the right *chercheur*," Michel says.

"What do you mean?"

"It's not exactly like *you* follow the safety precautions. You turned around the sign on the door and entered the *labo* to work anyway. What if there had been a chemical spill?"

I had to laugh. Michel hadn't been a *chercheur* here for long, but he understood me well. "It's my turn to say *touché*."

"Not to mention you ignore the warning signs about your very person."

"What do you mean?"

He points to the desk at the entry to the lab, where the results from our film badge dosimeters are laid out. We all wear these radiation monitoring devices, created by Ernest Wollan to protect the scientists working on the Manhattan Project, and at week's end, the film within the device is developed to measure the amount of radiation to which we've been exposed. I'd forgotten to check the desk when I entered the *labo* earlier today.

I walk over to the desk. There, among all the films showing safe levels of radiation, I see one where the numbers are extremely high. Squinting to make out the owner, I see my name listed on the bottom of the film.

If anyone finds out, I will be barred from the *labo* for weeks—for my safety, I'll be told. I cannot have that, especially since there's no categorical proof about the harm the radiation can cause. Certainly we are all familiar with the horrific fates that befall those with serious overexposure to radiation—most famously one of Thomas Edison's glassblowers, Clarence Dally, who had regular bombardment with X-rays and consequently lost his life, a much harsher result than Edison himself experienced with his eyesight and digestion issues—but regardless of the dosimeter readings, I'm certain I am fine. I've never experienced the sort of intensity or duration of X-rays that people like Edison or his workers did, or the almost unimaginable exposure that the scientists laboring on the Manhattan Project during the war experienced. It was *that* sort of exposure—large-scale or, in some cases, severe—that led to the creation of safety monitoring equipment, not the sort of small, daily encounters with X-ray beams that I have.

Glancing over at Michel, I slide the film into the pocket of my dirty lab coat. His eyes widen at my action, and I remember that he's new to our *labo*. Many of us disregard—or, as in this case, actively hide—the radiation films. We don't want our experiments to be derailed by the dosimeters. But I cannot risk Michel actually reporting my behavior; Monsieur Mering may turn a blind eye to his *chercheurs*' disregard of the safety rules, but he cannot be so lenient if this sort of conduct is called to his attention.

"Do you mind if we keep this as our little secret?"

CHAPTER SEVEN

November 17, 1947
Paris, France

Racing up the three flights to the widow's flat, I hastily stick my key in the lock and then slow my pace as I cross the main rooms to the narrow staircase up to my attic space. Although I do not worry I'll run into Madame Dumas—she keeps largely to her own rooms, a decision prompted by her husband's death not my arrival—she is the essence of propriety and would be horrified to hear me running across her flat. Even though I have confidence in my abilities and had hoped my research would make its way into that journal's pages, I am giddy at the thought that Monsieur Mering holds my work in high enough regard to submit it to that esteemed publication. That alone might be compliment enough.

As I practically skip up the final steep steps, I replay the scene that just transpired in the *labo*.

Monsieur Mering approached me as I was finishing up for the day. "Mademoiselle Franklin, how's the project coming along?"

I handed him the chart I had just completed in which I categorized carbons that graphitize, turning into graphite upon heating, and those that don't.

He scanned it and said, "Impressive identification of patterns across carbon types. Have you formulated a theory on why some types of carbon transform and some don't?"

Pointing to a particular column, I said, "It all goes back to the structure—the sort of molecules that construct the carbon."

"What do you mean?"

Closing my eyes, I described to him what I saw in my mind's eye. "I believe that the carbons that don't graphitize are rich in oxygen but poor in hydrogen, with a strong interior, cross-linking structure that prevents the graphitization. The opposite is true of the other type." When he didn't respond, I added nervously, "But I'd have to do additional tests and take many more images, of course. This is all just speculation based on the initial results. And as I believe I told you, I dislike speculation. Experimentation and objective facts have always driven my theories."

"How would you feel about publishing these results in *Acta Crystallographica*?"

I believe my mouth all but dropped open.

He continued. "I envision a series of papers, beginning with one summarizing these results, once they're finalized of course. Then maybe one to two subsequent articles in which you delve into the X-ray crystallographic techniques you used to obtain these numbers, and perhaps a final paper laying out your theory."

"I'd like nothing m-more," I stammered, incredulous at this offer.

"Excellent," he said, that irresistible wide grin overtaking his angular face. Then he stretched his hand out toward me, and for a minute, I thought he was going to caress my cheek. Instead, he gently rubbed my nose. "Can't allow my star *chercheur* to walk around with graphite on the tip of her nose."

Once I reach the top stair, I fling open the door to the landing, eager to spring inside my room and change for the theater tonight. Alain, Geneviève, and I are going to see *Henry V,* starring Laurence Olivier. It will be my third time watching this most patriotic of Shakespeare's plays with Olivier at the helm, and I'm delighted that some of the *chercheurs* have finally agreed to see it with me.

"Ow!" a voice cries out from behind me.

Who in the devil is that? The maid is gone for the day, and the widow would never consider climbing to the attic. I am *always* alone on this floor.

I turn to see a gangly, dark-haired, olive-skinned man standing in the landing, clutching his nose. A delicate, fair-haired woman comes rushing out of the attic spare room. "Vittorio, *est-ce que ça va*?"

"*Ça va, ça va,*" he says, lifting his hand from his nose. "No blood," he adds with a smile.

"Oh, I am so sorry!" I cry. "I had no idea that Madame Dumas had taken in more lodgers. I thought the other room was empty. Otherwise, I would have never—"

"Please, don't worry," he says. "I should have forewarned you."

"I feel terrible. Are you quite all right?"

Holding his hand up in the air, he proclaims, "As right as this nose will ever be!"

How could I not laugh at this gregarious, outlandish man? And anyway, he does have a distinctly hawklike nose. "What an unorthodox introduction!" I say. "Please allow me to apologize again and introduce myself. I'm Rosalind Franklin."

"Vittorio Luzzati, at your service," he says with a courtly bow, then gestures to the woman. "And this is my lovely wife, Denise."

As we exchange handshakes, I notice that while his French is impeccable, Vittorio has a hint of an accent. His wife, however, must be a native speaker. "Have you just moved to Paris? Or are you relocating within it?"

"Neither and both!" Vittorio declares, to which both Denise and I laugh. "I emigrated to Buenos Aires from Genoa at the start of the war—"

"Ah, not a fan of Mussolini?" I interrupt, then chastise myself for blurting out my question. In politics, one never really knows, and we are to be neighbors.

But he is kindly in his response, as well as brutally honest. "No. And, like Hitler, Mussolini was no fan of my people, the Jews."

"I understand. They are my people as well."

We share a nod of recognition before he continues. "While I was in Argentina, I met this stunning French creature"—he reaches for his wife and kisses her on the cheek—"who was there for medical school. When the blasted war finally came to an end, we returned to Paris where Denise grew up. And here we are!"

"Well, I'm delighted that you both are here. Welcome to Paris and to your new home." I gesture around the landing.

They stand side by side, their arms wrapped around each other's waists, exuding an air of contentment and collegiality. How fortunate I am that *they* landed here.

"How did you convince the widow to rent the room to you? She's notoriously fussy." As soon as I make this statement, I realize how they might interpret it, and I begin to backtrack. "Not that I mean—"

Vittorio holds up his hand. "I think we secured our room the same way you did. Adrienne Weill."

"You know Adrienne?"

"Indeed. And I know you."

"From Adrienne?"

"Adrienne mentioned you, but she wasn't the one who gave me real insights into you. That was Monsieur Mering."

"Oh, what a coincidence. How do you know Monsieur Mering?" I ask, feeling the heat rise in my cheeks at the mention of his name.

"I'm an X-ray crystallographer as well. In fact, I'll be working alongside you at the Laboratoire Central des Services Chimiques. And our mutual boss described you as the *chercheur* with the golden hands."

CHAPTER EIGHT

March 9, 1948
Paris, France

I SLIDE ON MY LIGHTWEIGHT BLUE GABARDINE COAT, GIGGLING uncomfortably at Geneviève's remark. "I am not puritanical."

"Really?" Geneviève teases me. "Then why don't you agree with Simone de Beauvoir's central thesis, that women have been subordinate to men historically because they are enslaved by their reproductive role?"

"It's not that I don't agree, but—" I squirm as I try to answer. The fact that women's status is bound up with maternity is one reason I've decided to eschew marriage and children, but the very topic of sex and gender makes me viscerally uncomfortable. And my *chercheur* friends know it, so it's become a good-natured sport to make me flail.

"But what?" Vittorio asks with a grin. My housemate has joined the *chercheur* ranks so seamlessly—in work and in teasing—that I cannot remember what it was like before his arrival.

"B-but—" I stutter as we all walk toward the *labo* exit. I am trying to refrain from blurting out something embarrassing, as they know well. It's disconcerting that at twenty-eight, I have not shed my childish discomfort with the matters of sex that my colleagues label basic biology.

Suddenly, I hear my name. "Mademoiselle Franklin?" It is Monsieur Mering. He alternates equally between *Mademoiselle* and *Docteur*, but does so with such a pleasant tone, I can never be irritated.

"Saved by the boss," Geneviève whispers with a giggle.

"May I have a minute of your time?" he calls out.

"Of course," I say to him. Then, turning to my friends, I add, "Go on ahead. I'll meet you at Chez Solange."

I feel nervous as I pass our worktables and equipment and walk toward Monsieur Mering's office, which opens up into the *labo*. Not only am I unaccustomed to being alone with him, but it is unusual for him to seek a confidential conversation with any one of us. The *labo* is an informal, friendly place, remarkably free of controversy and competition, and I cannot recall a single instance when he's needed privacy to speak his mind. Even the conversation we had about the possible publication of my results took place in the wide open area of the *labo*, with *chercheurs* and assistants all around.

"*Oui,* Monsieur Mering?" I ask, trying not to stare into his green eyes.

"Mademoiselle Franklin, I'm certain it hasn't escaped your notice that we're very pleased with your progress here."

I am confused by his praise. Not that he fails to acknowledge his staff; it's just that he typically delivers his commendations spontaneously, out in the workplace for all to hear.

"You've been very generous, as has Monsieur Mathieu," I say, for lack of a better response.

"It's only what you deserve. Obviously, you've become expert in the crystallography equipment in short order, and I feel confident that your paper will merit inclusion in the *Acta Crystallographica*."

"Thank you, sir," I stammer out, still perplexed. Is this some sort of impromptu review?

"For all those reasons"—he clears his throat—"I'd like you to accompany me to the conference in Lyons in May."

"Lyons?" I am astonished. Many of my colleagues have been here for some time without receiving an invitation to any of the scientific conferences that are beginning to reassemble across Europe in the wake of the war. "Me?"

"Yes, you," he answers with that disarming grin of his. That smile I cannot help but return. "You've earned it. I'm looking forward to showing you off."

Brightly colored tips of tulips peek up from the thawing soil as I walk the few short blocks to Chez Solange, but they barely register. I am torn between elation over the message Monsieur Mering sends by selecting me for this conference and nerves over any misstep I might make. Not that I feel anxious about attending speeches, making presentations of my own, or chatting with fellow scientists. I worry only about the sorts of admissions I might inadvertently let slip when he and I are alone.

Tucking the tendrils of my hair that the spring breeze has loosened back into my combs, I step into Chez Solange. The familiar checkered tablecloths and the warm glow of the fireplace at the restaurant's center calm my nerves. Perhaps I'm reading too much into the invitation; perhaps some of the other *chercheurs* took turns at attendance before I even arrived.

"What did he want?" Geneviève asks before I even sit down in the chair they've saved for me. The coq au vin in front of me looks appealing, but I have no appetite.

"To ask me to accompany him to the Lyons conference."

My friends are uncharacteristically silent, and I realize that it is indeed significant to be singled out for a conference. Are they angry at not being chosen? Do they think I'm not worthy of the honor? Or has the jealousy endemic to science finally surfaced in this rare supportive environment? Attending the conference in Lyons isn't worth any negative impact on this tightly knit group or my place in it, of that I'm certain.

"Congratulations, Rosalind. Well done." Vittorio is the first to offer.

Geneviève reaches across the table to squeeze my hand. "You're a genius," she says, and a round of "well dones" makes its way around the table.

As I dig into my coq au vin, the group's usual animated exchange takes hold and spills over into much broader subjects than my accomplishment. I allow my mind to ride the exhilarating waves of their conversation—from the terrible assassination of Gandhi in India, to the possibility of America adopting the Marshall Plan to aid the European nations in their economic recovery, to the likelihood that Israel will be made into a state, to the prospects of Patrick Blackett winning the Nobel Prize in Physics for his investigation into cosmic rays. I've just about put aside any concerns over their reaction to Lyons when I hear Monsieur Mering's name.

"Do you think the rumors are true?" Gabriel, at the far end of the table, asks Alain quietly.

"Which ones?" Alain practically snorts.

Geneviève's voice becomes louder as she argues with Lucas over who should win the Nobel Prize, and I cannot hear Gabriel's answer. *Bloody hell*, I think to myself. *Why can't Geneviève and Lucas talk a little more quietly, just for once?* Other than the oft-repeated story of his wartime decision to hide his Jewish identity and his desertion of Paris to work in a more remote, and thereby safer, region of France, both of which are understandable, I have been privy to no gossip about Monsieur Mering. Nothing. But then again, when a conversation even touches upon him, I do my utmost to change the topic or engage in something else. I worry that my feelings, so long repressed, will rise to the surface unbidden.

I strain to hear Alain and Gabriel's exchange, but the Nobel Prize debate rages on. As we rise and begin the brisk trek back to the *labo*, even Gabriel and Alain get swept into the friendly dispute, and I am left wondering: what are these rumors floating around about Monsieur Mering?

CHAPTER NINE

May 10, 1948
Lyons, France

I STAND ON THE HIGHEST HILL IN LYONS AND STARE DOWN AT the confluence of the Rhône and Saône Rivers, just south of the historic center of the city. The rivers glisten gold and coral in the mounting light of dawn, a glorious shade emphasized by the terra-cotta roofs of the city's buildings. *How happy I am that I travelled to Lyons a day early*, I think. *Otherwise, I would have missed this stunning sight.*

I begin the walk down the cobblestone streets toward my hotel, passing six churches that, from the style and materials, appear to date from the Middle Ages and Renaissance eras. The deep and varied history of the city—from its roots as an ancient Roman colony to its Renaissance commercial heights to its seventeenth- and eighteenth-century silk manufacturing success—is evident everywhere. It is as if the city is trying to reach back to more illustrious times, past the stain and heartache of the Nazi occupation, to an era it could be proud of. I reach too, focusing on Lyons's more recent past as a hub for the French Resistance instead of the many Jewish people deported to camps from its city streets.

Two hours later, I am dressed in my usual uniform of a crisp white blouse, dark-blue skirt, and a double strand of pearls, no New Look styles here if I want to ensure I am taken seriously. I await Monsieur Mering on the steps of the building where the Congrès de la catalyse de Lyons will be held today and tomorrow. A sea of dark-haired, dark-suited men begins to rush up and around the step where I stand, but I do not see his familiar chestnut hair, combed carefully across his forehead to mask the thinning patch, or those twinkling green eyes, always crinkling at the corners with his readily offered smiles. *Would his presence alleviate or exacerbate my nerves*? I wonder, knowing full well that it isn't the conference itself that's making my stomach flutter.

Suddenly, I spot a well-known face in the crowd, but it isn't Monsieur Mering. Waving, I call out, "*Bonjour*, Monsieur Mathieu."

The wild-haired scientist quickens his pace. "Ah, Docteur Franklin! I was delighted when Jacques told me he'd chosen you for the conference. You are the rising star of his *labo* after all."

Relief and disappointment course through me simultaneously, but I work hard to maintain an even, professional veneer. "Well, I am delighted to have been chosen. I was actually waiting here for Monsieur Mering."

Monsieur Mathieu waves his hand dismissively. "He'll find us. Let's go in and secure seats before the good ones fill up. We'll save one for Jacques."

We file into the auditorium where the first speech of the day will be given. Chatter in French, English, Spanish, and Italian surrounds me, and I feel swept up in the excitement of the new developments and the scientists around me. Monsieur Mathieu and I settle into chairs in the second row with an excellent view of the podium, leaving one empty next to us near the aisle for Monsieur Mering.

A speaker tests the microphone, and the light dims. Monsieur Mering still hasn't arrived, and just as I assume he's found another seat, he slides into the chair next to me. We nod in greeting as the speaker begins.

As Dr. Paul Emmett lays out the parameters of his study, I find myself lulled by his sonorous voice and distracted by the proximity of Monsieur Mering's leg to mine. While we often stand near each other as we use the crystallography equipment or study films, somehow this feels different. Whether it's the darkness or my wishes, I do not know.

Even when slides flash on a screen and Dr. Emmett points to particular results, I find myself unable to concentrate. And then Monsieur Mering leans close to me. I feel the warmth of his breath on my neck as he whispers, "Isn't he talking about the same sort of studies you ran at BCURA?"

Suddenly, my focus returns and I narrow in on Dr. Emmett's speech. His project and presentation *do* relate directly to the studies I conducted and papers I published at BCURA.

At the next pause in the presentation, I clear my throat and raise my hand. "Dr. Emmett, may I comment?"

"Of course," he answers. Several other scientists have made remarks or posed inquiries over the past half hour; it seems quite normal discourse for the conference.

"I believe an interesting correlation can be made between your experiments and the investigations I conducted on coal and charcoal while serving as assistant research officer at the British Coal Utilisation Research Association," I say in French, the primary language of the conference.

"Would you mind sharing with us?" Dr. Emmett asks.

I stand and speak about the parallels that can be made between the two studies. The room is silent as I finish, and I worry that I've spoken too much or perhaps too authoritatively, as is my wont. But then I hear a voice from the back of the room. "Would you mind repeating that in English, Mademoiselle Franklin?"

An hour later, the lecture draws to a close. Messieurs Mathieu and Mering and I are joining the fifty or so other scientists leaving the room for the lift of a midmorning coffee when a hand claps Monsieur Mering on the back. "Jacques, it's been too long."

We pause as introductions are made with this Dr. Haisinski. "You raised some excellent points, Miss Franklin. In fact, I think you elevated his whole talk."

"*Merci.*"

Dr. Haisinski turns back to Monsieur Mering and says, "It seems you've chosen well in your protégé this year."

This year? Does Monsieur Mering choose a different favorite each year, almost like a rotation? I've been hoping that he made his selection based on a unique set of qualities—certainly professional and perhaps even personal. Have I been inaccurate in my read of this sunny, supportive man? It certainly wouldn't be the first time. How wrong I'd been in my assessment of Professor Norrish—thinking he'd be fine to work for when, in fact, the opposite was true—not to mention several schoolmates over the years.

"We are fortunate that Docteur Franklin chose our institution. Not only has she become unbelievably proficient in our techniques but her application of crystallography to carbon is nothing short of miraculous." As he says this, careful to use the formal 'Docteur,' Monsieur Mering's eyes linger on me, and an unfamiliar chill surges through me.

Monsieur Mathieu chimes in. "Her deep understanding of carbon—on a molecular level—could be revolutionary in its application." He smiles over at me, with an almost paternal pride on his face. "Our Docteur Franklin could change the world."

CHAPTER TEN

May 11, 1948
Lyons, France

"SHOULD WE SNEAK AWAY AND DINE AT ONE OF LYONS'S FAMOUS *bouchons*?" a voice whispers in my ear.

I turn away from my conversation with a group of scientists and look up to see Monsieur Mering. Or should I say Jacques, as he has insisted I call him since the conference began. Using his first name felt uncomfortable, even forbidden, at first, but once I realized that everyone at the conference referred to one another by their given names, except for that one formal instance by Jacques at the beginning, I understood that calling him Monsieur Mering would only single me out. Unfavorably.

"Leave the cocktail hour and skip the dinner, you mean?" I ask, confused. The conference culminates with drinks followed by a formal meal for all the scientists, a final opportunity to meet others in our field and discuss our projects. I've been looking forward to it, and anyway, I've never been one for spontaneity.

"Exactly. The food at the conference meal will be abominable, like last night," he says, and he does not exaggerate. The chicken was so tough I began to suspect it wasn't chicken at all, not uncommon in these days of rationing. "But I know two exquisite little *bouchons* that are somehow able to serve traditional Lyonnaise fare—sausages and roast pork—not to mention delicious local Beaujolais red wine."

I know access to a broader array of fresh ingredients is easier outside Paris, and he does make it sound delectable. Still, would it be appropriate? Not only skipping the formal meal but also dining alone? Monsieur Mathieu—Marcel, I mean—has already left for Paris, and it would be just us two.

"Oh, yes, well," I say, hesitating because, of course, Jacques is my boss, and I must follow his lead. But a latent part of me also wants to be alone with him. "Anyway, I don't eat pork. Even though I don't keep kosher, my grandfather would roll over in his grave if I ate it."

His eyes widen just a little, and he says, "My Jewish upbringing has never stopped me from sampling the Lyonnaise pork specialties, but I respect your wishes. Still..." He grins and asks, "Your dietary requirements don't require you to eat stewed cat for dinner, do they? Like last night?"

How can I do anything but laugh when faced with such a question? And how can I say anything but yes?

The candle at the table's center has burned down low, leaving the exposed wick and droplets of white wax on the table. Our plates are bare; Jacques wiped every last scrap of the scrumptious duck from *both* our plates with the last piece of baguette. And the second bottle of Beaujolais is almost empty.

We spent the entirety of dinner talking about the molecular world of carbon. Imagining ourselves in that realm, navigating that minute universe. Wondering if other crystalline materials looked and felt the same. It had been magical, the sort of conversation I constantly carry on in my own mind but never imagined I could have with another human being. Let alone a man as magnetic as Jacques.

As he signals the waiter for another bottle of Beaujolais, I say, "I'm not certain that's a good idea." I've grown used to wine with meals; it is the French way. But usually, I limit myself to a glass or two with my *chercheur* friends or Adrienne. Tonight, I have had many more glasses than two. Jacques is very persuasive.

"Another bottle of delicious Beaujolais is *always* a good idea."

I giggle, surprised at how natural the unfamiliar noise sounds in my throat.

While the waiter pours two glasses of the purplish-red wine, Jacques says, "So tell me about you. You are such a compelling mix of formidable intellect and innocence. You're an enigma, Rosalind."

"Me, an enigma?" This time, I do not giggle but guffaw. "I don't think anyone has ever called me that before. Although"—I take a sip—"my father has probably thought it over the years."

"In what way?" Jacques leans across the table, and his face is only inches from mine.

"My father always had a very specific idea about how his children should live their lives. We were raised to be well-educated, generous members of our extended Franklin family first, our

Jewish community second, and England third. Giving back was inculcated in us from our infancy really. All this was possible because, of course, we had a certain amount of family money." I wince, thinking how that must sound. "Not that we are rich. I don't mean that; we are comfortable. It's just that Papa harangued us constantly about the focus our lives should take given that certain needs had already been and would always be addressed."

"How does being a scientist fit into that?"

"Well, that's the conundrum, isn't it? Papa seems proud of my success at school and at work, but he doesn't exactly understand the life of a scientist. And that life certainly doesn't fit into his worldview, particularly since science—as you and I practice it anyway—is all-encompassing. He doesn't appreciate that it's the lens through which I view the world and that our discoveries are a way of giving back." I tear up, thinking about the divide between Papa and me. Almost immediately, I feel embarrassed about surrendering to such an emotional display. *The wine made me lower my guard,* I think. I wipe my eyes as discreetly as possible given that Jacques is inches away from me.

He reaches for my hand. "My family's expectations for me aren't quite the same as yours—Russian immigrants are more concerned with survival than giving back—but I understand how hard it can be. How others can misunderstand our lives as scientists."

As I allow his fingers to intertwine with mine, I wonder if this gesture is one of platonic comfort or more. And for the first time, I consider whether I've been wrong all these years: could I have a personal relationship *and* work as a scientist if it was with someone like Jacques? *Stop*, I tell myself. There's no reason to make such a wild leap of logic from a simple, tender touch, the kind any compassionate person would give another human being.

I slide my hand away and reach for my wineglass instead. "Science doesn't allow room for philanthropy or family of your own really. And these are Papa's two primary objections." This feels both too intimate for our professional roles and perfectly appropriate for this exact moment. I dare not meet his gaze. Instead, I glance down at the nicked, wooden table, allowing my index finger to trace a deep groove in the surface.

His fingers inch toward mine until they nearly touch my fingertips. In that space between them, I can visualize the nitrogen and oxygen atoms that loosely comprise air colliding as his hand progresses toward me. Do our hands technically touch if an atom ricochets off his finger and collides into mine?

"Do you know, Rosalind," he finally says, "that being a scientist doesn't mean you have to be alone?"

Even though my eyes haven't left the tabletop, I can feel him staring at me, almost as if he's willing me to glance up. Finally, I can resist no longer, and I look into his green eyes, more jade than emerald close proximity reveals, and I allow my hand to fold into his. *Has my hand ever been held so tenderly?* I wonder. Then, much to my surprise, he leans across the table and brushes his soft lips against mine.

CHAPTER ELEVEN

January 14, 1949
Paris, France

I adjust the microscope lens to peer more closely at the carbon sample. The section I've prepared must be spread at the exact angle I've projected or I will not get the calculation I need for the study. So intense is my concentration that when I hear a noise—a sliding sound—near me I allow it to register and then disregard it entirely. Only when I hear a loud clearing of the throat do I look up.

It is Jacques, and his hand is on a thick manila envelope, approximately the length and width of a piece of paper. The object is within reach, but he pushes it even closer to me. "Open it," he commands in a whisper. His words sound like a directive, unusually authoritative for him, but his tone contains only exhilaration.

"I'm nearly finished with this slide. Can it wait, Monsieur Mering?" I ask. Funny how strange his full name sounds to me now, after struggling to say Jacques for so many weeks last summer.

"No, it cannot." Again, this sounds like an order, but I can see the excitement on his face. Reading expressions has never been easy for me, and even though I've come to know Jacques unusually well, I'm still unsure how to interpret this exchange.

"*Bien*," I say, remove my gloves, and reach for the envelope. Opening a pair of scissors, I use the sharp inner blade to slice open the top of the envelope. I reach inside and find the latest copy of the *Acta Crystallographica*. Why would he interrupt my work to give me this? A good-natured barb forms on my lips, but then I notice the sidelong glances of the other *chercheurs* upon us, Vittorio among them, and I hesitate. Instead, I say, "Thank you, Monsieur. I'll read it straightaway."

"Turn to page forty-two," he insists with a smile.

The entire *labo* has paused; now, no one is even pretending to work. Flipping through the journal, I reach page forty-two, and I see it. There is my name—in the *Acta Crystallographica*. I can hardly believe it. I've published papers in respected science journals such as *Fuel* and *Transactions of the Faraday Society*, but the *Acta Crystallographica* isn't a typical journal. Although relatively new, it has quickly become one of the most esteemed scientific journals. Even though Jacques told me he would soon submit my paper for publication, and even though my experiments were good and my findings solid, it is a far leap from those factors to publication in the highly competitive *Acta Crystallographica*.

"You thought the paper was ready for submission?" Although he'd told me he wanted to submit it, he hadn't actually informed me that he'd done so.

"I knew it was, and so did the editors of the *Acta Crystallographica*." He is very pleased with himself, and if possible, his smile grows even broader. "And they understand that it will be the first in a series."

I want to jump with glee. I want to wrap my arms around him and kiss him hard on the lips. But I see that every *chercheur* eye is upon us, so I must fight against every instinct and simply nod at the man I've come to love. "Thank you for your support, Monsieur Mering."

"It is no less than you deserve." He beams at me, and then something occurs to me.

I glance down at the article and then up at him. "I am listed as the *only* author."

"That's because you are the only author."

"But you supervised. And it is traditional to include the supervisor's name alongside the author's."

"Not this time," he says with a delighted grin. His voice then dropping to a whisper again, he adds, "Look at the envelope." Only I can hear this, and he starts strolling back toward his office, stopping off at Alain's station to ask him a question.

Scanning the room, I receive several nods of approval and a cry of congratulations from Vittorio, but I know any actual celebration will happen over lunch. I wait until each *chercheur* returns to his or her project, and then I turn the envelope over. There, in Jacques's scrawl are the words "Champagne. Bistrot des Amis. 20 heures."

The champagne bubbles tickle my nose. "Enough," I protest half-heartedly as Jacques tries to fill my third glass of Taittinger to the top, marveling that this delicious 1942 champagne escaped the oversight of the Nazi *weinführer* Otto Klaebisch, whose job it was to prevent the soldiers from looting and reserve the best bottles for the senior Nazi officers. *How can Jacques afford this bottle?* I wonder; our positions are lofty but our salaries are anything but. "I won't be able to work tomorrow from the headache."

"I think your colleagues would understand."

I laugh. "You don't know your *chercheurs*. They might excuse me if I'd been out toasting the journal article with them, but if they knew I'd declined their offer in favor of a tête-à-tête with you? Well, I don't think the reception would be as pleasant."

"Why not? I know you are very private, some might even say prudish," he says with a smirk, to which I pretend to slap his arm. "But romantic encounters abound among the *chercheurs*. Flirtations and escapades, to be sure, but also several on-and-off couples and even one permanent relationship has resulted from time spent together in the *labo*. Why shouldn't we enjoy each other's company? Why should we skulk around?"

"I would never want the other *chercheurs* to think you were favoring me. What if they thought you were partnering with me on the *Acta Crystallographica* article and pushing it forward to publication because of feelings for me?"

"No one would think that, Rosalind. *Ma chère,* everyone recognizes your brilliance and your dedication. No other *chercheur* comes into the *labo* on the weekend except you."

"It isn't simply a matter of my intellect or my hard work. It's also a matter of how you allocate your time and resources among the *chercheurs*. They're not only my trusted colleagues, they're my friends."

"You must know by now I can support you as a brilliant

scientist *and* be attracted to you. The two things are not necessarily causal." He pauses. "Is that the only reason why you haven't wanted anyone to know about us?"

The way he says *us* could almost make me agree to anything. Like announcing our relationship to the world. Like following him into bed, as he's suggested before. Almost.

"It's complicated, Jacques. There's my family to consider. And there's my work as a scientist."

"Why are we talking about your family and science in the context of *us*? Those things have nothing to do with *us*." His finger traces the length of my exposed forearm, slowly and languorously, until I shiver. "They have nothing to do with right now."

There is that *us* again, in that low, irresistible French voice, as if *us* is an actual, tangible material that could be analyzed with a powerful microscope. The tone that makes me want to throw propriety and caution to the wind and kiss him right here at Bistrot des Amis, just like we did eight months ago at the *bouchon* in Lyons. But while these eight months have passed with stolen touches at the *labo* and secret dinners at out-of-the-way bistros and breathtaking kisses in alleyways, they've also elapsed with long, empty weekends without a word and the entire month of August spent with "family" in which I did not receive a single letter. What does Jacques mean when he says *us*?

I don't dare ask. It isn't only the presumptuousness of such a query. It's also that I don't know how *I* feel about the idea of us. How can I long for this man and yet still believe that science and commitment do not belong together?

His finger continues its sinuous progress up and down my arm. "Tonight, I will be alone in my flat. Please come home with me."

He's made suggestive remarks before but nothing this forward or specific. And nothing this peculiar. "Aren't you always alone in your flat?"

He looks over at me quizzically. "No, or I would have made many more invitations. Particularly since I know there isn't a shred of privacy at your room at the widow's flat, especially with Vittorio and his wife right across the hallway. Not that you've ever invited me..."

I am still confused. "Do you have a roommate?"

"What do you mean?" He slides his hand away from mine.

I suddenly feel sick. I have to ask the question, but I'm terrified of the answer. "Who is usually in your flat?"

"The flat is often empty." He is dissembling; even with my limited faculties for reading people, I can tell that.

"Who is there when you're *not* alone?"

"Oh, Rosalind, I thought you knew." He sounds remorseful. And ashamed.

"Who is there when you're *not* alone?" My voice is shaking. I need him to say the words.

"My wife."

CHAPTER TWELVE

June 24, 1949
Paris, France

My parents will arrive with Colin this evening, and I still haven't finished the computations necessary to conclude the experiment. The next stage in my analysis of the structure of carbon is nearly complete, except for the measurements of the diffuse X-rays from the last batch of samples. If I am to meet the schedule of studies and subsequent publications I worked out with Jacques several months ago—and release upward of five papers on the topic in the next year or two in not only *Acta Crystallographica* but also the *Journal de Chimie Physique*—then I have got to speed up. *Imagine the mark I can leave on science if I meet this goal*, I think. It is heady stuff.

Jacques—Monsieur Mering, I remind myself to think and say—passes me in the *labo* on the way back to his office with a small "*bonjour*," and without looking up, I return the acknowledgment. This cordial, businesslike sort of exchange has been our pattern since that night at Bistrot des Amis. I remember little of the evening's end; only flashes of memories remain. Shoving Jacques's hands off me as we left the restaurant. Stumbling alone down the streets to the widow's flat. Climbing up the stairs to my room, the steps practically swimming through the lens of my tears.

Vittorio tells me that I was hysterical, and I'd chalk that up to his usual Italian hyperbole, except that Denise agreed. "Rosalind, *ma petite chou*, we didn't know what to do with you," she said a few days later. "You entered the flat with tears streaming down your face, but you wouldn't speak to us. When we heard you sobbing in your room, we insisted you let us in, but you still wouldn't tell us what was wrong. By the next morning, you rose with the sun and got ready for work as if nothing had transpired. Then or since."

In a tense voice, Vittorio had added, "Although I can guess what happened." He never elaborated, and I never explained.

Although the subject has not been brought up since, I have noticed that Vittorio is constantly watching me in the *labo*. His entire body tenses if he sees Jacques anywhere near me, and the warm rapport the two men once shared is gone. For several weeks after our disastrous final date, Jacques would stop me in the empty hallway outside the *labo* and plead for me to reconsider. "Rosalind, you cannot live your life as a scientific problem to solve, dispassionately excising the parts that don't fit your theories and standards—you must allow yourself to feel and experience," he would say. But now we all pretend at normalcy, and I find that if I do not allow the softer emotions like love and regret to creep in, if I keep myself occupied, I can carry on in my pleasant life with my *chercheur* friends and my work. But constant vigilance has become a hallmark of my days.

I glance up at the *labo* clock, catching Vittorio's eye as I do. "Less than three hours to Operation Franklin," he calls out, using the military moniker we've bestowed on my parents' visit. I have coached him and Denise well in the Franklin family dynamics, and I'm grateful for their assistance. *What marvelous friends they are*, I think. *Almost like a chosen family.*

"There is no backing out," I call back, not minding if the other *chercheurs* hear *this* bit of gossip. Vittorio and his wife had offered their services as a shield against the onslaught I expected from Papa.

"We will flank you throughout the meal, not to worry," he promises, and while he says this in jest, the presence of the Luzzati cavalry tonight will be a huge relief. Because Colin certainly did not need my parents to escort him to Paris so that he could then travel with me on holiday, I suspect their presence here is a battle in the making. Although I'm not entirely certain what fight I'll be facing.

Just as I settle back into my work, unfamiliar voices echo in the hallway leading to the *labo*. Along with every other *chercheur*, I glance toward the entryway and see a man and a woman walking with purpose toward Jacques, who greets them with an outstretched hand of welcome. Who are these people? I can tell from their attire—a charcoal suit for him and a straight-skirted dress for her—that they're not French, but they don't appear to be English either The *labo* doesn't often receive visitors about whom we haven't been informed in advance, and even those are usually governmental sorts.

I return to my computations, or pretend to at least, but keep an eye on the strangers in my peripheral vision. Jacques leads them around the room, introducing them to *chercheurs* as he does. Both the man and the woman engage in animated exchanges with my *labo* friends, and I wonder if they are considering positions here.

"Docteur Franklin?" Jacques asks when he finally rounds the room to me, uncharacteristically using my formal title. As usual, my heart flutters at the proximity of him and the sound of my name on his lips. I feel so different in his presence that I wonder if it's possible that the very molecules surrounding us alter with these variables. *Silly*, I think, *to even speculate that emotion might affect the laws of chemistry and physics.*

"*Oui*, Docteur Mering?" I ask, turning to him as if I've just become aware of his presence and that of the newcomers. It might be my best bit of playacting, something with which I usually struggle. But I've had to hone these skills over the past six months in the *labo* with Jacques, and I've been given plenty of opportunities to practice. How challenging it's been to simultaneously be attracted to him and yet know I must resist him.

"I'd like to introduce you to David and Anne Sayre. Monsieur Sayre is an American physicist who's touring our facilities as well as some other European laboratories that undertake work in X-ray crystallography as he makes his way to Oxford, where he'll be completing his course of study with Dorothy Hodgkin," Jacques says in his heavily accented English.

"It's a pleasure to meet you both," I say while shaking their hands. "I'm happy to answer any questions you might have about our *labo*. I came here to learn crystallography myself and—"

Jacques interrupts, saying, "Docteur Franklin is too modest. She came here to be a student of crystallography and, in short order, became quite the expert. She's publishing a course of papers in *Acta Crystallographica* on her work," he says, his eyes lingering on mine.

I remind myself to stay unmoved in the face of Jacques's praise, although I give him a polite nod of thanks. Even though I see his words for what they truly are—an effort to ingratiate himself with me again, to what end I do not know—I am privately susceptible to him. Over the past six months, he's made several similar attempts in the *labo*, but the watchful eye of Vittorio has always served as a deterrent to Jacques and a reminder to me.

David Sayre's eyes widen at the mention of the prestigious *Acta Crystallographica,* but I do not want to fall prey to Jacques's entreaties. I change the focus of the conversation back to the Sayres. "Monsieur Mering is too kind. As I said, I'd be delighted to answer any questions you have—"

This time, Anne Sayre interjects, but with a wide smile, "What a relief it is to speak in English. We've been trotting out our college French, but it's been a challenge."

I laugh a little and ask, "Are you a scientist as well, Mrs. Sayre?"

She answers, "No, I'm not, and please call me Anne. I don't profess to have any formal training. Although David always claims that with my years spent with scientists and at scientific institutions, I should be awarded an honorary degree."

We all chuckle, and Mr. Sayre says, "Anne is a talented and successful writer." He gazes over at his wife, and his pride is evident.

"What sort of writing do you do?" I ask.

"Short stories primarily," she says. "And I'm to be an editor at the Oxford University Press once we get settled there."

"How fascinating," I say, meaning the compliment. I've long been curious by the endeavor of creative writing; it seems an almost magical act of creation, although, of course, I know magic couldn't possibly exist. "I'd love to hear more about your writing."

We begin to chat about her themes, but then Jacques blurts out, "Perhaps Docteur Franklin and I could take you dinner tonight?" He doesn't look at me but keeps his eyes fixed on the Sayres. Still I know this is a sly action on his part to connect with me outside the *labo*, an attempt on his part to woo me after I'd made perfectly clear that I wanted him to stop. He may be my superior, but I find his statement to be very presumptuous; he has no right to speak for my time apart from the office.

Jacques's overture is unfortunate, because I like Anne Sayre and I would otherwise enjoy going to dinner with her and her husband. Her forthright manner and her intriguing work draw me to her, and I could imagine a friendship with this woman. But I cannot acquiesce to Jacques's machinations, and anyway, my family has provided me with an excuse tonight.

"My apologies. I would so like to join you all for dinner, but my family will be arriving this evening from London, so I must excuse myself," I say, then turn to Anne. "But if you and your husband need any help navigating Paris during your stay, I'd be delighted to be your guide."

CHAPTER THIRTEEN

June 24, 1949
Paris, France

"Where *do* the French get their supplies?" Mama asks, dabbing the edges of her mouth with the cloth napkin. "The rationing in England makes it nearly impossible to get the basics like eggs, milk, or butter. But here, I can taste the fresh cream and cheese in that *gratin dauphinois* and in this exquisite tarte tatin."

"The French are wizards at whipping up a dish with limited ingredients," Denise offers.

"Yes, Mama. The widow's maid, Albertine, has been giving Denise and me cooking lessons, and it's astonishing what she's able to create with three items," I add.

My mother nods appreciably. "I never thought I'd see the day when *you* would be interested in cooking, Rosalind."

I chuckle, trying to ignore the criticism implicit in her words. That I should've had an inclination toward the domestic sphere long ago. That the life I've chosen is a disappointment because it's different from hers and all the Franklin and Waley women who came before her. "It's not so different from science actually."

Vittorio chimes in; he can see where this conversation is heading, and he wants to intercede on my behalf. "Speaking of science, you should see Rosalind at work, Mr. and Mrs. Franklin. It is nothing short of inspirational." It is the first time that the subject of my work has been broached at the table, and I watch Colin shrink down into his chair. Undoubtedly, he's heard Papa engage in many a diatribe about my voluntary exile in Paris, my rebellion as a scientist.

"So we hear," Papa says, with firmness mounting in his voice. "But there is more to life than science. There is family."

Vittorio will not be deterred by Papa's minimization of my talents, even when a certain amount of pride does shine through his eyes at my success. And Vittorio somehow maintains his sense of humor. "No one understands the importance of family more than me—I'm Italian after all." He offers my parents his infectious, wide smile. The grin slowly fades as he imparts his message. "But of course, the scientific gifts that Rosalind has to offer the world can impact the *entire* human family. Not one family alone."

My parents are silent as they sip at their espressos and pick at their tartes tatin, and I can see Vittorio is perplexed. He isn't used to people being unmoved by his frank charm, so he tries again. "Rosalind is too modest to brag on her own behalf, so will you allow me leeway to share a little of her successes?"

My mother inclines her head in Vittorio's direction, a sort of half nod of assent. But my father doesn't move. Instead, he continues to glower.

"You know, of course, that she recently published a paper in *Acta Crystallographica*, the most prestigious journal in our field. But she probably hasn't told you that it will be the first of *five* such papers, and once her findings are released, the world will have a completely new method for ascertaining the molecular structure of materials of all sorts, not just carbon. In effect, she will be offering scientists the keys to uncovering the very stuff of almost any material. It is the ultimate philanthropy."

Glancing over at Papa, Mama says, "How beautifully put, Mr. Luzzati. And of course, we are very proud of Rosalind."

But her expression hasn't softened, and I can see that these are the words of the consummate hostess and social creature. They are not heartfelt. Papa says nothing; his face remains glacial.

I add, "Achieving this goal would allow me to leave a significant mark on science, one that transcends mankind's understanding of the smallest building blocks of inorganic materials, and maybe one day even organic matter. The living and nonliving alike."

Without replying, Papa stands up abruptly. I assume he will excuse himself to *les toilettes*, as Denise and Colin have not yet finished their desserts. Instead, he says, "Shall we walk to the hotel?"

I shoot an apologetic glance to Vittorio and Denise as Papa places a pile of francs on the table, ignoring Vittorio's protests that he would like to contribute toward the meal. As Papa heads out the front door of Café Louise, we get up quickly and follow in his wake. Once my friends take their leave at the entrance to the hotel, Papa suggests to Mama and Colin that they retire to the room. I brace myself for the conversation to come, knowing that the Luzzatis' efforts to bring peace via Operation Franklin have failed.

"Rosalind." His expression and tone are gentler than I expected. "Please understand that we have been pleased with the success you've had as a scientist here in Paris. Since you declared your profession at the age of twelve, I expected nothing less given your gifts and your determination."

"Thank you, Papa." This is the closest he has ever come to approval of my professional choices; science was his passion at university before duty pulled him toward the family business. And apparently, my great-grandfather Jacob had been so brilliant at mathematics and science, he'd gone to University College on a scholarship at the age of thirteen, which has always left me curious about the origins of my own passion. But I know it is a mere preface to less pleasant statements to follow, the calm before the storm.

"But surely you can secure meaningful scientific work in London. You've been in Paris for three years. It's time to come home. Our people have been decimated by the war, and we must band together even more closely now."

With his reference to the attempted annihilation of the Jewish people by the Nazis, Papa uses his most serious weapon. Oh, how he loathes me staying in France. But I cannot allow guilt to sway me, just as I have not permitted my disappointment in Jacques—or my heartbreak—to displace me from this otherwise idyllic scientific position.

I inhale deeply before speaking. Papa has taught me to stand by my beliefs; more than anyone, he's instructed me in the art of debate and argumentation through regular practice. Even still, a familiar dread settles upon me whenever I take a position that will dishearten him; the last, most significant time was my refusal to serve in the Women's Land Army during the war, instead insisting on continuing my Cambridge education and performing scientific work that would help in the war effort. And what I'm about to tell him will certainly disappoint him, perhaps even more than that decision.

"Papa, I am not sure I can replicate the sort of working environment I have here in London. I am permitted to investigate whatever topics interest me, to their natural conclusion. Support for the pursuit of pure science is rare, as is the encouragement of women as scientists, which I have in spades here in Paris."

"What are you saying, Rosalind?"

"Papa, I'm saying something that I know is hard for you to hear and even hard for me to say, given how much I love our family."

"What is it?" His eyes are steely, and his stance is closed off. I'd be put off by his appearance, except that I know it's his way of bracing himself. Papa is one of the few people I've learned to read.

"I'm not certain I want to return to England. Ever."

CHAPTER FOURTEEN

July 1, 1949
Calvi, Corsica

"Come on!" I yell to *la bande de Solange,* who lag far behind me. *How poky they are*, I think, *and tired*. Even pre-dawn espresso, brewed over the campfire in the roofless section of the partially bombed-out pension, couldn't rouse them to alertness or dampen their complaints this morning. I ignore their grumbling; I know they will thank me when we reach the summit.

Twenty minutes later, we near the peak of the highest hill in Calvi, where the chapel of Notre-Dame de la Serra rises before a vivid sunrise. We have an almost three-hundred-and-sixty-degree view of the area, a stunning region on the northwest coast of the island of Corsica. From my exploration yesterday morning at dawn—long before anyone else had arisen—I know the path becomes a trifle rocky and uneven ahead, so I turn to inform the others. I nearly bump into Colin, who is the only one who can keep my pace. Childhood summers with Papa spent on difficult backpacking holidays in France and England prepared him well for this relatively short trek. I call back climbing instructions to the rest of the band straggling behind me—Alain, Gabriel, and Michel, followed by the two female *chercheurs* who arrived over the past six months, Rachel and Agnes. Jacques, the last to retire and the hardest to waken, trails at the back.

I'd been annoyed, even angry, when I learned that Jacques was coming. He'd been invited as a courtesy, of course, because the group consists entirely of *chercheurs*, apart from Colin. No one thought he'd accept; he had never attended our holidays or weekend jaunts in the past. What made him join us this time? I certainly don't think any real desire to reconnect with me romantically fuels his presence here, no matter his canny efforts over the past few months to see me outside the *labo*, most recently with his proposed dinner for the Sayres. I've made my intentions clear, and perhaps, they've finally been accepted. And he's certainly made no overtures on this trip.

I station myself to assist anyone who needs a boost over the rocky outcropping at the peak. One by one, the *chercheurs*—more at home in a lab coat under the fluorescent lights of the *labo* than in shorts and hiking boots under the unrelenting Corsican sun—hoist themselves over the final hurdle to the crest.

After Colin, Alain, and Gabriel comes a red-faced, sweating Michel. "Rosalind, you—" he says between pants, "you are relentless. This is punishment, not holiday—" He pauses to catch his breath again as I help him over the final hurdle. "Especially at this hour."

I laugh, knowing that Michel's fussy exterior hides an amiable core. Ever since that day he agreed to keep my secret about the radiation readings, there's been a stronger bond between us; each of us feel more comfortable and authentic in the other's presence. I am certainly not the only one to discard my dosimeter results, though I've seen several other *chercheurs* toss them in the garbage from time to time. Not that anyone discusses this, of course. "You will thank me when you stand at the top of the hill and see Calvi unfold before you, with the golden rays of the sun around you."

When Calvi was first suggested as the destination for our summer holiday, I wrinkled my nose. All I knew of Corsica was that it was Napoleon's birthplace. I hadn't expected its white sandy beaches, ringed by azure waters, to enchant so thoroughly, or its historic center, towered over by the infamous citadel, to beguile. Oddly, I find that Calvi's ancient walls, riddled with bullet holes from Mussolini's men and countless early skirmishes, to be comforting; they telegraph the message that mankind will prevail against the worst of our kind, as we have before.

Pulling Agnes and Rachel over the top, I hear Michel call out to me, "Rosalind, I do thank you! It is every bit as beautiful as you said!"

Alain chimes in, "Yes, Rosalind, it is worth you waking us before dawn!"

The sound of chuckling floats down to me as I stretch out my hand to assist the final climber—Jacques. We lock hands and eyes, and I realize it's the first time we've been alone outside the *labo* since that night at Bistrot des Amis, even though our colleagues are within earshot. I freeze for a moment and then help pull him over this final peak on the trail.

Before he returns to our colleagues, he pauses and says quietly, "I've wanted a moment alone with you for months, Rosalind, but you always slip out of my grasp. I have something I want to say to you."

He is winded and stops to catch his breath, and in that moment, my stomach clenches. What will he say? What do I want him to say? The impossibility of our situation has meant that I don't allow myself to imagine.

Finally, he speaks. "I'll never forgive myself for our misunderstanding, Rosalind, and I understand if you never accept my apologies. But I will be forever grateful for the honor of knowing you a little more intimately than most and experiencing the brilliance of your mind. No matter what happens."

I step out of the cerulean Mediterranean and face the last remnant of the day's sun, allowing its rays to dry my skin. The ten days spent in Calvi have passed in an exhilarating blur of hiking and swimming and laughter and glistening sun. My exchange with Jacques, however brief, has given me a sense of peace that I hope extends past this holiday, even though I may have misunderstood his earlier efforts to meet with me outside the *labo*. Perhaps, with this sort of understanding and respect, I really could stay in Paris for the long term, even at the Laboratoire Central des Services Chimiques, where I feel so productive, so supported in work and friendship.

"Rosalind, come over to the fire!" Alain calls to me just as a gust of wind blows in from the sea over my still-damp skin. Goose bumps form on my arms, legs, and exposed belly—I've worn my first bikini on this trip—and I race to pull my shorts and shirt on over the wet bathing suit.

Pulling my towel around me, I sling my beach bag over my right shoulder and walk toward the roaring bonfire my friends have built on the beach. I lay my towel down next to Colin and Alain and accept the bottle of wine that is being passed around. The burgundy rushes through me, warming me almost instantly, and I pass it over to Gabriel, who's settled on the other side of me. Michel arrives with a fresh catch from a local fisherman working the lines just down the beach, and as he prepares to grill them over the fire, I recline on my towel. I watch the sunset while enjoying an arcane scientific debate among the *chercheurs,* my band.

The sun begins its precipitous descent, and sooner than I'd imagined possible, it is dark on the beach. We decide not to return to the pension for dinner. While the Hôtel di Fango, owned by a friend of Adrienne's and still digging itself out from the ruinous state in which the Germans and Italians left it after the war, has served its purpose, a cozy nook for a delicious meal it is not. Instead, Michel volunteers to secure more fish, Alain agrees to purchase several bottles of wine, and Colin and I offer to visit the *boulangerie* and *fromagerie* we passed earlier today for bread, cheese, and fruit. If the stores are still open, that is.

When we return with arms full of baguettes and a bag of grapes and fragrant cheeses, the group seems to have diminished considerably—only four of our eight remain. Although Michel seems to have done his duty by delivering a basket of fresh fish, I spot his silhouette alongside that of Agnes, strolling down the beach. This accounts for six of us—Agnes, Michel, Colin, Gabriel, Alain, and me—but not everyone.

"Where are Jacques and Rachel?" I ask.

Alain snorts with laughter, and Gabriel practically spits

out the wine he's just swigged. "Where do you think they are?" Gabriel asks.

I shrug. Had Colin and I passed them on the street, unawares? I glance over at my brother, who looks as mystified as I feel.

"They went back to the pension," Alain offers. "To enjoy their hotel room in our absence, I imagine."

"*Their* hotel room?" I am confused; I thought that Jacques and Alain were sharing a room. Have Rachel and Jacques struck up an affair on this very trip? Is that why Jacques felt the need to offer an admiring olive branch? To soften any anger or hurt I might feel?

Gabriel tries to explain. "Where have you been, Rosalind? Jacques and Rachel have been a couple since the first week she began working at the *labo*."

Alain says with a laugh, "He doesn't wait long, does he? How could you not notice, Rosalind?"

I feel sick at the idea, but realize—from their open manner—that they have no idea about *my* former relationship with Jacques. I say a silent thanks to a God in whom I don't believe.

As Gabriel and Alain chuckle, Gabriel says to Colin, "That's our Rosalind. Brilliant in the ways of the atom but oblivious in the ways of the world."

I do the calculations. Rachel started her job as *chercheur* just after the New Year. My last night with Jacques was the week *after* that.

I'm such a fool.

PART TWO

CHAPTER FIFTEEN

January 8, 1951
London, England

How I wish the Strand was more like the avenues bordering *the Seine,* I think as I make my way down the busy street facing my new laboratory at King's College. The din of honking vehicles and screeching trains is so loud I nearly cover my ears. I pause, thinking that I could see the Thames if I approached my new buildings from the rear, as they border the river to the north. But then I'd have to pick my way around the sixty-foot crater in the King's College quadrangle formed when a bomb was dropped on it during the war. Piles of rubble still scar the Thames Embankment and I'd have to walk around construction equipment working on the new Department of Physics, of which the Biophysics Research Unit was a part. *No*, I decide. It will only remind me of how London pales in comparison to Paris, how empty it can be without my fellow chercheurs, Vittorio, Adrienne, and in some ways, Jacques. I only hope that my new work does not pale or seem empty as well.

Am I right to take this position at King's as the Turner and Newall Fellow? To return to London? This is the question I've asked over and over to my younger brother Colin, my cousin Ursula, and my trusted Parisian friends since I learned about Jacques and Rachel and the idea of staying at the *labo* became impossible. A life without Jacques I could withstand; a solitary existence is what I'd always imagine for myself anyway. A life watching Jacques with someone else—day in and day out—I could not.

In my vulnerability over discovering the affair, I'd succumbed to the twin pressures of the compulsion to flee and my parents' constant insistence that I return home. And when an opportunity *finally* arose at King's College for a fellowship utilizing my expertise in X-ray crystallography—jobs were aplenty for everyone but me, I felt—it seemed a predetermined decision. But now, facing the reality of a makeshift laboratory on the Strand instead of a *labo* overlooking the Seine, I worry that I've made the wrong choice.

Leaving the Strand behind, I pass under the archway through the King's College quad to my new laboratory. I suppose the building's materials—white Portland and Yorkshire stone paired with Scottish granite streaked dark gray—are lovely in their way. *Would they be as attractive under the scrutiny of my crystallography equipment?* I wonder. Broken down into their component crystalline parts, would they lose the cohesive beauty they present in the wan light of this winter morning?

Scanning the quad, I spot the doorway for the temporary Biophysics Research Unit. I'd been confused by its location when I visited for my interview—it occupies a hodgepodge of rooms—but I'd learned that the department, which had previously been housed in a basement under the quad, was completely destroyed by the same German bomb that had left the enormous crater. The only saving grace was that the scientists had already moved out to make way for the Auxiliary Fire Service that inhabited the quad in the war, and no one was harmed.

I push open the door. While not Oxford or Cambridge—which weren't exactly knocking down my door, in any event—King's College has a well-established reputation in the sciences, and it is singular in its creation of the first interdisciplinary biophysics laboratory in England, an important step as scientists have begun to acknowledge the importance of tackling queries across disciplines. As I walk into the reception area, I try to ignore the many clerics I passed en route and forget about the other facet of its reputation—its fierce Anglicanism, which rose up in direct response to the decision by its more tolerant collegiate neighbor, University College London, where my great-grandfather had attended school, to admit not only Roman Catholics but Jews. This is the reason Papa blanched when I told him about my new position, despite his excitement over my return to London. I had my own reservations about the Anglican background of King's College: the very maleness of its institution.

Before I can even introduce myself to the receptionist, the head of the unit, Professor John Turton Randall, marches into the room. He is immaculately turned out in crisp white shirt, pressed suit, bow tie, and a sweet white flower in his buttonhole. This short, debonair, angular man—all jutting elbows and sharp cheekbones—peers at me through his circular glasses and calls out jovially, "Miss Franklin!"

"Professor Randall," I say. "Nice to see you again." We shake hands, and I hope my words sound more bullish than I feel.

"We've been anxiously awaiting your arrival," he replies, still the hint of a northern accent in his speech, a surprise after his years moving from different universities across England, including a stint in Scotland. He offers a smile, then begins marching again, this time out of the room. "Come and take a gander at your new digs! We've got it kitted out with that laundry list of gear you ordered!" Randall is as rumored—brisk, brilliant, and charismatic, a quality he needs in droves as he assembles the funds for this new venture.

I follow in his wake, a little in awe of this energetic war hero. He and fellow scientist H. A. H. Boot created the cavity magnetron during the war, and by use of an electromagnetic beam, this instrument helped our country immeasurably by helping the military find German submarines and locate bombs at night. To my mind, however, his most heroic act is populating his staff with women—in male-clubby England of all places and in male-centered King's College at that. Of his thirty-one biophysics professionals alone, he's hired eight women, a remarkable act for a male physicist and one of the reasons I decided to work for him.

We continue through the warren of hallways and offices until we reach a laboratory. Professor Randall gestures around the space, which is fairly large but feels cramped because of the low ceiling. "This will be yours. And you'll note that the instruments you requested are here, with the exception of your specially constructed camera within a vacuum chamber." He tuts, then adds, "Ingenious move that. Keeping the sample outside the vacuum and the camera within, to control the temperature."

"And the humidity. That's sometimes more important than the temperature."

He gives me a quick, satisfied nod. "Right. Excellent idea. You know your stuff."

"Presumably, that's why you hired me," I blurt out without my usual pause, and he gives me a brief, confused stare. In the Paris *labo*, my fellow *chercheurs* would've laughed at the sharp retort, recognizing it as part of my well-meaning but sometimes awkward banter. Here, however, I may have overstepped, and I will have to tread more cautiously in the more exacting, subdued English world. It seems that I have become a Parisian-sized scientist trying to fit back into an English-sized hole, and I only hope the effort doesn't make me too small.

Fortunately, the busy Professor Randall moves past the remark, perambulating around the room and pointing out the various items he procured on my behalf. His motions are quick and disjointed, almost like a bird, and he seems desirous of moving on to his next task. "Come, come. Don't want you to think this an ambush, but I've assembled a little welcome group. For once, nearly everyone is in the office and available, so we'll have tea in your honor to talk a bit about the unit and your mission."

Once again, I follow him down a corridor until we reach a rather large office where three people are seated in a half circle of chairs facing a wide mahogany desk. From the framed diplomas, certificates, and awards on the wall behind the desk, I see this is Randall's room. One seat—the closest to the door—is empty, and Professor Randall signals that I should take it. How carefully orchestrated is this meeting, with nothing at all like the casual warmth of the *labo*. For what have I sacrificed that rare camaraderie?

As I settle into my chair, my new superior begins the

introductions. "Miss Franklin," he says, "welcome to the Biophysics Research Unit, the first of its kind, and as you know, it is this interdisciplinary approach that holds the future of science. Or so I believe, and I've managed to convince the Medical Research Council so that they'll fund us." Everyone chuckles at Randall's humorous little boast so readily I imagine they've heard this before, and I see that the uncertainty of financing will be an undercurrent of my days here. I notice, of course, that he calls me "Miss" instead of "Doctor" as they had in formal situations in France, but I say nothing.

"Each of the scientists here is handed his or her own specific charge, one I believe will yield critical discoveries. And your mission is the most important of them all." He claps his hands, and the sound is so loud and startling that I jump. "Let's meet the talented people who'll be helping you during your Turner and Newall Fellowship." He gestures to the round fellow sitting next to me, with fair hair and eyebrows so light they seem invisible, and booms, "Please meet your assistant, Mr. Raymond Gosling. This bright young doctoral student will be your right-hand man."

The amiable-looking young man smiles and says, "Pleasure, Miss Franklin. I've heard great things about you and your time in France, and I cannot wait to get started on—"

Randall interrupts him, pointing to the next person in the half circle. "Here we have Alec Stokes, gifted physicist and mathematician. He knows his way around the X-ray crystallography equipment, but he primarily serves as our go-to person for theoretical problems presented by the patterns on X-ray diffraction film. Feel free to consult him as your work requires."

The seemingly shy Mr. Stokes, who has kept his eyes firmly

fixed on the carpet under his feet until now, glances in my direction and nods toward me, but before he can speak, Professor Randall again interjects. "Last but certainly not least, this is Mrs. Louise Heller. She's a Syracuse graduate, here while her husband studies in London on a Fulbright Scholarship. She serves as an odd body around the labs, in case you have a need."

The pleasant-faced, chestnut-haired Mrs. Heller smiles and ekes out a "Happy to meet you, Miss Franklin" before Randall begins talking again. I am going to have to learn how to deal with his charming but domineering manner.

As he pours me a cup of tea, he says, "These folks will assist you—like a band of pioneers—as you use your X-ray crystallography expertise to help map *the* critical part of a living cell." He announces this rather dramatically and then sits back in his chair, beaming at each of us in turn. I feel as though he expects a round of applause.

"Pardon?" I ask, thinking I have misunderstood. Surely, he didn't just say that I am to study biological matter—living substances, not the nonliving crystals with which I'd become expert. I sip at the weak tea, a sickly concoction that makes me long for the bracing *café* we made over the Bunsen burners at the *labo*.

"Oh yes. I thought we went over this." He glances at me with a quizzical expression, and when I shake my head, he says, "You'll be using your talents on biological materials."

"Not crystalline substances?"

Ignoring my question, he says, "We were extremely fortunate to have received biological materials from Professor Rudolf Signer of Bern, Switzerland. These fibers of deoxyribose nucleic acid, which he placed in a specially prepared gel, have an incredibly concentrated molecular weight, which makes them excellent for study to see if they hold any secrets about genes. Gosling here has been working to create images with some success already, an endeavor that will be magnified by your experience and intellect." The ear-to-ear grin reappears. "Just think. With your skills peering into the microworlds of cells and this material, we might uncover the structure of DNA and win the great race."

Race? What is Randall on about? My head is still spinning from the news that I'll be studying some aspect of the cell. "DNA is deoxyribose nucleic acid, correct? That's what I'll be working with?"

"Yes, Signer's beautiful brew of DNA, to be exact. It's quite unique, very distinctive from any other DNA preparation we've come across."

While I loathe saying anything that would make me sound less than expert in my field, I need clarification desperately. Especially since Randall has just upended my expectations about my role. Of course, I am generally aware of the history and developments in the field of cell research, genes, and DNA—beginning with Gregor Mendel's first identification of heredity through his pea-flower research in the 1800s, to the intersection of that research with Charles Darwin's theory of evolution, to the more recent debate about where genes might be found, namely the actual physical location of genes within the cell—but there are many areas of investigation upon which I could focus, none of which I am intimately familiar with. Which of them has taken Randall's particular fancy?

I fashion a question that I hope gets me the answers I need without revealing my ignorance. "Pardon, but would you mind expanding a bit on this great race for genes? From your insider's vantage point, of course."

"Ah." Randall sits back in his chair, his hands effortlessly forming a triangle as he launches into what seems to be a well-prepared lecture. Perhaps his efforts to raise money for the department have provided many opportunities for this exact speech. "Yes, the great race to uncover the secrets of the gene, with its elusive questions about how humans pass their characteristics and instructions about life from one generation to another. The answer, of course, is one of the most central questions of science. This inquiry about how genetic data gets from one chromosome to another one has been bandied about for almost fifty years. It started, as I'm sure you know, with an understanding that the cell nucleus contains chromosomes, those structures holding genes that are made up of two sorts of substances: proteins and nucleic acid. Up until recently, scientists were certain that the more complicated proteins—which have twenty kinds of amino acids and perform all kinds of cellular functions—were the drivers in sharing information from the old chromosome to the new and therefore the location of the genes. But the chromosomes also contain nucleic acids, chemical chains of bases, which most scientists had previously dismissed as only binding agents for the proteins and too simple to pass genetic information compared to the more complex proteins. So when the American microbiologist Oswald Avery published a paper in 1944 proposing that DNA—not protein—carries the genetic messages, well, you can imagine the reaction of the scientific community." He pauses, shifting his gaze from the ceiling to our faces with a start. Had he gotten so lost in his little presentation that he'd forgotten he's talking to a room of scientists? That we were, in fact, part of the scientific community? "Pardon me. I don't mean to launch into a lecture."

Stokes, Gosling, and Heller glance over at me, gauging my reaction. From their faces, I surmise that they've heard this talk before but don't dare object. But how can I object when my new supervisor is clearly building to the heart of his speech? Even though I find his tone more than a little patronizing.

"Please continue, Professor." I hold my tongue and say what is expected of me.

"Avery's paper left scientists with more questions than answers. How can DNA store vast quantities of genetic information, and then how can it transmit and create more genetic information? Confusion and some resistance arose in the more traditional scientific community, but among those of us who have a broader view, excitement mounted. What an opportunity to grasp on to this discovery. We threw our hat into the three-ring circus forming to understand this substance with its life-carrying abilities, and we've been determined to unlock the architecture of DNA ever since with the thought that we will find the elusive genes there. Understanding the structure of DNA will unlock the puzzle of how DNA undertakes this formidable task—as we assume it does undertake this task—and will prove, once and for all, the exact location of our genetic material. Once we identify the location and structure, well then, won't that structure help us solve the questions around the nature and function of genes? And your job will be to discover this structure."

What on earth have I signed up for?

"This will be your task, Miss Franklin—not just to map the molecular structure of DNA with an eye toward discovering the location of genes with your brilliant skills as an X-ray crystallographer but to beat anyone else who enters the race. Together, we will be seekers in the secret of life itself." His smile overtakes his small face. "Welcome to the circus."

CHAPTER SIXTEEN

January 13, 1951
London, England

"YOUR NEW DIGS ARE TOPPING!" URSULA CRIES OUT, ALWAYS the one to use the latest slang. She meanders around the high-ceilinged four rooms—an airy bedroom, spacious kitchen, along with a generous living and dining room—which seem like a palace to me after so many years in a single room in the widow's flat. I've decorated the space carefully with the few elegant objects I collected in Paris—a painting of hillside trees gusting in the wind, framed photographs I've taken of my mountain climbing expeditions, a metallic vase from a bric-a-brac store that I filled with fragrant greenery—and I tell myself that the spareness is intentional, even sophisticated. I know if I'm wrong, Ursula will be blunt in her assessment.

But instead of commenting on the decor and furniture—a comfortable sofa and complementary armchair as well as a Victorian dining table and chairs—she asks, "How did you ever land such a place? Good flats are harder to come by than sugar these days."

My cheeks feel warm. Somehow Ursula always hits upon my sensitive areas, even though she doesn't intentionally seek them out. She'd never want to hurt me. I'm embarrassed about the way I secured this space.

"Well, initially I tracked down one that I overheard two people talk about in the autumn, while I was traveling with the Luzzatis in the Haute-Savoie. But when that turned out to be a dud, I was forced to rely on—"

Ursula calls out, "Let me guess! The family."

"Spot-on," I answer.

"Did Aunt Mamie work her magic?" she asks. As part of the London County Council, our aunt had some pull in these matters, and various Franklins have appealed to her in times of need.

"I'm ashamed to admit that she did," I answer. There is no sense in denying it. How else would I come by a flat this large with a lovely view of Thistle Grove at this desirable location, in Drayton Gardens in Chelsea near Fulham Road? While I feel conflicted about the way I secured this space, I adore the location and the flat itself.

"There's nothing to be ashamed of, Miss Rosalind. Everyone else is using all the means at their disposal to get flats, and you'd be caught out if you didn't do the same."

"I appreciate your attempts to make me feel better, Miss Ursula," I say with a twirl of my emerald-green New Look skirt, which Ursula alone among my English acquaintances appreciates, and she squeezes my arm. One of the delightful rewards of returning to England is the proximity to my dear cousin and friend, who can help heal the wound left by Jacques, I think. Periodic holidays together do not compare with the regular visits we will enjoy now. And I hope reconnecting with old school friends and cementing my friendship with the now Oxford-based Anne Sayre will help fill the gap left by my wondrous array of *labo* friends. "But I do hate to ask for favors."

Just then, the door shudders with my father's distinctive knock.

"Already?" Ursula asks. "I'd been hoping for a bit more time together."

"I did ask them to come at eight o'clock," I say with a glance at the brass clock on the living room mantle, which shows seven thirty. "But you know my parents—"

"Always ridiculously early." Ursula finishes my sentence for me, pastes a wide smile upon her face, and opens the door. "Aunt Muriel! Uncle Ellis! What a pleasure. We've been eagerly awaiting you."

"What on earth is this flavor, Rosalind?" Papa says, his upper lip curled in distaste.

I glance over at his fork, which holds the remains of a bite of *lapin à la cocotte*, or rabbit stew, a recipe I'd altered to remove any trace of pork. "I imagine it's the garlic."

"Garlic." He practically spews the word. "Why didn't you tell me you'd be cooking with garlic tonight?"

"Well, I did mention that I'd be making you one of my French specialties, and I think you know—from the many French holidays of my childhood—that the French are fond of garlic."

Mama tsks. Ever protective of Papa, she says, "Oh, Rosalind, you know your father can't abide garlic."

"Yes, I am your father, and I am not fond—"

Colin's wife, Charlotte, interjects, "Well, I think it's marvelous. With all the food rationing, every dish is mystery meat with two bland vegetables and no flavor at all. This is fantastically savory." She takes another bite of the rabbit from her plate and follows it up with a nibble of the artichoke dish I'd prepared as a side.

"I agree, Ros," Colin concurs, a more and more frequent occurrence these days. Since he's relaxed into marriage and a position at Routledge, the family publishing establishment, instead of the banking he loathed, he's become quite content to side with his slightly more outspoken wife.

Thank goodness we are a small group tonight, I think. My other married siblings couldn't make it, Jenifer had a school function, Ursula's new banker beau had a work commitment, and while I'd wanted to invite Aunt Alice for this first family meal I'm hosting at my new flat, Ursula advised against it. Papa and his socialist older sister aren't exactly on speaking terms at the moment. And that meant I could not invite Papa's other siblings. Now I see that a small dinner party was probably for the best, as I would not welcome a barrage of complaints over my methodically prepared *lapin à la cocotte.*

Ursula takes the reins, hoping to steer the conversation away from food and my father's disdain for my French fare. "I've been trying to get Rosalind to tell me about her new position at King's College, but preparing this feast distracted her."

"Yes, Rosalind," Mama says, although she really isn't terribly interested in the details of my work. She simply knows that it's polite to ask. "What can you tell us about this new job of yours?"

As I begin to explain, I realize that my father is the one actually paying attention. He's always been the only Franklin both intrigued by my work and able to comprehend it, even if he proclaims not to fully accept my path, a declaration I sometimes doubt. After all, there was a brief moment during his early adult years when he dabbled with the idea of becoming a scientist himself. Not that his youthful passion for science ever stops him from needling me about changing my course to undertake family philanthropy instead or to start thinking about a husband and family of my own, which only ever prompts me to think about Jacques. And upon his arrival in my apartment, he complained bitterly about its walking distance to any synagogue, even though he knows well that I don't believe in God. Only science.

"I'll be leading a team under Professor J. T. Randall. You might have heard of him. He and another scientist—a Dr. Boot—invented the magnetron, which was incredibly helpful detecting subs and bombers at night during the war."

"Is that what you'll be doing, Rosalind?" Mama asks, half-horrified. "Making weapons? I thought you were vehemently opposed to this buildup of weaponry happening in England, America, and Russia."

"I am, Mama," I say, surprised that she remembers that. "My work will have *nothing* to do with the military. I'll be taking all the X-ray crystallography skills I developed in France and applying them to biological material."

Papa's eyebrow is raised in that familiar quizzical and challenging manner. "It sounds as if you are switching fields—from physical chemistry to biology. Haven't you already sunk enough of yourself into physical chemistry to change focus now?" he says, sounding half-curious and half-skeptical. "To what end, Rosalind? Science won't give you a family, and it won't give you faith. These things are what matter, what last."

In my peripheral vision, I see Ursula comically rolling her eyes at this oft-repeated diatribe, and her humor softens my anger. Instead of going head-to-head with my father over science and family and faith for the millionth time, I decide to share a vignette with him. "To what end indeed, Papa. Have you ever heard of Schrödinger?" I ask.

When he shakes his head, I say, "Erwin Schrödinger. He's a physicist who won the Nobel Prize, but I want to tell you about a book he published called *What Is Life?* Schrödinger wrote that it was time for us to end this view of the sciences as separate, that we needed to understand that the sciences overlap—to view biological subjects through a physicist's lens, for example. After all, biological organisms are constructed from molecules and atoms and all sorts of material we can't see, aren't they? In understanding their structure, mightn't we better understand our biological subjects? Approached from that perspective, life as embodied by biological organisms like humans is physical matter undertaking some kind of activity—eating, drinking, breathing, *living* by the rules set forth in physics. And interestingly, life is also about passing on the genetic information somehow imprinted upon us as biological organisms. Look around the table here." I gesture to myself, Mama, Papa, Colin, and Ursula. "Somehow, Colin received the Franklin nose, Ursula got the Franklin eyes, and I received your tendency to argue and debate." Everyone laughs at this oft-repeated truth.

Papa's face softened when I was speaking, and while I can see that my words move him and speak to the youthful part of him that viewed science as a sacred quest, he won't relinquish his role as critique-wielding father figure. "Sounds very mystical and very French."

I ignore his comment and continue, finding myself more and more seduced by the science with which I've been tasked as I speak. "So to answer your question, Papa—'to what end' is my work? I'll be researching how life itself replicates in endless, observable permutations, how life continues rather than ends with the biological organism when it dies. Papa, the science I'll be conducting is the study of life itself."

CHAPTER SEVENTEEN

January 30, 1951
London, England

The weak sun is streaming through the windows when I return to my laboratory after mandatory safety training, providing a surprising amount of natural illumination. Still, my King's College work space is no *labo*, with its high ceilings and spacious, brightly lit work room, enough for twenty *chercheurs* to pursue their independent projects simultaneously with Jacques overseeing them all. *Stop*, I tell myself. If I am ever to embrace the calling I proclaimed to Papa and this new life in London at King's College, then I must stop comparing my promising new situation to my old impossible one. I cannot pursue a future that constantly comes up wanting; I must blaze a new path.

What could be more novel than the application of my knowledge and skills as a physical chemistry scientist to *the* quintessential biological material, I ask myself. What could be fresher than accepting Schrödinger's invitation? Even in my few short weeks at King's

College, I can understand why Randall wants to focus on this intoxicating research, no matter the manner in which he'd framed it. I only wish it wasn't a race; science performed at a rush—with the goal of outperforming others—isn't undertaken for the right reasons.

Pinning the dosimeter, doled out to me at the training, on my lab coat, I turn to Ray Gosling, my assistant, who's busy reviewing the sketch of a tilting microcamera I just drew. I'm hoping this approach will allow for unusual angles and consequently unprecedented images. "What do you think?"

He turns to me, agape. "I think it's bloody fabulous."

My eyes must have widened at his words, because he immediately exclaims, "Pardon!"

"Please don't apologize, Ray. I'm used to a lab full of swearing French scientists. They don't hold back in the presence of women," I say with a laugh that I hope assuages him. I have no desire to stand on ceremony with Ray; I want him to experience some of the collegiality I'd come to appreciate and receive it in return. And I don't want gender getting in the way of that.

"It's not because you're a woman," he says, blushing at the word. Funny how a scientist, also formally trained as a doctor, can be so squeamish about talking about basic biological differences. Myself among them.

"No?" I ask, chuckling.

"It's because you're so posh."

"What?" I am well and truly astonished. What on earth is Ray talking about? I've never said anything about my family or our background; while we were trained to be proud of our Jewish heritage and the Franklin family success, we were also taught to keep quiet about it.

"The way you talk, where you grew up. I mean, you even went to St. Paul's," he says. "You're practically an aristocrat. It just makes me more conscious of my language, that's all."

I'm not certain how to feel. In France, my social standing was blurred by my status as an outsider, so it's been a long time since I thought about the class differences ubiquitous in English life. But I *am* sure that I don't want those distinctions in my lab. I want free speaking, a comfortable exchange of ideas, and hard work.

For once in my life, a quip comes to me, one that might help defuse the tension and prevent this situation from occurring in the future.

"Well, I *bloody well* don't want you to feel that way," I say with a smile.

Ray appears surprised, then bursts into hysterical laughter. "God, it sounds hilarious coming from your mouth. I never thought I'd hear you say that word."

"And you may never again." I laugh along with him. "But I never want you to hold back based on codswallop like that. We're on the hunt for something far bigger than ourselves—far more important than silly class distinctions, true or imagined. Deal?"

"Deal," he says, with that infectious smile of his.

"So back to work, no holds barred?" I ask.

"No holds barred," he says with a nod.

"Before we talk about the microcamera design, let's back up a moment, shall we?"

"Of course."

"You've managed to get the best image of DNA yet, incomplete and hazy though it is, and I applaud you for that. It was exciting to see the hints of a crystalline structure in the DNA material." I gesture to the X-ray photograph he'd taken several months before, one he hadn't managed to reproduce. His X-ray crystallography skills are limited, having been self-taught, but I aim to teach him. "But in order to flesh out any real three-dimensionality—or any real structure, for that matter—we need more data. Loads more data. And that means many images—clearer ones—and then many, many calculations to see if we can derive a three-dimensional structure from the two-dimensional image."

"Exactly. I'm excited to learn from you." He nods eagerly, and I'm impressed with Ray's lack of ego. Many scientists are less concerned with making discoveries that benefit large swaths of the population than with protecting their reputations. "You're so knowledgeable about these techniques. It's impossible to think you just learned them yourself in the past few years."

"I look at it this way, Ray. Whatever problem I'm faced with, I will pick up any technique necessary to get me the answer. And since we can best get at the nature of DNA through crystallography, we will become proficient at that technique." I pause and give him a brief smile before returning to the task at hand. "To me, it seems that the barriers to gathering that data are twofold. First, we've got to collect many more angles of the DNA, which, I hope, my camera design will help with. Second, we've got to tackle this tricky problem of stabilizing the humidity in the camera to get clearer images. I've been noodling on a fix for that, but let's talk about that camera first. What do you think about the design I mapped out?" I pause, then add, "Be honest—as we just agreed."

Pointing to the sketch, he says, "The mechanism here would allow the camera to capture angles that were previously out of reach. Perspectives I couldn't get when I was working with the DNA before."

"Good. That's what I'd hoped. You've worked with these samples and this equipment firsthand. I haven't had the chance to do that yet, so I welcome your insights."

"King John keeping you too busy with his social agenda?" he asks with a smile. Always trying for a laugh, Ray has a host of nicknames for our leader—the "Old Man" or "King John." Not that he'd ever say them to Randall's face. Unless they were at the local pub and each had several pints.

"He does like to keep his people occupied and not necessarily with work," I admit. Since my arrival at King's College nearly three weeks ago, Randall has organized several drinks parties—which always seem to begin in the afternoon rather than the evening—a group outing to the Royal Albert Hall for a Sibelius concert, and near-daily lunches at the mixed King's College union, where both men and women may dine together. While lunchtime is not the vibrant Parisian affair I'd adored with my fellow *chercheurs* at Chez Solange, it is by no means the desultory brown bag meal of my time at BCURA and at Norrish's lab at Cambridge. For that, I am both surprised and grateful.

"You're lucky to have been spared the cricket so far," Ray adds, laughing. "That is a bridge you'll have to cross come springtime."

"I'll do my level best to sidestep the cricket." It's difficult not to laugh along with my good-natured assistant, and I enjoy him so much I already invited him and his lovely wife, Mary, over for a group dinner last weekend. "Seriously, though, would you make any adjustments to the design? Or shall I go ahead and submit it to the college workshops to build?"

"It's spot-on, Rosalind." His face is serious.

"Thank you, Ray." I nod. "With a lot of work and a little luck, we'll get Professor Randall his elusive Holy Grail yet."

"Holy Grail indeed," he echoes, his smile returning.

Just then, the door to the laboratory flies open. I nearly jump at the sound of the door slamming against the wall behind it. A tall, angular man with light-brown hair swept back from his forehead steps into the room. He isn't *un*handsome, but his demeanor and facial expressions are strangely off-putting.

"Hallooo. Did I hear mention of King Arthur and the knights of the round table?" he calls out jovially. Not waiting for us to answer, he says, "I know what role I shall play—I'll be King Arthur to your squire and maiden! After all, you've served as dutiful squire to me before, haven't you, Ray? And we cannot have our maidens unprotected, can we?" he asks, looking at me with a grin, as if he's done me an enormous favor.

Does this stranger actually expect me to smile back at that remark?

Ray jumps up and shakes the man's hand. "Good to see you back. Nice holiday, I hope?"

"The best." He turns his gaze on me, but I cannot see his eyes behind the glare of his thick glasses. "I am pleased to finally make your acquaintance, Miss Franklin. I've heard a lot about you."

While I've gotten accustomed to it when Professor Randall addresses me as "Miss" rather than "Doctor," for some reason, I dislike it when this man calls me "Miss." Who is this man? And what does he think he's doing storming into *my* lab, ordering about *my* assistant, and informing me he's about to take charge like King Arthur? Not to mention I am nobody's maiden.

"I'm afraid you have me at a disadvantage, sir," I say, doing my utmost to restrain my temper and instead use the etiquette instilled in me by Nannie Griffiths long ago.

He takes a step back and then pauses for a long moment. Then, after an unusually long deliberation, he says, "Strange, that." His eyebrows rise above the rims of his glasses and then knit in confusion. "Well, we will get it all sorted. I can't have the newest member of my team in the dark, can I?" Stretching out his hand in greeting, he says, "I'm Maurice Wilkins."

CHAPTER EIGHTEEN

February 8, 1951
London, England

"Am I interrupting you?" Ray asks as he steps into my small office. Having never had an office of my own, I've been delighting in organizing the space to my liking. The only area I cannot claim is the bookshelf alongside one wall, which contains shared scientific journals. While I've found myself flipping through the journals to peruse recent articles on the creation of drugs to battle leukemia, the discovery of an orbiting cloud of planets on the edge of the solar system by Dutch astronomer Jan Oort, and Dr. Jonas Salk's efforts to develop a polio vaccine, there's another reason why I like these publications; they provide a reason for my colleagues to access my office. I quite enjoy the impromptu discussions when members of the staff I've not yet met pop in for a journal, giving me the opportunity to meet several other women on Randall's staff, including Dr. Honor Fell, Dr. Marjorie M'Ewen, Dr. Jean Hanson, and laboratory photographer Freda Ticehurst.

"Never," I answer, pivoting away from the paper I was drafting for the *Proceedings of the Royal Society* on my Parisian work. Randall had insisted that while I was getting settled in and setting up my new laboratory, I write up the results of my prior research, with the goal of having at least one paper published in that esteemed journal. "It will cement your status as one of the scientific community's experts in the structure of carbons," he said. While I hate to have my attention diverted from the intriguing new work at hand, I know that to move forward, I need to lay the past to rest. *All facets of it*, I remind myself when an image of Jacques Mering comes to mind. Just when I think I've successfully banished him from my mind and heart, he surfaces.

"Now that the microcamera is underway at the workshop, I thought we could get started on the humidity problem," Ray says, pulling a chair closer to my desk.

"My thoughts exactly," I say, forcing my thoughts to the task at hand. "Especially since we've got the X-ray equipment cleaned and reassembled and we are nearly ready to go." Last week, Ray and I had put the X-ray gear together with the prototype Ehrenberg-Spear tube that allows for fine focus of the X-ray beam; once we fitted it with the new microcamera and readied the DNA sample, we'd be prepared to actually experiment.

"Let's talk it through, shall we? When we extracted the DNA strand, we affixed it to a small metal frame to better stretch it out for analysis."

I smile. "By metal frame, you mean the unbent paper clip, correct?" How amusing that a perfectly ordinary office supply had been ingeniously repurposed for such an important objective.

Ever ready with a smile, Ray returns my grin and says,

"Exactly. Once we had the sample elongated for study on that paper clip, we knew we had to keep it moist. But we kept running into problems."

"I have an idea for a solution, but I'm wondering if I could see your notes or records about the moisture problem. Yours and whoever else you were working with on this—you mentioned a 'we'?"

"Oh, I thought you knew. I worked on this with Wilkins."

"Maurice Wilkins?" The tall stranger who came barreling into my office a week ago after a prolonged skiing holiday is now ever present in the department offices. Randall finally introduced him as the assistant director of the biophysics unit—much to my embarrassment—and I learned that Wilkins had been educated in natural sciences and physics at Cambridge and then spent much of the war in America working on the Manhattan Project. He and Randall were chums from earlier university postings. Because of this, I'd decided to ignore Wilkins's overly familiar, presumptuous behavior and brash comment about being the "maiden" to his King Arthur. All part of my resolution to hold my tongue in this less tolerant English environment.

But Ray's statement that Wilkins worked on DNA is news. Randall never mentioned this when he held the welcoming tea for me in his office, never mind that Wilkins wasn't present. To the contrary, he made clear that DNA was my project alone, that he alone would supervise me, and that Ray and, to a lesser extent, Stokes and Heller would help me as needed.

"Yes," he says. "We need to get some of the humidity out of the camera to get the images we want, but I'm not sure how to do that while keeping the sample moist enough. We ran out of ideas. You have some?"

"I have a sense of what went wrong, although I'll need to confirm it with your notes. But my guess is that if you'd tried a salt solution and some drying agents, you might have had more sustained success."

"What do you mean?"

I pull out a blank piece of paper and rough out a diagram of the experiment, showing the specimen and the new microcamera in the tube. "We could try first taking out the moisture from both the sample and the camera with either a vacuum pump or a drying agent or both. Then we could carefully control the humidity within the camera and specimen by creating a series of salt solutions through which we could bubble hydrogen."

"Ingenious. It would allow us to dictate the moisture levels. How did you know how to solve for this when we haven't even started the experiments?"

"I used these techniques in Paris. Most scientists have several tricks for hydrating fibers at their disposal. I'm surprised Wilkins didn't try some of them. I would have thought these methods quite familiar to him. Or to someone here at King's."

As I say this, I become more disillusioned by Wilkins. Irritated too. A man with his level of experience *should* have been able to solve for the humidity issue. If he couldn't even manage that problem, he wouldn't have gotten very far with the bigger questions and issues at hand. Good thing Randall handed the project over to me.

As I begin to map out the sorts of salt solutions we could utilize—explaining that it will be a trial and error until we obtain the sort of image that will lend itself to true three-dimensionality—Wilkins pops his head in the room, as he has several times recently.

He hovers for a long moment but does not enter. I assume he's here for a journal from the bookshelf, so I wave my hand toward them, indicating his freedom to enter. Instead, he lingers in the doorway, listening.

"Sounds like you're talking about my famous picture of DNA. Need any help?" His arms are crossed, and a rather smug grin forms on his narrow lips—as if he's doing us a favor—as he mentions the only respectable image of DNA during his tenure in charge of the material. And even that one, Ray took.

His "famous" picture indeed. He couldn't get it right the first time except for that one, rather tepid image, and now he's here to proffer advice?

Thinking of Nannie Griffiths, I force a smile and say, "While I appreciate your offer, I think we have it in hand."

Wilkins recoils as if I've slapped him. Why should he have such a violent reaction to a colleague politely declining an offer of assistance? It wasn't as if I'd utterly rejected him. I wonder with whom I'm dealing.

An hour later, Ray and I are still planning our first experiment, and I notice his eyes keep drifting to his watch. "Shall we head to lunch?"

Bundled in our coats, we rejoin and walk the long corridor to Randall's office, expecting to see him gathering his troops for lunch as he does several days a week. I've come to particularly enjoy Freda Ticehurst, who runs the photographic lab, and hope she will be joining us. But the hallway outside Randall's office is uncharacteristically empty and quiet.

His secretary explains, "Professor Randall had a meeting at Birkbeck today. He brought Mrs. Heller and Mr. Stokes with him, but they'll return in time for afternoon tea." Tea is another of Randall's daily rituals for his staff.

Ray and I resolve to dine ourselves. As we leave the building, passing several of the black-robed clerics who are ubiquitous at King's, I bump directly into Wilkins, who is walking with a gaggle of five boisterous men. These particular fellows also work in the biophysics unit but almost as a separate team on their own project. From what Ray explained to me, they are former military men who took advantage of an intensive college course offered to ex-soldiers and accepted positions with Randall almost in the manner of a military posting.

The men greet Ray with several good-natured punches on the shoulder but say little to me other than a few wan "good days." The conversation centers on evening plans at a pub called Finch's, and I feel utterly out of sorts with this athletic crew. I'm relieved when we near the building that houses the dining rooms. As I step to the right toward the communal dining area that serves as the student union as well, I notice that the men drift left, toward the all-male dining room. It is the sort of division that assures women are left out of the casual conversation and rapport that fosters the sort of companionable, productive work environment I experienced in Paris.

Ray freezes in the middle. Wilkins glances over at me and, with a shrug, says, "Sorry, the gents and I had plans to dine together." There is none of the smug assistance and friendliness he offered earlier today.

I do not move, and neither does Wilkins. Clearly, he will not alter his plans to include me, and I cannot follow along with his. He is forcing Ray to choose between us. Is this punishment for my earlier lack of submissiveness? Is it retribution for failing to acquiesce to his "offer"?

Nodding to Ray, I say, "Go ahead and join the others. I should finish up that paper for Professor Randall anyway."

"Are you quite certain?" he asks quietly, visibly torn. I can only imagine how he must feel—pulled in one direction by his current superior who oversees his thesis and tugged in the other direction by his former boss and assistant head of the department. I don't envy Ray's position, and I don't want to make this moment harder for him than necessary.

"Of course." I force a smile on my lips, even though I want to scream. "I'll see you at tea."

With reluctance, he follows after Wilkins, who's already on the heels of his mates. And I am left alone.

CHAPTER NINETEEN

March 23 and 24, 1951
London, England

"DO YOU SEE THAT?" I ASK.

Ray and I are examining the images of two sets of DNA fibers: one that I'd hydrated and another that I'd placed over a drying agent. To my eyes, the moister DNA fiber is visibly longer and thinner than the dryer one, which is shorter and more crystalline. How could these two fibers be so very different? I study another set of images and make the same observation.

He stares from one image to the next. "I do. But I'm having trouble believing my eyes."

"I know," I say excitedly. "It's hard to fathom."

"Almost impossible."

"There are *two* forms of DNA." I clap my hands in awe.

"One wet and one dry." Ray's voice is an incredulous whisper. "Utterly distinct."

"This could be transformative."

"That's an understatement," Ray says with a burst of laughter. "Should we name them?"

I laugh, giddy at this breakthrough. "I suppose we should. How about Rosalind and Raymond?"

He roars. "There's a claim for posterity! And I do believe that's the second joke you've told me."

I beam at him. "I wish we *could* name the DNA forms after ourselves, but sadly, I think we must be more professional. Shall we go with the classic A form and B form?"

"A form and B form it is," he concurs, shaking his mane of fair hair. "When I think that we could only get blurry images of these fibers before your arrival—"

"I'm glad I could sharpen things up—"

Ray interjects, "Another understatement."

"You must come to my flat tomorrow night for a French meal I'm hosting for some friends. Let's celebrate."

I hear footsteps behind me, and someone asks, "What are you two celebrating?"

It is Wilkins, of course. His tone is suspicious. How long has he been standing there? He has sprung up on Ray and me so frequently by now that I feel him around us questioning and judging even when he's not actually present.

The table gleams with Mama's castoff china, Aunt Alice's unwanted silver, and a crystal vase full of snowdrops and crocuses. The scent of chicken, mushrooms, garlic, and wine wafts through the air as the *coq au vin* simmers in the kitchen. The clock nears seven, and the guests should be arriving any minute.

This is the exact moment I adore most about hosting, the anticipation of the evening unfolding around me. It is the same anticipation I feel when embarking on a new scientific endeavor.

The doorbell buzzes, and I open the door to find Freda, my favorite Biophysics Unit employee apart from Ray. She squeals to see me in my aquamarine New Look dress rather than my usual white blouse, dark skirt, and lab coat, and as I pour her a glass of burgundy, Ray arrives, his second time here. A few minutes later, Alec Stokes knocks on the door, followed by my friends Simon and Bocha Altmann from Argentina who were, respectively, a physics graduate student at King's and a biochemist at University College. I bring the shy Alec and the outsiders Simon and Bocha to the circle of King's College guests drinking in my parlor, and soon they are all chatting and laughing. By the time I add David and Anne Sayre, who are in town from Oxford for three nights, the group is merry and welcoming. The group doesn't have the ease, frankness, and warmth of my *chercheur* companions, but I've come to accept that will never be replicated.

By the time we sit down to dinner, a fine mood has settled upon us all. Freda and Ray exchange quips about Randall's departmental cricket game last spring, warning me about the season to come. Simon becomes animated sharing tips about which entrées to avoid at the coed union, and even Alec chimes in when we talk about the makeshift lab space and the plans for our new departmental wing, currently being built in the bomb crater. Anne and her husband share some amusing vignettes about being Americans at Oxford. Everyone compliments me on the meal.

Ray, a little wobbly on his feet, stands and says, "A toast to our hostess. We thank you for a gracious evening with some of the most delicious food any of us has had for some time."

A chorus of "hear, hear" sounds out, alongside a subtle chant of "no more meat and two veg," a not-so-subtle reference to the usual tasteless fare offered at restaurants in these ongoing days of rationing. I laugh alongside my guests, wondering how I can gather such an affable, lovely crew together here and yet manage to feel disconnected from the rest of the scientists at King's. Is it attributable to Wilkins and his influence, or is there something different about me when I'm at work there?

Ray remains standing. "And another toast for our discovery yesterday." He lifts his glass high. "To Rosalind Franklin and the secret of life!"

"Hear, hear!" Freda calls out, while Alec looks on quizzically. Though his words are vague, I wonder if Ray has said too much.

Freda volunteers to help me clear the dinner plates to make way for the tarte tatin I prepared for dessert. I like this bright woman, and I wish our work brought us together more frequently. As the kitchen door swings behind us, we stack dishes, and she whispers, "I need to tell you something."

I am not used to being anyone's confidante, except Ursula and my sister when we were much younger. "All right," I say, hoping the information she wants to share isn't too intimate.

"Did you and Ray make your big discovery yesterday afternoon?"

"Yes," I answer warily, not wanting to reveal too much at this early stage.

"I'm not going to pry into what the discovery was—I know

you'll tell me when you're ready—but is it possible that Wilkins is aware of what you and Ray found?"

"Possibly. He does tend to surprise us in our laboratory. Why?" I think about the many times I've sensed eyes on me, only to turn and find Wilkins standing in the doorway with that irritating smirk on his face. I've tried my best to be civil in reply—while making the boundaries clear—but I've been accused of unintentional terseness in the past. What reaction, intentional or otherwise, might these exchanges have elicited in Wilkins?

"Well, around four o'clock, he came storming down to Randall's office where I was dropping off some images. He launched into a rant as if I wasn't even there."

My heart pounds faster, and I don't want to think about what Wilkins might have said. But I need to know. "What did he say?"

"Wilkins wanted to know why he was being shut out of the research conducted on the DNA samples prepared by Dr. Signer. He also demanded an explanation as to why *you* seemed to be in control of it, especially since he thought you'd been hired to be *his* assistant."

"How did Randall respond?" Did he explain that he'd promised the DNA investigation to me from the start? I want to ask this of Freda but cannot be so blunt. If Randall was straightforward about the division of labor, it could lessen the friction between me and Wilkins—and lay to rest his repeated efforts to check in on our work. But perhaps that would never be possible if Wilkins thought that I'd been brought on to assist him, an unimaginable thought. Why would a scientist of my experience and training ever want a position to "assist" someone working at my own level, except for the title designation? Why would I ever leave behind the Parisian *labo,* with the autonomy and support and productivity I experienced there alongside a group of dear friends? Never mind my troubles with Jacques.

"He told Wilkins to stop whining and get on with his own work, that it would all work out in the end."

"Thank you for telling me, Freda," I say with a pat on her arm. But I do wonder about Randall's words and why he didn't explain to Wilkins that he's allocated the DNA work for me, why he didn't tell Wilkins that I was *not* brought on to assist him. I worry about Wilkins's anger, and I don't like it one bit.

CHAPTER TWENTY

June 30, 1951
Uppsala, Sweden

I FOLLOW THE PATHWAY ALONG THE FYRIS RIVER THAT DIVIDES the picturesque town of Uppsala in two. Sunlight glints off the water, warming me on this crisp June afternoon and allowing me to unwrap my arms and soak in the sun. How pleased I am that we decided to break free from the schedule at the Second Congress and General Assembly of the International Union of Crystallography and travel by train from Stockholm to this university town, with its medieval cathedral and sixteenth-century castle, for the day. After months of grinding work at the King's College laboratory, overlaid with tension from Wilkins's increasingly proprietary behavior, this escape with my dear friends the Luzzatis and the Sayres, with whom I'd planned to attend this conference, is a welcome release.

"How are you finding King's College?" Vittorio asks as the pathway widens and we can walk two across. It's not quite expansive enough to accommodate Anne, with whom we've been walking as well, so she strides ahead of us and joins the rest of the group. While I've been enjoying Anne's company on this trip—she and I took a solo jaunt to the pastry shops of Stockholm where I found sticky cakes and desserts in abundance, quite in contrast to the sugar-rationed status of England, and stopped by a literary reception hosted by the publisher of a magazine for which Anne wrote—it is a gift to have a rare, few moments alone with my dear friend Vittorio, who understands me so well.

"Is it enough to say that it's not Paris?" I answer with a chuckle.

He laughs. "More than enough. We miss you terribly at the *labo*."

"*Everyone* misses me?" I ask, and I can feel one eyebrow arch quizzically. It's not that I've ever heard Vittorio lie, but he can stretch the truth with his overarching desire to please. And I find it hard to believe that Jacques misses me.

"Yes," he insists, "even *him*. He doesn't say as much, but he talks of you and your skills frequently to those of us who know you." Neither of us need to say Jacques's name aloud to know about whom we speak; Jacques hovers in and around our conversations. "You absolutely made the right choice, Rosalind—even if London isn't Paris."

In Vittorio's shorthand, this signifies that leaving was the best move for me, because Jacques and Rachel Glaeser are together. "He's still with her?" I half whisper.

"Very much so. Never mind the mysterious wife who no one has ever seen but certainly exists," he replies quietly and sighs. Then, in a brighter tone and louder voice, he says, "I hope the research, at least, is going well in London."

"Incredibly well," I answer in a similarly sunny voice, banishing any upset over Jacques and Rachel's ongoing relationship from my mind. I will not allow Jacques Mering to spoil this stunning setting with my treasured friends. "You recall that I'm working with DNA now instead of carbons?"

"Of course," Vittorio answers, walking a little closer to me on the path so he can catch every word. "It's a brave new world for you."

"True, but science is science no matter the world in which it operates. I've refined the high humidity techniques I learned at the *labo* and applied them to this new material, and I've made an astonishing discovery."

"What?" Vittorio's eyes widen.

I've been itching to tell someone about my enormous find, but I've counseled Ray to keep it quiet until we're absolutely sure. Vittorio, though, I know I can trust. "I've learned that there are actually two forms of DNA."

"No!"

"Yes!"

"That's revolutionary."

"I know. But there's more."

"More? As if one science-altering finding isn't enough!"

The words tumble out of my mouth in a jumble; I am so overjoyed to share this news. "The images I've gotten are of such crispness and detail that I can see the structure emerging before my eyes. Before I even do the mathematical analysis."

"What do you see?"

"It is crystalline in shape—"

In his excitement, Vittorio cannot help but interrupt, "So familiar to you!"

"I know." I return his delight with a broad grin. "I think it's a helix."

"My God." He shakes his head in amazement. "Have you shared your findings with anyone yet? At your laboratory or elsewhere?"

I shake my head. "Other than my assistant. Once I finalize the images, I'll do all the calculations to confirm it. But I don't want to share my suspicions with anyone else until I do."

"I can understand keeping your discovery from the larger scientific community until you are absolutely certain—look at the attention and press Linus Pauling is getting over his announcement about the helical nature of proteins. And he hasn't even verified his findings with the necessary X-ray crystallography images, as Professor Bernal from Birkbeck so slyly pointed out at this very conference. Imagine what they'd say about your work; it would be headline news because you have the proof in your images, and it's no mere speculation." Vittorio stops talking, and his heavy eyebrows knit in confusion. We attended Pauling's lecture together a couple of days ago, and the Caltech chemist's presentation had been crowded and scintillating with loads of intriguing data points for my own work. "But why would you hold back from sharing with your colleagues? We always discussed early findings at the *labo*—"

"King's College is not the *labo*," I snap. Then, realizing that my voice is unexpectedly sharp, I say, "I'm sorry, Vittorio. I don't mean to make you the brunt of my frustrations."

He stops walking. "What's going on, Rosalind? Talk to me."

Aside from Anne, with whom I'd discussed this at a very high level and who found the developments deeply upsetting on my behalf but didn't quite grasp the full extent of the scientific betrayal, I have not reviewed this with anyone else in detail. Against all my efforts to the contrary, my eyes well up with tears.

I take a deep breath and begin. "The head of my unit, Professor Randall, is fine and actually has hired other female scientists for his staff. But I cannot get along with the assistant director, Maurice Wilkins. He is every bit as alienating as I'd expect a traditional English scientist to be—excluding me from team lunches by arranging them in the all-male dining room and the like. But the worst part is that he insists on inserting himself into my designated area, the X-ray analysis of DNA, which had been promised to me exclusively by Randall. I'm worried less about claiming a scientific territory—"

Vittorio interjects, "You were never concerned about ego like so many scientists."

I nod at his compliment and then continue. "—than I am worried about what a mess he'd make of my work if he got his hands on it. He didn't even use some basic techniques when he had the DNA samples initially."

"Oh God, I'm sorry, Rosalind." He reaches for my hand and gives it a quick squeeze. The effusive Vittorio would probably prefer giving me a tight hug, but he knows me well enough to withhold.

"There's more." I pause. "A friend told me that Randall and Wilkins had some sort of a row over the ownership of this DNA research. I expected Randall to defend my area and leave Wilkins no doubt that the work was mine, on Randall's order. That would put an end to this interference on Wilkins's part—he's always checking in with my assistant, Ray Gosling, to find out what we're working on, and I swear through he goes through my office when I'm not there. But Randall waffled and apparently changed the subject when Wilkins raised his voice."

"I'm not surprised that this Wilkins fellow wants to worm his way into your area. These sorts of discoveries are big news in science and—"

I interrupt with what I believe is a salient point. "Plus he failed to make any significant progress when he was in charge of the DNA analysis, and I can see that he'd hit a wall in any event—"

Vittorio takes his own turn at interrupting. "There you have it. He is resentful that a woman is succeeding where he failed, and most likely, he will either continue to encroach on your territory or try to take credit for your work. Be careful."

For such a relentlessly optimistic man, this is a surprisingly dark warning. I take heed, but I'm not certain how to proceed. "I don't think I can go to Randall with my concerns. He didn't defend me when Wilkins directly launched his attack on this same issue, and he specifically said he doesn't like complainers."

"You have only one choice then, my dear Rosalind. Protect your science at all costs."

CHAPTER TWENTY-ONE

July 24, 1951
London, England

This is a sad excuse for a conference, I think. The summer conference season is meant to provide both a respite from our laboratories and an easy means to connect with like-minded scientists—by luring us away with the promise of exotic locales. Although the Cavendish Laboratory at Cambridge, founded by the esteemed Professor James Maxwell, among others, as a center for experimental physics originally and now biology as well, is certainly impressive with its peaked roofs and ancient building on Free School Lane, Sweden it is not. Surveying the crowded, humid lecture room, I recognize several other scientists and nod in their directions but keep to myself as I await the first lecture. Given the loose agenda and informal nature of this "conference," the speakers have not been officially announced, but I'm looking forward to seeing what insights the Cavendish's research into the structure of proteins can bring to my own work. Never mind the relative bleakness of the venue.

A balding man with a long chin and dark-rimmed glasses stands and clears his throat. "Good morning, and thank you all for making the long and arduous journey to Cambridge to join me and my cofounder of the Cavendish Unit for the Study of the Molecular Structure of Biological Systems, John Kendrew, to hear about our work on protein structure," the man says, and the largely English audience chortles at his little joke about the local conference. He speaks with a thick, Germanic-sounding accent, and I realize that he must be Max Perutz, the molecular biologist who'd been recruited by Cambridge from Austria in the 1930s. His demeanor is remarkably lighthearted, despite the rumors that he'd been exiled to Newfoundland on Churchill's orders for part of the war because of his Germanic background. Unfortunate that he had to suffer through deportation even though he's Jewish and plainly not a Nazi sympathizer.

"I'll be your first speaker today, sharing the most recent developments of our study of hemoglobin, the protein in red blood cells that transports oxygen. As you undoubtedly know, we've been studying the most significant protein in red blood with X-ray diffraction for some time..." As he continues speaking, I quietly slide my notebook out of my bag and begin to take notes on his crystallography methods.

After an hour of nonstop lecturing followed by a half-hour period for questions, my hand is cramped from all the writing. Finally, Perutz comes to his conclusion. "Thus, I feel confident that in the days to come, we will definitely transform the clear patterns we've gotten on our images into a three-dimensional structure, supporting our initial hypothesis about the form. And hopefully identifying the location of genetic material in the process."

I sense the frustration in his words—and the defensiveness as well. From my own work, I know well the tedious labors involved in assessing and understanding the X-ray diffraction pattern of an image formed when X-rays pass through crystals, deflecting off atoms and interacting with one another. Perutz and his colleagues face an even greater challenge with the larger proteins on which they work than I do with DNA, because the number of deflections and interactions with the bigger crystals of this size is so vast that interpretation of the X-ray patterns requires much more knowledge. And time.

Stretching as they rise, the audience members stand for the midmorning break of tea and pastries, chattering as they queue to leave the room. I spot an old friend from BCURA, Samuel Kent, and we gravitate toward each other as we exit, catching up over the typically weak conference tea that no amount of milk, sugar, or lemon can doctor.

I notice Wilkins across the room, gesticulating rather wildly. He is deeply engaged in conversation with an unfamiliar man who matches him in lankiness, height, angular features, and frequency of hand gestures and facial expressions, although the other man has fairer hair. While continuing my own conversation with Samuel, I angle myself to watch Wilkins in my peripheral vision. I've never seen him so animated before, and I wonder why. Could it be the person he's talking to that elicits this reaction, or is it the topic they're discussing?

A bell softly rings, and we queue to return to the lecture room. I take my seat and watch as Perutz's cofounder, John Kendrew, stands at the podium. The bushy-haired fellow, bespectacled like nearly everyone in the room except me, seems a bit nervous, and when he speaks, his voice is calmer and quieter than Perutz's. "Welcome. Before I discuss the developments we've made this past year in the study of the smaller protein, myoglobin, through X-ray crystallography, I want to say a few words. We are entering a unique phase of scientific discovery, one that may well become competitive and even contentious in the days to come as revelations come to light. But let's remember that we are more alike than we are different and that we all share a common goal—scientific understanding. Like many of you, I gravitated to the study of molecular structure by way of another field, and I'm guessing that you shifted for the same sort of reason as did I, because you sensed that the answers to these enormous scientific questions didn't lie in one department but in the overlap of many. After all, I'm trained in chemistry but working on a biological issue in a physics lab—"

How insightful is his view of our scientific exertions, I think. *Even lyrical.* His perspective echoes that of Schrödinger as well as my own views about the importance of sharing developments with other scientists while respecting the time and space necessary for the reporting scientist to complete their own project before leaping in—and ensuring that we respect and honor one another's contributions. Instead of scribbling down Kendrew's every word, I put my pencil down and allow his ideas to wash over me.

My contemplative state ends abruptly when another fellow leaps up and races to the podium as soon as Kendrew concludes. It is the same man with whom Wilkins had been speaking at the tea break. Who is this overeager person?

"It seems our newest researcher is extremely eager to share his paper," Kendrew says with a tolerant half smile.

"For which you very kindly supplied the title," the other man adds.

"Well," Kendrew says with a sheepish laugh, "in a moment, I think you'll understand why I suggested he call his talk 'What Mad Pursuit.'" The audience laughs along with him, and he adds, "Allow me to introduce one of the newest members of the Cavendish, Francis Crick."

This spry fellow Crick confidently launches into his talk without hesitation, even though I'm guessing this is the most esteemed audience to which he's presented. As his long, lanky body curls into a series of emphatic poses and his hands gesticulate, he spews a load of data at first, but then, as he delves into the heart of his speech, his thesis emerges. He suggests that X-ray crystallography will never be able to solve the puzzle of the protein's structure. I am stunned. Could this Cavendish scientist actually be standing here telling his superiors—Perutz and Kendrew—that the years they've spent on this research are all for naught because they'll never discover the structure of protein through their chosen means? That their goal is Sisyphean?

What nerve, I think. How dare this Crick fellow assert that X-ray crystallographers have no chance of achieving their aim in the realm of proteins? Here, of all places. Lawrence Bragg, the head of the Cavendish itself, is one of the founders of X-ray crystallography.

Just as I consider leaving in protest, the luncheon break is announced. My friend sidles up to me in the queue for the buffet, whispering, "Can you believe Crick?"

"I can only imagine what Perutz must be saying to him right now."

"Never mind Perutz. What about Bragg?"

"Was he there?" I am incredulous that the famous scientist would have attended today's small conference.

"He popped in briefly and stood at the back, although I'm not sure he heard Crick's little diatribe. He might have left beforehand."

"Well, he's certain to hear of it regardless."

We muse on the situation until we are called back into the session. The room becomes uncomfortably warm as the day wears on, and I fan myself as I await the next speaker. To my shock and dismay, I see Wilkins rise from his seat in the front row of the lecture hall and approach the podium.

What on earth will he speak about? This is a conference focused on X-ray diffraction, and I'm handling that area of King's College DNA study now.

"Good afternoon." He mops his brows. I realize he's not only hot; he is nervous. I have to repress the urge to feel sorry for him. "I appreciate you sticking it out in this heat through the headliners to listen to an update of our developments over at King's College."

He fumbles a bit with the overhead projector. Finally, he manages to illuminate a chart of numbers that must be incomprehensible to almost everyone in the audience. Except me.

They are my numbers. Many of them anyway.

Wilkins points out that each series of numbers came from DNA samples from different animals, eventually reaching the calculations that I performed on the Signer DNA. It is then that he says these all demonstrate X-ray patterns with a clear central X. Then, quoting Alec Stokes, he announces that this consistent pattern and these results are very indicative of a helix. The audience breaks out in applause at this declaration, but all I can do is seethe.

How dare he.

I am so furious that I cannot hear the remainder of his lecture. All I can hear and see and think and feel are my results on that screen. Results that are in their nascent stages. Results that need to be repeated and refined over and over again until they are definitive. Results that must be rigorously scrutinized to find the pattern that emerges. Results that—only then—can be written up into a paper and presented to colleagues.

Wilkins's lecture is the last of the day. I wait until all the other audience members file out of the room and only Wilkins, Crick, and Kendrew remain near the podium. Staring at Wilkins, I stay seated while the men congratulate Wilkins on "his" findings and make plans to meet at the local pub. Only when Crick and Kendrew finally leave the room and Wilkins gathers his papers and slides from the podium and projectors do I finally approach. Vittorio's admonition to *protect my science* reverberates in my mind.

"You had no right to discuss those results. They are preliminary at best." Although I am trying to keep my volume low, it echoes through the now-empty cavernous space.

His eyes grow huge behind his glasses, and he takes a couple of steps away from me. "I–I was only giving a regular report of K-King's College's projects—one academic institution to other academic institutions," he stammers. "It's how things are done here," he says, as if my time in France turned me French and I'm only now learning the mysterious ways of the English.

"It's not that I'm being unduly territorial with my research. It's that I know the data is not ready for even this level of reporting." I am barely keeping a tidal wave of fury at bay.

"Yours *is* one of King's projects."

The wave lets loose. "The X-ray crystallography is my work, and I'll let you know when it's ready. Until then, please go back to your microscopes."

CHAPTER TWENTY-TWO

August 13, 1951
London, England

With each step along the Strand, growing closer to King's College, I become more tense. I'd achieved a clarity of mind and calmness on my holiday these past few weeks, and I'd hoped it would stay with me on my return. It certainly lingered during the weekend I spent in Oxford with the Sayres. But as I pass under the peaked archway toward the biophysics unit, I feel a rush of agitation as I anticipate seeing Wilkins for the first time since the Cavendish conference. I fight it; I want to imbue my regular life with that same peace I felt in Brittany.

Ah, Brittany. When I'd heard that an old friend from Paris, Margaret Nance, was planning a trip to Île de Batz, an island off the coast of Brittany, I asked to join in. Arriving later than Margaret with another woman, Norma Sutherland, because of the Cavendish conference, we struggled to find boarding at first, but with a little negotiation in my excellent French, we secured rooms. Once settled, our small group of women delighted in white sandy beaches, the clear blue ocean waters for swimming, and the stunning coastal hikes that ringed the island. Not everyone had the appetite for strenuous hikes, so alone, I satiated my desire for mountain climbing on the comparatively easy *le trou du serpent*, or serpent's hole, where the land was overtaken by vast granite boulders and, according to legend, Saint Pol de Léon defeated a dragon that had been tormenting the island. The pure concentration of reading patterns in the rocks—placing my hands and feet in the exact right crevices—is simultaneously the most intense and relaxing activity I know, and I long for its pacifying effect on my restless mind even now.

I stop short as I approach my department, thinking of something Norma said to me on the last afternoon of the holiday. After watching me haggle with a local fruit merchant, she had commented that I could be surprisingly brusque. When I defended myself by pointing out that I'd lived in Paris for several years and that I'd become accustomed to the contentious but good-natured sort of bartering used in the marketplaces, she said that wasn't what she was referring to. What she meant, she said, was that I could be astonishingly blunt and adversarial for such a kindly person—and not just with shopkeepers. Her words upset and shocked me at first, as her perspective didn't jibe with my sense of myself. Could it be her English view of me, I considered, since my French friends never took umbrage with my actions? But now, I am wondering. Could I have behaved the same confrontational way with Wilkins and been unaware of it? Perhaps, in my response to his superior deportment, I was too harsh? Especially for an Englishman to handle?

I'm willing to own my part in my hostile relationship with Wilkins, and if I take the first step toward conciliation, maybe he'll follow. Even though I don't necessarily believe he deserves it. I know I'll never have the camaraderie and trust of the *labo*, but could I have some semblance of collegiality at King's College beyond the lunches and events organized by Randall and my mentorship and friendship, I daresay, with Ray? Possibly even with Wilkins, and then perhaps his merry band of men would follow suit? Must protecting the purity of my science, as Vittorio put it, mean creating a barbed, impenetrable wall around myself and my work?

I walk downstairs to the cellar laboratories, keys in hand. Knowing I'll be the first person in the office is a solace, as I want to think about this conundrum in the quiet and clean whiteness of the lab. Pushing open the door to my office, I'm not surprised to see a pile of mail on my desk. As I sort through the more mundane correspondence and pin on my dosimeter as I plan on doing some experiments later, I spot a note from Wilkins, affixed to a series of calculations by Stokes and a copy of a letter he'd sent to Crick.

What on earth is this?

Clearing my desk of the detritus so I can focus on these missives without distraction, I read the scribbled note to me first:

Asked Stokes to look into the kind of X-ray crystallography patterns a helix might throw off. In the abstract, of course. And it seems to comport with your notions. Also, I've been experimenting with the DNA fibers and have come up with some ideas on the chains. Hope the holiday was good—

How could he do exactly what I asked him *not* to do and then write me this breezy note? I take a deep breath, trying to remind myself of my desire for harmony, and look at Stokes's math next.

He used the elegance of the mathematical device known as a Bessel function, and I see that his calculations might ultimately be helpful to support my images—when I am done taking them, not before—but that Wilkins wants to skip my process entirely and draw conclusions without the necessary infrastructure of definitive crystallography to prove them. *But,* I tell myself, *maybe I'm overreacting;* perhaps the communication to Crick elucidates a different motive altogether. Benefit of the doubt must become my maxim with Wilkins, and I skim the Crick letter with that in mind.

When I finish, I crumple the typewritten letter in a ball and throw it to the floor. Wilkins shared everything he'd done with Crick, including details about the clarity of my new images, all in an effort to impress upon him the importance of DNA study rather than the protein investigation that Crick insists is paramount. But that wasn't the totality of his offenses. He had also penned a handwritten note to me across the bottom of the page: *Shall we collaborate on this, Rosalind? Me, you, and Stokes?*

The audacity of the man—inviting me to collaborate on *my* own work. And then sharing my work too early *outside* our own laboratory.

I begin pacing my office and running my fingers through my carefully combed hair. What am I going to do? Any notion I'd had this morning of putting aside any brusqueness on my part and initiating a more pleasant relationship with Wilkins has been utterly jettisoned. I want to scream, and I nearly give in to the impulse, but then I hear the hallway outside my office come alive with the sound of footsteps and chatter.

A knock sounds at my door, and before I can answer, Ray

sticks his head inside. "Let me guess—Brittany was topping?" he half asks with a wide smile.

"It was indeed, Ray. Thank you for asking." Keeping the admonitions of Nannie Griffiths top of mind, I try to force a return smile, but my emotions are a torrent. I cannot imagine how my face must look.

"Everything all right?" he asks.

"Pardon me. It's just that I returned to something rather"— I hesitate, not wanting to draw the ever-affable Ray into the fray between me and Wilkins once again—"unexpected."

He stays affixed to the doorframe, as if he's afraid to come any closer. "Is it about Pauling?"

"Pauling?" I'm thoroughly confused. Even though I don't want to name the source of my anger, I assumed Ray knew that I'm fuming over Wilkins. What does the Caltech biochemist Linus Pauling have to do with anything? I know that this spring, he published a revolutionary paper in which he proposed that the primary structure of proteins is the alpha helix, an assertion he'd made without the benefit of X-ray crystallographic evidence but using a speculative model. But we work on DNA, not proteins; only the specter of the helical nature of DNA is a true overlap in our work. So what does Pauling have to do with us? Why would Pauling upset *me*?

"Yes, haven't you heard?" When I shake my head, he explains, "Pauling wrote Randall and asked him to send copies of the DNA X-ray crystallography images, as Pauling heard from Wilkins that he wasn't going to be interpreting them. Pauling felt that science deserved their interpretation. Imagine the nerve."

"He wanted *our i*mages because Wilkins told him that *he*

wasn't going to be deciphering them? And that if Wilkins wasn't interpreting them, no one else was?" I'm incredulous. Not only at Pauling's audacity at demanding another institution's scientific work but at Wilkins's suggestion that because *he* wasn't in charge of assessing our images, they wouldn't be interpreted well or at all.

"Yes," Ray answers, and for the first time ever, I see anger simmering beneath his placid surface. "But," he says, the optimism slowly returning to his face, "Randall would have none of it. He was furious at Pauling's presumptuousness and told him his scientists had it in hand."

"That's something at least," I say, relieved at Randall's response. But this does nothing to diminish my fury at Wilkins. If anything, it has intensified.

"It's something." He stares at me, waiting to see if I'll tell him about the original source of my discomfiture. When I say nothing, he says, "Well then, shall we reconnoiter later this morning?"

"Let's," I answer, feeling very grateful to have Ray for my assistant. His kindness and empathy at this moment, and his brilliance at other moments.

He leaves me, but before I can gather myself and sit back down at my desk, I hear another knock. Assuming it is my assistant returning with a brief question, I call out, "Come in."

But it's not Ray. It's Wilkins.

Staying in the doorway as if I've erected an invisible barricade to the interior of my office proper, he asks, "Good holiday in Brittany?"

How can he stand there and ask me about my holiday as if he hasn't perpetrated multiple deceptions upon me? His disingenuousness is legend.

I cannot speak. I can barely look at him. I don't think of him as a particularly perceptive man, but he must sense my state, because he's retreated and now practically stands in the hallway.

"You're preoccupied, I see. Perfectly natural on return from holiday." He chuckles nervously. "Once you've settled in, perhaps you could take a peek at the note I left you."

I walk toward him and watch as he visibly recoils. For a second, I almost enjoy myself. "I already have."

"Ah, I see. What do you think?" He takes another step back.

"You want to collaborate?"

"Yes?" His response is more of a question of himself than anything.

"What does collaborate mean to you? Does collaborate mean telling people like Linus Pauling that I'm not doing my job—that I'm not interpreting the data I'm collecting? Or does collaborate mean looking at my results while I'm away on holiday, having Stokes examine them, and then sending the whole package to a scientist at a completely different institution? Perhaps collaboration means trying to usurp the work that's been assigned to me and that I'm making headway with—after you couldn't make heads or tails of it when it was yours—so that you can make a muddle of it?"

Wilkins's eyes are round as saucers.

"You are caught up in an invisible competition with unknown challengers for the structure of DNA," I continue, "but you forget that this is science, not a race." Then I slam my door shut.

CHAPTER TWENTY-THREE

August 13, 1951
London, England

Somehow, I maintain my composure on the train north to Hampstead. A prim, elderly woman sits on the banquette across from me, embroidering and periodically glancing over at me. Her stern demeanor as well as the drape of her cardigan are so reminiscent of a strict St. Paul's librarian that I cannot fathom a display of the emotion I feeling welling up within me.

I manage to remain calm as I walk from the station to Colin and Charlotte's home near Hampstead Heath. The bright August daylight has waned, casting a diffuse, golden glow over the park, and despite my despair, I am able to note its exceptional loveliness. By the time I ring the bell, I imagine I'll be able to lay claim to this composure for the entirety of the family dinner.

But when Colin opens the door of his multistory, redbrick house to greet me, the soft caring in my brother's eyes weakens my resolve. I burst into tears. I don't think I've ever cried in front of a family member, at least not in recent memory, and I surprise myself. Colin freezes, because he hasn't a clue how to respond, and I am left sobbing on the doorstep. After a long minute, Charlotte is summoned and finally arrives. I am passed into her care.

She leads me through the entryway, past the dining room table with china and silver carefully laid out for the family meal, and into my brother's library. We must weave through the stacks of books—mostly old, some quite valuable—on the floor and on every surface. Although Colin has been working for the family's publishing business, Routledge, for some years, his true passion lies with incunabula—rare, early printed books—and manuscripts, and he longs to be an antiquarian. If I'd ever leave science for a husband and a family, this messy, beloved place is the sort of domestic haven I'd want for myself.

Once Charlotte has me settled on Colin's library sofa, she asks, "What on earth has happened, Rosalind?"

My chest heaves, and my breath catches. I cannot speak through the sobs.

Charlotte reaches out for me, taking me in her arms. My brother enters the room and stands behind her, as if he's embracing me by proxy. Given our stoic, unaffectionate Franklin upbringing, I'm certain his discomfort is extreme in the presence of this wellspring of emotion. The fact that he's managing to stay in the parlor attests to his loyalty to me. And love.

My sobs begin to subside, and my breathing slowly returns to normal. Only then does Charlotte pull back slightly to examine me. "Are you quite all right? Should I fetch a doctor or call for an ambulance? Do you need an ice pack?"

I almost laugh. Young mother that she is, she chalks all crying jags up to cuts and bruises and assumes that a good bandage will patch me up.

Pulling away from her arms, I pull a handkerchief from my pocket and dab at my eyes. "No, I think my bout of weeping is quite over."

"Whatever is the matter, Rosalind?" she asks.

"How long do you have?" I ask with a half laugh.

"Is it that Wilkins fellow?" Colin asks. My mild-mannered brother's voice sounds even, but I can see that his fists are clenched. I've mentioned my irritation with Wilkins from time to time but have purposely chosen to spare my family the most egregious of his actions. I don't need to provide Papa with any more ammunition for his arguments that I should leave science for a family business or an altruistic endeavor.

"Yes, it is him. But it is also the entire scientific community that allows someone like him—for there are many—to rise up."

A deep furrow appears between Colin's light eyebrows. "Is he abusing the power he has over you?"

"He is certainly trying. But not in the way you're imagining," I say, but Colin's fists don't unclench. I've always imagined that Colin saw horrors during his war service about which he's never spoken aloud, and I'm guessing that my histrionics have triggered those recollections. "Not physically. He's trying to undermine my work, but not in any way I can officially complain about."

Colin's hands loosen a little, but Charlotte leans toward me. "How so?" she asks, undoubtedly more attuned to the daily abuses women suffer, now that her first instincts to heal my wound with a plaster have been proven wrong.

"He used my absence to insert himself into my work, even

though I explicitly asked him to do the opposite just before I left."

"To what end?" Colin asks.

"He's calling it collaboration, but in truth, he means to stage a coup. He wants to take back the area that was explicitly given to me on my arrival—an area I feel honor bound to pursue because he made a dog's dinner of it when he had it. He's all caught up in this scientific race to be the first to map the structure of DNA. But I don't know who he's racing against." I take a deep breath to calm myself. "And it's not a race that I signed up for, in any event."

"The bastard," Charlotte whispers.

"Charlotte!" Colin cries. I doubt he's ever heard his lovely wife utter such a phrase.

But she doesn't back down. "This Wilkins fellow deserves it, Colin."

"I suppose he does," Colin agrees with his wife.

She turns her attention back toward me. "Can we help in any way?"

I smile at my surprisingly fierce sister-in-law. "I wish I could let you loose upon him, Charlotte. That might set him straight."

We all laugh at the thought, and then I continue. "No, but I will have to make a plan. Perhaps I'll leave King's College. I cannot deal with Wilkins."

"Where will you go?" Colin asks. My brother has been listening and watching out for me, it seems.

"I'm not certain yet." I push myself to standing from the depths of the cordovan leather sofa and say, "I must look a fright. I've got to pull myself together before the parents arrive." I feel the area around my eyes to see how swollen they are. One look at me and Mama and Papa will go on the offensive, and I cannot risk that tonight of all nights. I couldn't bear another lecture about leaving behind the long hours and demands of science for a life of philanthropy and family after I've already made the sacrifice of coming to London. I'm too vulnerable. I'd do it.

"There's a mirror on the hallway wall," Charlotte points out.

"Rosalind," Colin says before I leave the room. "You deserve to finish your science. Don't let this Wilkins force you to finish your work prematurely or run you out of King's College."

I'm astonished. My amiable, even-tempered younger brother is taking a firm, almost combative stance on my behalf. It's so unlike him that I'm speechless.

"What I mean to say is this. You're onto something. I can hear it when you talk about your DNA discoveries. Don't let Wilkins's desire for a share of your glory knock you off task. Hold firm. And fight for your science if you must."

CHAPTER TWENTY-FOUR

October 25, 1951
London, England

"I had hoped that this meeting would not be necessary," Randall says while removing his glasses and wiping them vigorously with a handkerchief. I wonder whether he's chosen this exact moment to clean his spectacles so he cannot see us clearly. Given his loathing of confrontation, I'm certain this meeting is painfully uncomfortable for him, and avoiding our gaze is one way of managing his discomfort.

But it cannot wait any longer. This showdown has been in the making for nearly two months, if not longer. Since Wilkins's ill-fated invitation for "collaboration," I've tried every tool at my disposal to avoid this—ignoring Wilkins, chatting pleasantly with him, even lunching with him at the student union, where women are allowed, as I made a point to mention. But time and time again, I would find that he'd undertaken some insidious action either to chip away at my work or to peer inside my research, and I cannot stand it any longer.

Protect your science. Fight for your science. The nearly identical admonitions of two of the people I treasure most—Vittorio and Colin—have steeled me for this occasion when I have wavered. Not from fear of an argument but from concern at appearing as a complainer. I have chanted their words to myself when I hesitated, and I think them now.

"As had I, sir," Wilkins chimes in.

My blood boils. Wilkins only calls Randall "sir" when attempting to manipulate him or to close ranks alongside him. While I like and admire our department head, he does have a weakness for flattery.

"It doesn't befit my position," Wilkins adds.

I take a deep but hopefully silent breath to calm myself and provide that extra beat I often need to frame a proper response. "I wouldn't think this a question of position but rather of designated areas of research," I finally say in a measured voice.

"Really?" Wilkins asks a question he doesn't actually want me to answer. "When you object to my sharing your research at a conference where I am appearing on behalf of our department and reporting on our unit's work, then it most certainly is a matter of position."

I know he's slyly raising my outburst after the Cavendish conference as a way to obfuscate the matter at hand. I can almost hear him think: *Maybe if I keep Randall focused on the disrespect Rosalind has shown to her superiors at King's, then we won't have to focus on my acts impinging on her work.*

For once, I manage to hold my tongue. I will only play into Wilkins's hands if I speak before Randall has his chance to weigh in. I wait for Randall to finish his overly thorough cleansing of his glasses and replace them on his nose.

Randall then straightens his tie, forms his hands into a careful triangle, and sighs in our direction. "How unfortunate. I find all this wrangling to be beneath us as scientists and as people."

Wilkins and I both nod but say nothing.

"But the acrimony between you two is poisoning the unit and the work. Not to mention the toll it's taking on poor Ray Gosling. So here I am."

"Yes, sir," Wilkins mutters, as I say, "I am sorry that you've had to get involved, Professor Randall." I am careful not to apologize for anything I've done.

"Maurice, you are correct that—to the extent you are reporting on the unit's progress overall and acting in my stead as a representative of the unit—Rosalind should not object to your discussion of her research," Randall finally pronounces.

Wilkins shoots me a triumphant look, which I pointedly ignore. He's such a child. I keep my gaze fixed on Randall, who's still speaking.

"But, Maurice, just because you are assistant director of the unit does not mean that you can overstep your bounds into her research, as it seems you've been repeatedly doing. As you know, when I brought her on, I promised her the X-ray crystallography work on the DNA given to us by Professor Signer."

"W-what?" Wilkins sputters. "You never—" He sounds in earnest.

Randall raises an imperious-looking eyebrow. "You would not be suggesting that I'm speaking an untruth, would you?" He's no louder than he's been during the entire meeting, but his words are imbued with such animus, I feel as though he's screaming.

Wilkins feels it as well. He scrambles and says, "No, no, sir. That's not what I meant at all."

"Good. I would certainly hope you—of all people—would refrain from such accusations."

"Of course, sir. But why me 'of all people'?"

"I haven't forgotten the stunt you pulled with Linus Pauling, telling him we weren't interpreting Rosalind's stellar images when we clearly were. Or at least Rosalind has plans to assess them in totality. I'm still scratching my head trying to understand why you'd speak such a blatant untruth and what you'd stand to gain from it."

"S-sir, as I told you earlier, I never said that to Pauling. He misunderstood something I said to another person about whether or not I personally was—"

"We've been over this, Maurice. You may not have said it to Pauling directly, but you said it to someone." He inhales deeply. "And I cannot have that." Wilkins quiets, and Randall takes center stage. "Even though I'm certain Rosalind's realm was clear from the start, it seems I must dole out territories like some medieval lord. Believe me, I have no desire to treat you brilliant scientists like two of my subjects."

My heart pounds. Randall has taken my side so far, but will he ultimately side with Wilkins? After all, they've been working together at various institutions since before the war, and Randall has only known me for a year or so. Will old alliances prevail, or will he keep his promises?

"Rosalind," Randall says as he turns to me, "you will focus on the research that brought you to King's College in the first place—X-ray crystallography study of DNA. You'll use the Signer DNA as we discussed from the outset."

I cannot believe it. Randall has stood up for me, staking out the claim I'd always thought was mine. My relief is so palpable I wonder if it has a molecular structure of its own.

But what will Wilkins have? Will it keep him busy enough that he'll be far out of my hair?

"But the Signer DNA—" Wilkins begins to protest until Randall cuts him off. I don't need to hear his full complaint to infer his meaning. The Signer DNA is special in the clarity of the images it yields—we all know it—and he doesn't want to relinquish it to me.

"Maurice," Randall says, plowing ahead without regard to Wilkins's objections, "I'd like you to use your considerable talents on that excellent pig thymus DNA provided by Erwin Chargaff. I have high hopes."

Wilkins's cheeks flame red, and I can see he's furious at this division of labor. Randall's compliments have done nothing to placate him. Given the promise I've already demonstrated, Wilkins has gotten the short end of the stick, and he knows it.

I feel like I've been given wings.

CHAPTER TWENTY-FIVE

November 21, 1951
London, England

Randall's edict yields a new dynamic in our unit. Wilkins erects a barricade between us, amassing scientists loyal to him on his side and ensuring that no communication passes directly between us. I believe he means it as some sort of punishment for raising our rift to Randall. But what he fails to realize is that isolation suits me well.

Without the distraction and drain of Wilkins and his interferences—actual and anticipated—I lose myself in the research. With Ray at my side, I create even crisper and more astonishing images of the B form of DNA, and we begin the hard work of the calculations to transform the patterns of the A and B forms into three-dimensional shapes. I find myself dreaming in scattershot black dots on a background of white, and I realize that even in my sleep, I'm trying to solve the question of the structure of life. I know that it's just within my grasp; I need only to stretch a little more.

Even when Wilkins unleashes his latest weapon upon me—his new office mate—it serves only as an irritation at first. This specialist in microscopes, an Irishman named Bill Seeds, fancies himself a comedian and delights in gags and tricks. He assigns nicknames to everyone in the unit, but I know Wilkins is behind the name I'm given—Rosy. It's the short form of my name, of course, and early on, I specifically told Wilkins I did not like it. I also know who is behind Seeds's biggest prank; when I flick on the lights to my lab early one weekday morning, I find the cloths covering my X-ray crystallography equipment decorated with a multitude of signs labeled "Rosy's Parlor."

While this bothers me, my primary concern is Ray. The poor fledgling scientist, ostensibly my assistant and advisee for his thesis, is increasingly used by Wilkins as a pawn. He is called into Wilkins's office at all hours, often to provide information about their past work on DNA, sometimes to assist in his current research on the pig thymus samples, and occasionally to send me messages about meetings. Wilkins exacts his rage passively through my assistant, until, once again, tensions are fever-pitched.

As we greet the scientists arriving for the King's College colloquium on nucleic acid structures, I purposely stand next to Randall instead of Wilkins. I want today to be a success, which means, in part, giving Randall no cause for undue concern. Consequently, I plan on avoiding Wilkins until I take the podium from him after his speech.

After greeting a nattily attired biophysicist from University College—and wondering whether I should have changed out of my usual lab attire of white blouse, dark skirt, and lab coat into one of my four New Look dresses—I feel Ray nudge me. "Is that the Crick fellow who Professor Wilkins is always going on about?" Ray whispers.

"What do you mean?" I ask, glancing in the direction that Ray stares. I'm trying to hide my surprise—he usually assiduously avoids the topic of Wilkins.

"Wilkins has been spending a lot of time at the Cavendish lately, even though they only work on proteins, and he even mentioned spending the weekend at the home of a Cavendish friend, who I assume is Crick. Unless it's the other fellow who started working there—Watson, I think, is his name. Wilkins really likes him as well," he answers.

I'm sure he is drawing on the deep well of information he learns from Wilkins during the regular trips Wilkins organizes with staff members to Finch's pub. I myself have never been invited; I'm only included in the official outings organized by Randall himself.

Wilkins is chatting away with a tall, angular fellow, who is instantly familiar as the scientist from the Cavendish conference, the one who spoke so terribly out of turn about X-ray diffraction analysis of proteins. And here he is at King's College, chatting with Wilkins once again like old friends. "I do believe that's Crick. I recognize him from this summer."

"Why would he be interested in a colloquium about DNA structure? From what I understand, he thinks proteins are the bee's knees, not DNA," Ray says.

"I don't know. Maybe he's here for collegial support? Or to see if there's any light that the work at King's can shed on protein analysis? There are quite a few folks here from the Cavendish, and I went to their summer conference."

Before Ray can comment, Randall indicates that we should usher the group into the lecture hall, where the twenty or so scientists assemble. After a lovely introduction by Randall, Wilkins begins. He presents essentially the same speech he'd given at the Cavendish, and this time, I know I can raise no objections. It's been blessed by Randall.

We pass each other without incident as I take his place at the podium for my own speech. I stare down at my lecture notes and then back out at the crowd. And despite the fact that I've never struggled with public speaking, I freeze.

I labored for hours on my lecture, but still, I'm nervous to share even these initial results of my X-ray crystallography study of DNA with my peers. Haven't I heard the esteemed J. D. Bernal say that a good scientist doesn't speculate until he or she is entirely certain of their outcomes? Have I taken enough images and done enough calculations to make the assertions I plan to make today? I feel sick at the thought of saying too much, too soon. Randall clears his throat, and I realize that I have no choice but to begin.

"Thank you for joining us today to hear what we've got underway here. As many of you know, my focus since I arrived at King's is the X-ray crystallography study of DNA fibers." Step by step, I describe how I hydrated DNA fibers and then memorialized the changes between the wet to crystal to dry states with images. I know this methodical explanation will make clear the skill and experience I bring to both preparation of samples and crystallography itself, particularly in comparison to Wilkins's high-level descriptions.

I then reach one of the climaxes of my speech. "It was by using these methods that my assistant Raymond Gosling and I realized there are two distinct forms of DNA—what we call the A form and the B form. And we are just beginning to dive into their differing qualities and structures. Ultimately, we hope to discover their functions as well."

The audience members let out what seems like a collective "ah" and then begin chattering among themselves. I know that this discovery surprises and excites many of them, but I need to continue.

"I'll be happy to entertain questions about these two DNA forms at the end of my lecture."

Do I dare say what comes next? Even though the scientist within me craves more hard facts before I reveal what my crystallographic evidence is already telling me?

After taking an emboldening breath, I stare down at my handwritten speech. I skim the notes about methods I used to inject varying levels of humidity into the strands for X-ray examination and the observations I made when the DNA fibers were at different levels of hydration. And then I review my conclusion—that the results strongly indicate a helical structure with anywhere from two to four chains and the phosphate groups on or near the outside. I hesitate. Can I really share all three elements of my conclusion—the helix, the number of chains, and the location of the phosphates? Is it too much, too soon? These conclusions *are* revolutionary.

I make a decision, and then I meet the gaze of the scientists in the audience. "Although it is early days, it does seem from the initial results of my experiments that at least one form of DNA has the structure of a helix."

CHAPTER TWENTY-SIX

December 4 and 5, 1951
Cambridge, England

"It seems Kendrew wants the lot of you to visit the Cavendish *tout suite*," Randall barks out at the mandatory afternoon tea. "Tomorrow if possible."

Typically, Wilkins and I stake out opposite sides of the room at these compulsory events. He stands with his cadre of ex-military men, and I flock to Freda, while poor Ray bounces between the two groups. Today, just by happenstance of the timing and Wilkins's late arrival, we are practically shoulder to shoulder.

Why on earth would John Kendrew, who runs the Cavendish Laboratory at Cambridge with Max Perutz, want *us* to visit their labs with such haste?

As Randall completes his directive, Wilkins and I automatically glance at each other, then avert our eyes. Wilkins asks, "*All* of us?" gesturing to the room of a dozen or so people. "I can't imagine that Kendrew wants to be bombarded with all of us."

His group laughs, but what stands out to me isn't his joke but his failure to ask *why* Kendrew is summoning us. Isn't he curious about that?

"Well," Randall harrumphs, "now that you ask, Kendrew only mentioned Rosalind and Maurice by name. But it seems only right and proper that Raymond Gosling and Bill Seeds should go along as well."

"Did he say why he wanted us? And so urgently?" I ask the question I assume is on most people's minds. I cannot imagine what Kendrew and his team at the Cavendish would be working on that would merit an emergency visit. From my memories of the summer conference, Kendrew has been working—in an appropriate if plodding fashion—on the structure of proteins for years. What could possibly have happened that we need to be in his lab in Cambridge *tomorrow*?

"No, he did not. He simply described it as a matter of urgent professional courtesy, and a gentleman cannot decline such a summoning. So off you go!"

We assemble at the Liverpool Street station the next morning for our train to Cambridge. Even though it's early, only eight o'clock, I'd considered taking an even earlier train to avoid riding with Wilkins and the odious Seeds for two hours. But I didn't want to initiate a chain reaction of unpleasantness between Wilkins and myself that might reflect poorly on Randall. So here I am.

To avoid the awkward question of how close I should sit to Wilkins and Seeds, I board the train first. They choose seats six rows ahead of me, which sends a clear message but spares me from having to telegraph it. Ray sits next to me, but as usual, he is left in the disagreeable position of toggling between the two of us throughout the journey.

After a cab ride from the train station to the Cavendish, Kendrew greets us in the reception area. "Good of Professor Randall to send you all out to the Cavendish on such short notice."

"Happy, as always, to collaborate," Wilkins says, shooting me a sly look. I know he chose the word with great care.

"I wouldn't call this a matter of collaboration. It's more in the vein of courtesy." Kendrew starts toward the door at the back of reception. "If you'll follow me to the Austin Wing, I think it will become clear."

The four of us assemble single-file into a queue and wind our way through a warren of corridors until we finally reach a black door at the end of a long hall with the number 103 emblazoned on it. Kendrew pushes it open and ushers us inside a small, white brick–walled room decorated only with a few blackboards and a long table with chairs. But there, at the room's center, stand Crick and the fellow Ray identified as another Cavendish scientist, the disheveled, curly-haired Watson.

Without a formal introduction by Kendrew, Wilkins strides directly to each man. He gives them each a hearty, familiar shake and slap on the back in turn. It seems Ray was correct that Wilkins has a relationship of some sort with these two scientists.

"Ah, Dr. Wilkins, you know Francis Crick and James Watson, of course. They've told me as much. But perhaps your colleagues aren't as familiar?" he asks, nodding toward Ray, Seeds, and me.

"No, indeed," I answer, "but delighted to make their acquaintance."

He names each of us and our titles, then says, "Please meet Cavendish biophysicist Francis Crick, who you perhaps saw speak at our summer conference, and the newest member of our team, biologist James Watson."

We exchange pleasantries, but we still have no explanation as to why we're here. Ray looks at me with eyes askance, and I know he's asking himself the same questions as me. Oddly enough, Wilkins doesn't appear perplexed. What does he know?

As if intuiting our thoughts, Kendrew says, "I'm certain you are curious about the reasons I asked for you to visit the Cavendish on such short notice. I wouldn't have done so unless I felt it necessary." He clears his throat, signaling his discomfort with what he must say next. "The mission of our team at the Cavendish is to untangle the molecular structure of protein; by informal agreement, we leave it to you folks at King's College to noodle on DNA." The sort of verbal understanding about the clear areas of research between King's and the Cavendish—between the head of the Cavendish Laboratory, Lawrence Bragg, and the head of our King's unit, Randall, really—is quite common in the scientific realm. They'd agreed that the Cavendish would work on the genetic material in protein while King's alone would focus on DNA. Because the furtherance of scientific developments and thought requires that scientists share information to some extent, we operate by a set of unwritten conventions that include respecting boundaries around the subject of a scientist's or institution's investigations and giving proper acknowledgment for any assistance that one scientist or institution might give another.

Kendrew continues, glancing over at Crick and Watson with a less than pleasant expression. "By chance, I discovered what Drs.

Crick and Watson have been spending their time on lately, and I confess that they've gone far adrift of the Cavendish mission and the understanding between the Cavendish and King's College. So far adrift that I felt you should be informed."

The men look anything but sheepish, which I would have expected given the dressing-down they've just received. The angular, tall Crick has a supercilious grin on his face, and the too-youthful Watson appears strangely proud underneath his shock of wiry curls. I cannot imagine what these two have gotten up to that they'd be practically beaming in the face of their superior's clear displeasure.

Kendrew points to the far corner of the room, where a rickety structure made of odds and ends has been built. "Rather than working on their assigned projects on protein," he says, making clear that he hasn't quite forgiven Crick for his harsh words at the summer conference, "they've cobbled together a model of DNA. Apparently, your recent talks at King's College spurred them on." As we walk over to the strange design, he continues, "But of course, the structure of DNA clearly falls within King's purview." He's referring again to the gentleman's agreement between Randall and Bragg.

Kendrew turns toward us. "I thought you should know at once. And I wanted to give you the opportunity to see Crick and Watson's work in case it benefits your own—as they insist it will."

Without waiting a beat, Crick launches into a mini lecture on helical diffraction theory, about which he knows a surprising amount. But his didactic tone grates on me. Is it possible that he doesn't know about my experience as an X-ray crystallographer? I would never talk to another scientific colleague in such a know-it-all fashion, particularly if I was touching on his or her area of expertise.

Crick culminates with a sweeping gesture in the direction of their jerry-rigged structure. "You can see we've built a three-chain model of a helix. Quite along the lines of what the general thinking is at King's College."

While I appreciate the nod to King's, I wonder why he didn't address me directly when he made the comparison. In fact, he spoke to Wilkins rather than me.

I decide to assess the model in its entirety before reflecting on this peculiarity. I walk around the bits of wire, cardboard, and plastic stuck together to form the loose approximation of a curving staircase, albeit a rickety one I'd be terrified to climb.

"Here you can see that we have the replica phosphates on the inside with the bases—sodium ions—on the outside," Crick notes.

My heart beats excitedly, knowing that they've got it all wrong, particularly with respect to the location of the phosphates, which they *should* have known. Any chemist would know that hydrophobic substances like bases go on the inside where they are protected, but hydrophilic substances like phosphates go on the outside, and although neither Crick nor Watson are chemistry experts, they certainly could have consulted with one. Even putting that aside, I suppose it's no surprise that they got so much of it wrong, given the lack of independent research and scientific investigation they utilized in building this model. In fact, I would have been despondent if they *had* reached the right conclusion.

But I take that important beat and hold back from blurting out what I know to be the obvious flaw. Any critique will surely shut them down, and I want to learn all I can about them and their model before going on the offensive. So I calmly ask, "How did you arrive at your model?"

Watson chimes in this time. "Well, as Professor Kendrew said, the King's College talk really lit a fire under me—"

I cannot stop myself from interrupting. "You started working on your theory and this model just a little over a week ago?"

One week? These two think they can solve the mystery of the location and structure of genes—and ultimately the function—in one week? The hubris is hard to comprehend. Where is the doggedness and dedication to the slog of experimentation that is the hallmark of good scientists?

"Good work," Watson says, his tone dripping with condescension. As if he's surprised I'm able to work out that calculation for myself. "Yes, after the lecture. We started with the hypothesis that the DNA structure was a helix—"

I interject again. "So you began with the end in mind?"

"Exactly," he answers, again with that patronizing smile. Watson's approach to science contains such a vital flaw it nearly takes my breath away. How can one call oneself a scientist and begin one's investigation with a conclusion instead of building to one only after exhaustive research? Not to mention that he's in conflict with his own philosophy by cheating, in that he used *my* hypothesis and *my* research as I shared it at the meeting at King's College. Is this true of Crick as well? A lightning bolt did not strike them, delivering the answer to this key scientific riddle. Unless they consider me a lightning bolt.

Proceeding uninterrupted for the next fifteen minutes, Crick and Watson exchange excited remarks about how they constructed their flimsy model—of which they are unreasonably proud—and how they goaded each other onward to the next level of "insights," as they call them. And then they step back, awaiting our accolades. Or so it seems.

I glance over at Wilkins, who says nothing. If what Ray told me is true and Wilkins is friends with Crick and Watson, then I don't expect that he'll scold the two men for overstepping their bounds. But I do expect more than the half smile of pride I see on Wilkins's face. What is going on? Why isn't Wilkins irritated that they've overstepped their bounds? After all, their own superior is visibly annoyed with them.

If no one else is going to speak, I will, but in my own time. And I want to make them wait.

I walk around the model like a hawk circling its prey. "You do realize that DNA requires a lot of water, don't you?" I finally ask, without pointing out the structural flaws.

Watson shoots Crick a glance, and Crick says, "I suppose."

I hold back a smile, realizing that neither man recalled the requisite amount of hydration surrounding each strand that I'd shared at the meeting and neither understands what the nucleic acid needs.

"Where is the water in your model?" I continue with my questions.

"What do you mean?" Crick's brow knits in visible confusion.

"How does the molecule have enough hydration?" They look so blankly at me that I pose another query. "You have phosphates on the inside and the bases on the outside."

Neither man answers my questions.

I decide not to enlighten them. Instead, I want to leave Crick and Watson doubting their model and realizing that I alone comprehend its flaws and the means to fix it. Even though I don't relish being part of this man-made race, even though I wish I could work on science for its own sake, I'll be damned if I'll let these two upstarts enter the race late and win.

CHAPTER TWENTY-SEVEN

December 28 and 29, 1951
Paris, France

My heart swells at the sight of the Seine. Even though gray-blue clouds dominate the skies and some would call the day gloomy, I am elated. Every café I pass, every stylish Parisian I see, every gust of wind bringing scents of strong coffee and freshly baked brioche, delights me. Unlike my arrival in London, the place of my birth and the city most familiar to me, this return to Paris feels more like coming home.

"Why Paris again?" Papa had asked over dinner on the final night of Hanukkah. He and Mama wanted me to spend the winter holiday—when King's College closed for Christmas—with them and our extended family. I think they viewed every gathering as an opportunity to dissuade me from my course, and I watched as my other family members nodded along in agreement. Everyone except Ursula, Colin, and Charlotte, of course. But while I'd wavered early in December and considered staying in London for the holiday, after the Department of Physics's annual dinner, I'd committed to Paris.

I was pushed to my limits by the sight of Bill Seeds on stage singing parodies about everyone in the lab. His taunting, ribald song about the expansion of Randall's empire offended and worried me, and I noticed I wasn't alone. Even those professors usually tolerant of Seeds's antics and the bravado of the ex-military men in their ranks looked offended. The mood at King's College Biophysics Research Unit had grown tense recently, and for once, I wasn't the only one who was experiencing it. It was almost a relief to witness the near-universal discomfort.

Wrapping my coat around myself more tightly against the Parisian chill, I'm relieved to be close to Adrienne's flat. Although she invited me to stay with her and her daughter, I feel more comfortable staying with the Luzzatis. Anyway, it allows me more time to review my DNA images and plan with Vittorio, whose expertise with X-ray crystallography is superb.

The door to Adrienne's flat opens before I can even knock. "Rosalind, it has been too long!" she cries, enveloping me in her warm embrace.

How I wish for a scientific mentor like Adrienne—or even Jacques—at King's College. "It seems a lifetime," I say, and it does, although it's only been a year.

She pulls back to examine me. "You look wan. I see dark circles under your eyes."

Well, Adrienne is known for her directness. I'd noticed the circles myself but chalked them up to the journey to Paris and the sleepless night before my departure. But the truth is they've been present for months.

I wave her away. "It's nothing—just the travel."

She accepts this excuse and settles me with a strong cup of coffee in front the fire. I arrange the full skirt of my emerald-green wool dress so that she'll be pleased at my appearance; no one scrutinizes me like Adrienne. In a caring, if blunt, way of course.

"Otherwise, you look well. But you didn't have to wear your finest to visit me for coffee," she says.

"I'll be going to the *labo*'s holiday party afterward. That's why I couldn't stay for dinner."

"Ah, the *labo*," she repeats with an arched brow. "I assume Jacques Mering will be in attendance?"

I sip my coffee and avert my eyes. I've worked so hard to *not* think about Jacques since I left Paris that it pains me to have his name mentioned, and thoughts of him surface. Somehow Adrienne knows about the interlude between me and Jacques although I never discussed it openly with her. "I assume so, but I don't know. I haven't been in touch with him. I'm staying with Vittorio and his wife, Denise, and I'll be going to the party with them."

"Be careful, *ma chère*."

"What do you mean?"

She tsks. "You think I don't know the depths of your feeling for Jacques? I can see from your expression that you still carry—" She pauses, then asks, "How do the English say it? Carry the torch?"

"I carry nothing of the sort, Adrienne. Just because I haven't decided to replace him with some other scientist doesn't mean that I'm pining for him."

"I'm not accusing you of pining for him. But I can see he fills the space in your heart that you've allotted for love, and as a result, no one else can get inside."

How can she know this on first glance, after nearly a year apart? I want to protest, but even as she says it, I know she's right. It's just that I don't allow myself to think about this topic. No, it's more than that. I work tremendously hard to ensure that my thoughts never stray to Jacques.

"Adrienne, even if that were true—which it is not—there is no one in my life I'd even consider. And anyway, you know how I feel about combining science and family."

"Come now. There must be some gentle Englishman who adores science as much as you do with whom you could imagine a life. Someone like my late husband."

How did this conversation devolve so quickly? I'd been looking forward to sharing my science with Adrienne and getting guidance on my career. Lately, I'd begun fantasizing about leaving King's College and putting its poisonous environment behind me; I'd even contemplated a return to the *labo*, although I know it could be dangerous for me emotionally and certainly a step backward in my career. But must everything in life be a march forward and upward? Can I never make a decision that incorporates science *and* happiness? I think how Adrienne would use that sentiment as support for her argument that I consider having a personal *and* a professional life.

A tear streams down my cheek. I reach up to touch it and examine it on my finger, surprised to find it there. I don't want to have this discussion, don't even want to revisit my views on being a scientist and a wife.

Adrienne pulls her chair closer to mine, reaches for my hand, and says, "Tell me everything."

Hours later, Vittorio, Denise, and I burst into their apartment, our cheeks ruddy from the cold but laughing. "What a night," Vittorio calls out as he walks to the little table where they've set up a makeshift bar. "How about a warming drink?"

"No, not for me," I call back as I wriggle out of my coat but keep my scarf to wrap around my shoulders.

Denise says goodnight, adding, "No offense to either of you, but I'm guessing you're about to talk science, and my warm covers are calling."

Vittorio lights a fire in the ornate marble fireplace, so incongruously fancy in this simple flat. We drag two mismatched chairs to sit before the flames.

"Denise was right," I say, grabbing my bag with my images. "I do want to talk science."

"Let's see the pictures," Vittorio says, understanding what I want to show him and discuss before I even say it.

I hand over the precious manila envelope with my best DNA photographs. As he studies the images, I think about the evening, an informal gathering at a café near the *labo*. It was wonderful to see the *chercheurs* I knew from my years at the facility, exchanging updates about our respective research without worrying about what they might do with my results. How rare my collegial experience at the *labo* had been, a fact I only now truly comprehend. If only I hadn't started a relationship with Jacques, I might have stayed for the long term. I hadn't expected a loving embrace from him this evening, but I'd anticipated more than the perfunctory greeting he gave me. What had I done to deserve that reception? Left the *labo*? Had my own self-protective iciness prompted his behavior? *Stop thinking about him,* I tell myself. It doesn't matter.

"These are astonishing, Rosalind," Vittorio says, breaking me out of my reverie. His much-appreciated and hard-won compliment placates me. "The X-shape in the B form is vivid and, as I'm sure you know, is the hallmark of a—"

"Helix, I know." I know I shouldn't be so abrupt with Vittorio, but I didn't think I could stand hearing about the helix from yet another scientist. Just because I'm not shouting it from the rooftops and keep my discussion of it to a limited group doesn't mean I don't know the molecular structure of the B form of DNA is a helix. I simply want to ensure that I've taken every possible image from every imaginable angle and made every calculation before I do so. "Thank you, although I plan to get even crisper shots. What would you do next?"

"If you were a crystallographer, you mean?" he asks, half kidding. It is his little joke that I am a physical chemist primarily and only moonlight in crystallography.

"I am a crystallographer," I answer with a smile.

He laughs. "Of course you are. Well, if it were me, I'd apply the Patterson calculations to confirm the structure of the B form of DNA. It will help show the heavier atoms and make possible the measuring of distances between them. It will give you a good look at the molecular structure." He studies the A form images as well. "You could apply the same analysis to this trickier A form too. Though the pattern is so complex, I'm not sure the calculations will yield. Or when."

"I'd been considering it."

"I think it's your best bet to get definitive numbers for structural analysis. But I've got to warn you..." He trails off.

"What?"

"It's really taxing. The calculations take an enormous amount of time and concentration."

"Have you ever known me to be lacking in either?"

He laughs again. "Of course not. You've got both in abundance."

"I'd rather engage in these Herculean labors than take a shot in the dark with model building like some of my English counterparts who fancy themselves to be the next Linus Pauling."

"What do you mean?" Ever sensitive to my mood, the smile disappears from his agreeable face. "I thought King's College was the only institution focusing on the structure of DNA."

"King's is supposed to be the only one; that's the deal that the head of the Cavendish Laboratory at Cambridge, Lawrence Bragg, and the head of my unit at King's College, Randall, struck. But these two rogue scientists at the Cavendish have been playing around with the idea, even though Bragg has forbidden it as ungentlemanly. They're supposed to be working on proteins, not DNA."

"What would prompt them to try a model without any data?"

I could hug Vittorio for asking this question, the very one that came to me but strangely no one else. "Exactly. The one fellow, James Watson, said he was inspired by my lecture on the topic, but Watson and his counterpart, Francis Crick, have become pals with my coworker Wilkins—"

Vittorio sits upright in his chair and interjects, "The one who's been giving you such trouble?"

"The very one. Anyway, Wilkins has become close with Crick certainly and quite possibly Watson, and I wonder at the coincidence. I hate being part of this ridiculous race to be first. What happened to science being done properly for its own sake?"

"That doesn't sound like a coincidence. It sounds like Wilkins is sharing your data with his friends." He sighs. "I'm all for the sort of collegial sharing we have at the *labo*—we need cooperation in science—but this sort of exchange is not in keeping with that spirit, especially if he realizes the manner in which Crick and Watson are acting upon that information. In defiance of the gentlemen's agreement between the two institutions. While I wish I could advise you to leave immediately, I feel like you're on the brink of a major discovery, Rosalind, and for now, you must focus on the science. But as soon as you're done and you've published, you should get out of King's."

CHAPTER TWENTY-EIGHT

March 6, 1952
London, England

FOCUS ON THE SCIENCE.

I've followed Vittorio's advice since I left Paris in early January, and for two months, I've repeated the same routines. I set up the experiment for the hundred hours that the X-rays will be bombarding the B form of the DNA fibers. I adjust the tilting camera, finally ready from the King's College workshops, to precisely the correct angle. I finalize the positioning and turn on the X-ray. My results are getting closer and closer to optimal, and I feel as though this image might be the one I've been waiting for. My focus is yielding results.

Will this image display the definitive perfect X shape? Crystals diffract X-rays in distinctive patterns, depending on their physical qualities, often providing the key clue in ascertaining the structure. Seeing an X pattern on the photographic film after the X-ray diffraction of DNA—with the broad bands at the top and bottom—would be highly suggestive, if not dispositive, of a helical structure.

Each time I examine an image, this is the question I ask myself. It will certainly help lay to rest any lingering doubts about announcing the helical shape of the B form of DNA. And as soon as I capture that perfect image, I will turn my efforts to the A type of DNA, which has a sharper but more confusing picture, and then learn more about the two forms by comparison through the Patterson analysis Vittorio recommended. Only then will it be time for model building.

I hear a bang outside my laboratory door. I jump. Who could that possibly be? It is early evening on Saturday, and while I might run into the odd scientist or assistant before lunch, I'm usually on my own by the afternoon. Even the cleaning crew is finished for the day.

There's a firm knock on my door, and I get up, relaxing a little. I assume it must be someone from the unit. "Yes?"

Randall peeks his head in. "I thought I heard someone fumbling about in here. Glad it's you." He looks me up and down. "What are you doing without any protective gear on?"

I ignore his comment. One of the things I like most about working in the lab on weekends is not wearing my dosimeter or any of the protective shields for my face or eyes that make it hard to see my results or the equipment. In fact, when I find the prior week's dosimeter card lying about—usually showing elevated levels that would keep me out of the lab—I simply dispose of it. No one is the wiser, and I assume many of my colleagues do the same. As they had at the *labo.*

"And what in the name of God are you doing here so late on a Saturday, Rosalind?"

"I could ask the same question of you, sir."

"You've got me there," he says with a chuckle and straightens his tie. "Got me there. Always hunting for funds to keep this place alive and kicking. It keeps me here at all hours. I wish I could spend my time on the science like you, but I've got to keep the money coming."

"I'm sorry to hear that, sir. I wish I could help."

He sits down in the chair at the lab table nearest to the crystallography equipment and me. "You help more than you know, Rosalind."

"What do you mean?"

"If your discovery is half as good as I think it is, you will make my job a heck of a lot easier." He pauses, then says, "Particularly since the insulin research is turning out to be a bit of bore."

"Thank you, sir."

"Any news?"

I'm not certain what he wants me to say. I give him regular updates at our weekly departmental meetings, and of course, I see him multiple times a day at the compulsory lunches and afternoon teas. He does understand my reticence for a premature announcement, however, and I wonder if this is his way to get me to commit to my conclusions, to ask me more casually.

"Well, you're aware that I've been getting clearer and clearer images of the B form of DNA—definitely confirming its helical nature as well as the number of its chains. Although I'm not ready yet to provide details publicly."

"I understand your caution." He nods and then adds, "Although you may have that quality in overabundance."

I decide to ignore his remark, even though it sounds

suspiciously like something Wilkins would say. "I have high hopes for even clearer images, but I've also been using the Patterson calculations for further analysis."

"Those are a bear by all accounts."

"They are indeed, sir. But I wouldn't be a very thorough scientist if I ignored the A form and what it can tell us about both forms—so I assessed both with Patterson. Obviously, both are critical to DNA—and to understanding our genes."

"Agreed, agreed," he says, although his tone tells me that he wishes for a different answer. Then he stands up and begins walking around the room. "But I'm hoping that you might feel comfortable giving a preliminary report next week."

My shoulders tense at the very thought of it. It's too soon. Still too soon. "Next week?"

"The Medical Research Council is holding the annual meeting of all the biophysics units it funds. And I want to ensure we get the same amount—or more—this year. Your work might just be the ticket to inspire them." He clears his throat, and then his voice becomes stern, almost scolding. "Don't want our fellow biophysics institutions to get all the money, do we?"

"No, sir."

"Your research could be a showstopper. Especially if we give them a taste of what's to come."

"I suppose I could put something together, sir."

He smiles at my agreement, his shoulders visibly relaxing. Was his popping into my laboratory this evening really an accident? His appearance and request seem much too orchestrated. "I would greatly appreciate it if you'd put pen to paper, Rosalind. Especially now."

"Why 'especially now'?"

"Well, it's no surprise that there's friction between you and Maurice, and he's informed me that he won't play any public part regarding DNA while you're here. It's quite a quandary. So I need to put a name and face to our DNA discoveries."

My stomach lurches. What is Randall suggesting? I cannot imagine he'd want to oust Wilkins, with whom he's worked for years. Is he hinting that I should quit? While I long to exit gracefully from King's College, I want to do it on my own terms and in my own time. "Do you want me to leave, sir?"

"No, Rosalind. That isn't what I was suggesting at all. Wilkins can keep on with his project and you with yours. Although at some point, we must find some sort of resolution to the problem between you."

"I'd like that," I say even as I wonder what sort of resolution Randall would like me to find. One in which I serve as Wilkins's assistant? Because that's what Wilkins would like.

"Good. I'd hate to lose my key scientist in the discovery of the century," he announces and leaves the room.

And I am left wondering whether Randall has just given me a compliment or issued a threat.

CHAPTER TWENTY-NINE

March 18, 1952
London, England

The compulsory afternoon tea disperses on a higher note than usual. It's not that the tea is any stronger or the usually dry and tasteless biscuits any moister or sweeter. The mood lifts on the buoyancy of Randall's news.

I feel an unexpected lift in my step. The Medical Research Council meeting went tremendously well, according to Randall, largely on the basis of my work. I'd felt uncomfortable sharing the sorts of details I did with him, but now I am glad I did, especially since all official reports filed with the Medical Research Council are considered confidential until purposefully released to the public. When I leave here—and I *will* leave here—I'll have done so with a wealth of publishable research and a grateful employer. Regardless of how my relationship with Wilkins evolves.

Hands in the pockets of my lab coat, I allow the smile to linger as I walk down the corridor toward my laboratory, accepting a few stray congratulations as I do and an endearing arm squeeze from Freda. After all, good news about departmental funding is good news for everyone who works here.

I quicken my pace as I approach the office Wilkins shares with Seeds. I saw the look on his face when Randall made his announcement, and I have no desire to come face-to-face with him at this moment. Or ever again, if truth be known.

His door is open a crack, and I take care to walk softly. As I creep past that ominous opening, Wilkins's voice spills out into the hallway. "This whole agree to disagree thing is a farce, Seeds. A farce, I tell you. She's meant to get all the good stuff, and I'm supposed to soldier along with the bad? Randall thinks it's perfectly fine that she's got the legendary Signer DNA and the new camera and I'm left with the Chargaff material and the old Raymax tube? Am I not her superior? Haven't I been working for Randall for years, following him wherever he goes and doing whatever he asks?"

I freeze. I know exactly who "she" is—me, of course. Part of me wants to race down the hallway, away from this excoriation, and part of me wants to stop and listen. I want to know my enemy, for that is who Wilkins is proclaiming himself to be.

"It's not fair, mate," Seeds agrees, but his voice sounds a little lackluster and half-hearted. As if he's heard this rant many times before.

"Meanwhile, she does nothing to further the cause of science. She tinkers with those images over and over again, and then she dawdles with the calculations; all this delay and she refuses to admit that both the A and B form of DNA are helixes. Says she needs more time. Hasn't she learned anything from Pauling's success with model building? He made huge strides in understanding molecular structures without a single X-ray crystallographic image. We could make our own bloody model and announce the helical nature of DNA to the world now! We'd be the toast of the scientific community—maybe even get ourselves one of those Nobel Prizes!"

Now Wilkins is practically screaming, and I'm surprised that no one else scurries down the corridor to identify the source of the commotion. Is it possible that they've grown used to this tirade? I creep around the corner so that I'm far enough away if someone does arrive but close enough that I can still make out the hateful sentiments. I've known of his dislike of me for some time, but the vehemence of his loathing is unnerving, and I am left shaking.

"I hear you, mate," Seeds says, but his voice is curiously flat, as if he's bored by this diatribe. I wonder how many times Wilkins has made these same complaints about me. The situation is worse than I'd believed. Much worse. "From Randall's little toast today, it sounds as if she's tricked him into thinking that she's toiling away on the mystery of DNA—feeding him little tidbits of information to keep him believing that."

"She *is* working on it, Bill. I've got no doubt of that. I don't think she ever leaves the damn lab, as a matter of fact; she's a bloody spinster after all. It's just that she's working at a snail's pace—overturning every stone and all that nonsense—before making any public statements or moving into the model-building stage. All the while, our competitors are getting closer to the discoveries that should be ours. She might as well not be working on it at all."

"Why don't you ask Randall to have her give you some of the

good DNA back? Seems like a reasonable enough request, and you'd move this project along."

Strange, I think, *how none of them say my name.* Only "she" and "her," as if I'm a nameless stand-in for all women. I wonder if it makes it easier for Wilkins to think of me that way, to direct his anger at some anonymous woman he doesn't speak to and doesn't name, rather than me, Rosalind Franklin, fellow King's College scientist, a human being with whom he's talked and worked and dined.

"I can't do that, Bill. Randall made the division of labor clear—point-blank forbidding any intrusion by me on the Signer DNA—and I'll look like a bloody whinger if I complain again now. I've got to find another way."

Seeds says something inaudible. Even though I can't make out his words, I can certainly guess at them by Wilkins's response.

"My friends at the Cavendish are gobsmacked by this situation. They cannot imagine a woman getting away with this sort of dilatory behavior at Cambridge—certainly not with Linus Pauling's model-building success on the scene and other scientists in the DNA race breathing down our necks. They insist that this project would have been taken out of her hands at the Cavendish, and they keep asking me why something isn't being done here at King's. They believe the project should be handed over to me as I'll expedite matters, and barring that, well—" He pauses, as if even in the midst of this soul-baring tirade, he fears going too far.

"Well what?" Seeds asks, a note of genuine curiosity in his tone for the first time since this harangue began.

"Well, then they think the data should be handed over to them. They'll act on it expediently so that the world will learn the structure of DNA in a timely fashion."

"You think it should be given to the Cavendish?" Seeds's tone is skeptical, and I can tell he disagrees with Wilkins's idea. Is this the first time that Wilkins has made *this* proposal? "What claim do Crick and Watson—or anyone at the Cavendish for that matter—have to DNA? I thought their boss, Bragg, put a fence around DNA and told them to keep their noses fixed on protein. Have they been working on the molecular structure of DNA on the sly?"

"No, no, nothing like that." Wilkins rushes to reassure him, realizing that he has indeed gone too far. "I just want to make certain that we"—he pauses, and then in a rush, says—"King's, I mean, wins the race for DNA."

CHAPTER THIRTY

April 17, 1952
London, England

THE FLOPPY-HAIRED IRISH SCIENTIST SITS ACROSS THE DESK from me, and it takes everything in my power not to tell him how much his words at the Stockholm conference meant to me. *Any proposal about molecular structure of any materials—living or nonliving—has to be put to the test of X-ray analysis, as we should not rely on models alone*, he'd said or something along those lines, and I'd copied down what I could recall in my notebook as if the words were canon. This refrain has been rattling around my mind since then and has often served as a solace when I receive criticism or pressure at King's to abandon my methodical analysis and rush to construct a model or make public pronouncement about the structure of DNA.

This alone would have inspired me to work for Professor J. D. Bernal, a pioneer in the use of X-ray crystallography with molecular biology and the head of the newly established Biomolecular Research Laboratory at Birkbeck College, part of the University of London. But there's more. I've actually met Bernal before, in Paris at the *labo*; he's friends with Monsieur Mathieu, and this, too, makes me predisposed to like him, never mind that Anne Sayre has always found him distasteful for some reason. I know it's not scientifically supportable, but I have an affinity for anything connected with Paris, whether it's people, food, or science. Perhaps it's unfair, this adoration I have for France instead of my home country. But it is the only place I've ever fit in.

Bernal pushes away the lock of hair that keeps flopping onto his forehead. "We'd be delighted to have you here, Dr. Franklin." He smiles and says, "And not just because you come highly recommended by my great friend Marcel Mathieu. Your educational and professional shift from physical chemistry to biological materials is remarkably similar to my own, as is your training. I think you'd fit in wonderfully here at Birkbeck."

A weight lifts from me with these words, one that has been growing heavier and heavier but became overwhelming when I overheard Wilkins's rant about me. Bernal's words mean that I don't have to stay at King's College where I'm reviled and scorned by Wilkins and his cadre. I am welcome somewhere else, a place that might feel more like home.

I want to leap up and dance, but instead, I calmly answer, "I'd like that very much, Professor Bernal."

"Brilliant. I've got a load of viruses earmarked for you to study." He glances at some papers on his desk. "I see that your fellowship at King's won't officially finish until a year from January, but I've had success moving fellowships over here from other institutions. So it's really a matter of when Professor Randall will be comfortable with your research such that he can let you go."

"I'll speak to Professor Randall, but I'm thinking after the winter holidays might be a good time."

"That would work perfectly for us. Delighted to have you join Birkbeck, Miss Franklin. Whenever you're ready."

I practically skip down the front steps of the Georgian house on Torrington Square in Bloomsbury where Professor Bernal's laboratory is located. The thought that I can leave King's behind for this fifteen-person scientific research group where I felt immediately comfortable and wanted is almost too marvelous to believe. While I'm not operating under the misimpression that Birkbeck is a Cambridge or Oxford—or even King's College—there is something about Professor Bernal and the unorthodox nature of Birkbeck itself that attracts me to the position. The University of London, which Birkbeck is part of, was one of the first English colleges to admit women, almost forty years before Oxford and Cambridge, and I hope this signifies something about the atmosphere at the institution. Of course, the hiring of female scientists by Randall, which I'd thought boded so well for King's College, was no portent of that environment, but I don't think Randall and Bernal are cut from the same cloth. Either way, I'm hopeful.

I float the few short blocks to the tearoom near the British Museum. Since I'd taken the morning off to interview with Professor Bernal, I thought I'd make a day of it by meeting Ursula for the afternoon. As I step into the tearoom—its deceptively simple exterior masking some of the strongest tea and most exquisite biscuits and cakes in the Bloomsbury area—I shake the light rain off my serviceable tan trench coat and spot a bright flash of red in the back of the shop. It can only be Ursula.

"Miss Rosalind." Ursula leaps out of her seat as I walk toward her for an embrace; she's still the only Franklin comfortable with physical displays of affection. "Is that a smile I see upon your face?" she asks.

I could not wipe this grin off my lips if I tried. "Miss Ursula, it is indeed. Or shall I be calling you Mrs. Ursula these days since you are a married woman?" I very much like Ursula's husband, the kindly banker Frank Richley, but their marriage exists outside our friendship somehow. As if their union—for which I served as a bridesmaid and a witness—happened to a different Ursula.

"Very funny. We will always be Miss Ursula and Miss Rosalind. That will never change," she says with a smile. "It's been some time since I've seen you look so happy. In fact, it very nearly distracts from those dark circles under your eyes," she says, then makes a show of a scolding glance, an approximation of our grandfather's. "Why aren't you using that incredible cosmetic I told you about? It would do wonders to hide the circles." She shakes her head. "You look like you've got two black eyes."

I wave her away but with a broad smile. She knows full well that other than a swipe of bright lipstick and a dab of powder, I won't wear cosmetics. Not the array that Ursula wears anyway, even though I have noticed my persistent dark circles myself.

"Well, I'm happy to see that smile, but it doesn't make up for the fact that you've been hiding away from me. We haven't seen you at a family meal for over a month." This time, her scolding is real, as is her hurt. "And you haven't returned any of my phone calls or letters."

After I order my tea and cake from the waiter, I offer my usual excuse. "Oh, you know how it goes. The laboratory has been unusually demanding. I'm sorry, Miss Ursula. It isn't that I don't want to see you."

She adds some sugar to her tea and avoids my gaze as she stirs. "You know, your sister, Jenifer, says you hide yourself away when things aren't going according to your plans. I suspect you've been retreating from all of us because you can't put a brave face on something that's happening at King's College. What is it?" she asks, finally meeting my eyes.

How can I withdraw from my dear friend and cousin? How can I lie in the face of her caring inquiry? I've never told her an untruth in my life. The odd omission perhaps, but never, ever a lie. And I cannot do it now.

But I give deflection a valiant try. "You know you can't trust everything Jenifer says. She's still so young," I say, although in truth, I'm surprised at Jenifer's insightfulness about me. And then I give Ursula an approximation of a chipper smile.

Ursula gives me a skeptical glance in return, seeing right through this thin attempt at diversion. My facade crumbles, and tears well up in my eyes. Still, I refuse to let them fall as I recount my time at King's, the good and the bad. The elation over my discoveries. The kinship with Ray. The patronizing glares and comments by Wilkins. The refusal to abide by the boundaries Randall has set. The overheard diatribe.

"My God," Ursula says when I'm finished. "We've got to get you out of there."

"I think I've already gotten myself out of there. Remember that smile you saw on my face when I walked in?"

"Yes?" she says warily.

"I'd just come from Birkbeck at the University of London, where I got another job offer. Hence the smile."

Ursula sighs. "Thank God."

"I don't think your God had anything to do with it."

"That old kerfuffle—I know your beliefs and you know mine. Let's not allow those differences to get us off track from this wonderful news." She reaches for my hand and gives it a squeeze. "I'm so thrilled. When can you leave?"

"I've got to talk to Professor Randall, but I probably cannot leave until January."

"January?" Alarm sounds in her voice. "That's nine months away. How will you last until then?"

"It'll give me the chance to wrap up my work, Miss Ursula. And knowing that I'm leaving will allow me to shoulder the burden more easily. The time will fly by," I say, trying to convince not only Ursula but myself. Then I stand up, my chair screeching against the linoleum floor. "Shall we head to the museum?"

As we slip on our coats and chatter about whether we should see the Dutch prints and drawings exhibit first or the show on Leonardo da Vinci, I bump into a tall man walking into the tearoom.

"I'm so sorry, sir," I say, looking up. I know this man; it's Francis Crick from the Cavendish.

"Rosy?" he asks, a wide, welcoming grin on his face. "How funny to see you here."

Why is he calling me by that awful nickname Seeds uses for me? The one he and Wilkins use to irritate me? How does Crick even know it? The three times I've been in his company, no one used that name to address me. And anyway, since we hardly know each other, it would be more proper for him to call me Miss Franklin, or perhaps Dr. Franklin. I can think of only one reason why he'd call me Rosy—Wilkins must talk about me using that name.

"Why are you calling her Rosy? No one calls her that. Her name is Rosalind," Ursula says, never one to allow her favorite cousin go undefended.

"It's my turn to apologize, it seems," Crick says sheepishly. Then recovering his usual avuncular manner, he says, "What brings you out of the dungeons of King's?"

"A day with my cousin," I say, gesturing to Ursula. "If you'll excuse us—"

We begin to take our leave when he calls out, "How's that DNA research going, Rosy?"

I pivot back toward him. If he thinks he can cow me by calling me Rosy, he's about to be disabused of that notion. I flash him a smile and answer, "Brilliantly."

"Success with both the A and B forms? Not getting stuck on one of them, I hope?" His expression is open and affable, as if he's just making simple conversation with a colleague. But there is so much more to his words.

By his question, there is no doubt that Wilkins has told him all his complaints about my "overly thorough" approach and my "unreasonableness" in not moving forward with more haste with the two forms. "Research into both forms is proceeding as scheduled," I reply.

"You're not still stuck on that idea that the A form isn't a helix, are you? Because that's nonsense."

"Even if my measurements show nonhelical results? Not that I'm saying they do either way."

"Even so. There are many explanations that could accommodate a helix, even if the numbers point otherwise." He smiles, which I suppose he thinks is pleasing, but to me, it resembles the Cheshire Cat. "But the idea that the A form *isn't* a helix is pure rubbish."

I feel my cousin's arm slip through my own, wanting to extricate me from this awful exchange. "Come, *Rosalind*." She emphasizes the correct pronunciation of my name. "We have an appointment with some exhibits at the British Museum. Good day, sir," she says and pulls me outside. Never sliding her arm out from mine, she pulls us toward the famous behemoth of art and culture. "You must march right out of King's College and into Birkbeck at the earliest opportunity, Miss Rosalind. We cannot allow such condescension again."

CHAPTER THIRTY-ONE

May 2, 1952
London, England

"ARE THOSE THE NEW IMAGES?" RAY ASKS DISTRACTEDLY AS I walk into the lab with a packet in hand, late because of my annual physical with the college physician, a regular trial every scientist who works with radiation must endure. Ray is leaning over the sample that's been bombarded with X-rays for the past two days, and he doesn't move.

I'm surprised at his reaction. He almost always drops what he's working on and scampers over when he sees that a new batch of X-ray crystallographic photographs are finished.

"Yes. Do you want to review them with me?"

"I do," he answers, but he hasn't taken his gaze off the crystallographic equipment. "But I think you've got to come over and see this first."

"What is it?" I ask as I walk toward him.

"I'm not certain I can describe it to you. I think you've got to see it for yourself."

I stand next to him and peer through the microscope at the DNA sample hanging from the wire holder. Before my eyes, one of the DNA fibers changes from the A form to the B form so suddenly that the fiber falls off the holder. I jump back. "How on earth—"

Ray interrupts me. "I know! It changed, didn't it?"

"Yes, and then it leapt off the holder as I was studying it."

"No!" he says, incredulous, and then positions himself before the microscope again. "What would cause it to transform with such force that it would move vigorously?"

I shake my head and then ask, "Ray, do you mind writing up this development while it's still fresh?"

"I'd be delighted to," he says with relish. "What a sight!"

"I'll take a first pass at the images and let you know if I find anything special."

He doesn't even answer; he is lost in the dance of DNA.

I spread out the new images over the light box. We've been getting such incredibly crisp and elegant photos of the B form that I'm not hopeful for much more, even though I tell people otherwise to buy us more time for our calculations. As I slide a few of the images over the light, nothing stands out; they are all excellent in crispness and clarity. Until the very last one.

I catch my breath. There it is.

The most spectacular image sits before me. The bold and striking shape of an X formed by clear black spots—with nothing in between the arms of the X—materializes in my vision. I'd thought that the photographs of the B form of DNA that I'd been getting had been definitive, but I'd been wrong. The difference between the images I'd taken before and this one is the difference between a painting by the school of Michelangelo and the artist himself.

It's my turn to not believe my eyes.

"Ray, can you come over here?" I ask slowly, as if acknowledging this discovery might make it disappear, even though I know I need to get his input. *Silly*, I think. *Such a thought plays into superstitions and the same sort of thinking that gives rise to religion.* I'm a scientist, and I believe in the laws of *this* world, the testable, quantifiable, provable evidence before me.

"Can it wait?" he asks, not looking up. "I don't mean to be disrespectful, but this is such an intriguing scientific event, and I want to capture every detail."

"I'm not certain that it can."

With reluctance, he puts his fountain pen down and walks toward me. When he reaches the light box, I don't say a word. I simply sit back and give him access to the view.

"Good grief."

"It's as perfect as I think it is?"

"It's flawless, Rosalind." His tone changes from reverence to exhilaration. "Look at the way the arms of the X radiate from the center so symmetrically."

"I know," I say, shaking my head in near disbelief at the image.

"And there's not a single spot between those two arms. The space between them is empty."

"The fifty photos that came before it were excellent, but this is different. This is breathtaking."

He turns to me, his eyes bright and his face beaming. "It *is* breathtaking, isn't it?" He laughs and says, "I don't think I've ever said that about an X-ray crystallographic image before. Or any scientific results, for that matter."

"Neither have I." I laugh with him, then more seriously, I say,

"If we ever had a doubt about the helical structure of the B form of DNA—"

He interjects, "This picture has laid waste to those doubts. Should we stop our research?"

"Why on earth would we do that? We still have to back up our helical theory on the B form and come to some sort of resolution as to the structure of the A form."

Ray sighs. "It'll be hard to continue with all those laborious calculations after the excitement of today."

I pat him on the shoulder. "I know, but we'll be all the more certain when we publish our papers and make our pronouncement to the world."

His eyes flash at the mention of our papers, those all-critical components to his PhD. "All righty then." He pushes himself to standing and returns to the new development, passing by the special metal cabinet where we store all these astonishing X-ray photographs.

Turning back to the image, I drink in its marvelous shape and vivid details. Then I label it "Photo 51."

CHAPTER THIRTY-TWO

June 25, 1952
London, England

We are assembled in what was once a vast bombed-out hole in the ground in the King's College courtyard. The fact that this Blitz-wrought chasm in the center of the quadrangle is now filled with the pristine, state-of-the-art laboratories for the Department of Physics, including the Biophysics Research Unit, is meant to be symbolic of England's triumph over the evil of the Nazis. Progress seems to be the order of the day and Randall's greatest wish for my work.

Ray and I gaze around the new two-story underground space, with the underside of the quad serving as the roof. I'd been worried about the quality of light, but the presence of abundant light wells provides a surprising amount of illumination. We're eager to get settled in our new lab and are hoping for an early exit from the ceremonies, so we take seats toward the back of the crowded lecture hall.

I lift the pamphlet placed on each of the seats and flip through it as we wait for the first speaker to begin. To my surprise, I see a description of my work there, the same details I'd given to Randall for his very private report to the Medical Research Council for funding purposes.

I fume as I read about the *helical polymer chains of DNA* with a *parallel arrangement* and how Randall hopes the research will yield insights into DNA's function. My angers mounts as I read the names of the group responsible for this research—me, Ray, Stokes, and *Wilkins*. How could Randall break my trust and share this information with a very public crowd, including journalists here to report on the new buildings and celebration? And how could he suggest that Wilkins had participated in this project? Other than some very initial stage images, Wilkins hasn't been working on it for well over a year. I've reached my limit.

I will make an appointment to tell Randall about Birkbeck tomorrow. Now may not be the time, but it cannot wait any longer.

The sun has set, and somehow I've forgotten all about Randall and the pamphlet for the moment. All I can think and see and hear are the Patterson calculations, and slide rules spread fan-shaped across my new desk in the just-opened laboratory assigned to me. I feel as if I'm on the brink of unfurling the secrets of both forms, if only I keep at it a little longer.

When I hear a knock at the door, it is as if it's happening somewhere else, to someone else. It takes me a moment to rouse myself from science to the real world and say, "Yes?"

"Rosalind?"

It is Randall, and the betrayal and my anger come back in a rush. But before I can say anything, he pushes into my room, largely empty except for myself, my lab desk, and a mountain of boxes. "Your office is in the hinterlands, isn't it?"

I suspect that it's Randall who placed my office in the middle of nowhere, so I say nothing. Perhaps he thought if I'm out of Wilkins's sight, I might be out of Wilkins's mind. That would put an end to all his troubles, wouldn't it? Well, I am about to be out of both of their sights.

I remind myself that this is of no matter to me. I've already found my path to freedom. I need only persuade Randall to set me loose.

"Just thought I'd check in to see how the new digs are."

"Very nice," I answer, deciding not to pick a fight over the location of my lab. What does it matter? I won't be here long. I gesture around the room. "Spacious, as you can see. The lab is just through that door."

"Looks like the right spot to work your magic." He surveys the room, then nods. "Although this lab is long in coming. We eked it out patiently, didn't we?"

"That we did, sir."

"Well, good to see you settled. Time for you to be heading home, isn't it?"

I *am* tired. I could just say yes and put off the inevitable until morning when I make a formal appointment with Randall's assistant. Or I could seize this opportunity and take the first step out of King's.

"There's actually something I've been wanting to talk to you about, sir."

Randall stiffens and fidgets with his bow tie, the way he does when he's nervous. Has he anticipated a reaction over the pamphlet? I might have exploded over it if I hadn't already put my exit plans into action. I'm willing to overlook that betrayal; indeed, the fact of it might make this exchange easier.

"What is that, Rosalind?" he asks, rather formally and without his usual smile.

"I've spoken to Professor J. D. Bernal at Birkbeck, over at University of London..." Now that I've begun to say the words, they don't seem real, and I begin to worry. What if Birkbeck's offer doesn't come to fruition for some reason? All I have from Bernal is his word. I'd be without a position, and my parents would undoubtedly rise up and seize me for one of their charity projects. I'd become a charity project myself in the process.

No. That simply won't do. If Bernal doesn't come through, someone will; even Anne and David have offered to poke around at Oxford for me, should an opportunity not come through in London. And I will leave King's College regardless.

"Yes?" Randall prompts me along.

"Ah, yes." I return to the present and this important conversation. "He's offered me a position in his lab. Assuming we can arrive at a convenient time for my departure from King's, that is. One that is suitable for you."

He sits down in the chair across from me. Crossing one leg over the other, he leans in my direction but doesn't actually look at me. "This is what you want?"

"What I wanted was to make things work at King's. Under your direction, sir. But that would have required the atmosphere in the Biophysics Research Unit to change, and I do not see that happening anytime in the near future. Wilkins has turned the tide against me, and I cannot turn it back—with him or others."

Randall nods, so slowly that it doesn't register at first. Then, to my surprise, he says, "Then Birkbeck it is."

I am taken aback. Where is the insistence that I stay? Where is the disappointment over my departure? I hadn't expected histrionics, but I had anticipated resistance at least. Particularly since Randall has proclaimed that I'm his most important weapon in procuring funding. I thought I'd have to plead and make a case for my departure. Perhaps I am reading the reaction of this inscrutable man incorrectly. It wouldn't be the first time for me, since I struggle to read the nuanced phrases and facial expressions of people I know far better than Randall.

Business seemingly concluded, he stands. "Shall we settle on a date?"

There can be no mistake about his response to my departure now. I don't answer; I'm still reeling from his ready agreement. Can it be that my usefulness has waned since he received the most recent influx of cash? Or is it that Wilkins finally needled Randall into adopting his point of view about me?

"Hmm," I say, my thoughts a muddle. "What about January 1?" I throw out the first date that comes to mind.

"I will speak to the Turner and Newall Fellowship Committee to see if they'll agree to allow you to spend the third year of your fellowship at Bernal's lab at Birkbeck. If so, then January 1 is as good a day as any." He pauses, then adds, "Assuming you can finalize your research and write it up before you leave."

As he walks toward the door, his footsteps seem lighter. Or am I imagining it?

Just before Randall leaves the room, he turns back toward me and says, "I'm sorry you won't get to enjoy this fresh new laboratory for too long, as I don't anticipate the committee will have any objections."

CHAPTER THIRTY-THREE

July 18, 1952
London, England

"SHOULD WE PULL A PRANK OF OUR OWN?" I SUDDENLY TURN TO Ray and ask. He glances over, bleary-eyed from the hours spent at our Patterson calculations today. The fact that we are nearing the end has buoyed us for months and has bolstered us through this warm, humid day.

"Us, pull a prank? You?" He looks shocked, having heard me lament Seeds's unkind pranks since the chap started working here. "I thought I'd never see the day."

I hear myself giggle—actually giggle—and I'm so startled at the sound I actually clap my hand over my mouth. Since the Turner and Newall Fellowship Committee agreed to let me transfer my fellowship to Birkbeck in January, I have felt immeasurably lighter. An end to this uncomfortable environment is at hand, although I do feel poorly about orphaning my research. And Ray.

"The day has come, Ray."

He is beaming. "I'm guessing you have a specific prank in mind?"

"I do." I smile back at him.

"Please don't tell me it has something to do with peeling oranges."

One overly warm June afternoon in the laboratory, Ray had despaired of ever finishing the Patterson calculations and confessed that he couldn't see how the numbers would reveal the structure of the A form anyway. I froze for a long moment, unsure how to explain to him the three-dimensional shapes I saw so clearly in my mind. A vivid flash of orange appeared in my peripheral vision, and an idea occurred to me. I reached for the navel orange sitting on Ray's papers and asked, "May I?"

"Have at it," he replied and watched as I began skinning the peel off with a sharp lab knife. As the peel spiraled to the floor, I explained how our measurements and numbers would reveal a three-dimensional shape just like this. Or not, as seems ever more likely for the A form.

"For the B form, our structure will probably look like this orange peel. We don't know yet what design the A form will take, although it may well be similar."

We laugh at the memory of our day with the orange peels. "I wouldn't inflict that upon you again. No, this prank is more in the vein of a memorial service to our failing friend, the helical A form of DNA."

For the past several weeks, ever since early May when I achieved that perfect photograph—Photo 51—of the B form, we have been struggling to finalize our assessment of the A form, ever hopeful that it will be helical or, if not, that it will at least tell us something more about the B form of DNA generally. We know what we're dealing with in the B form—a helix undoubtedly. But try as we might, deep as we dig into the Patterson calculations, we cannot validate a helix with the A form images. The complicated myriad of crystals in the A form simply do not form patterns that conform to that shape. And finding the correct shape is absolutely necessary to understanding the function of it.

I need to put an end to the speculation. Not to mention the baiting Wilkins inflicts on me and on long-suffering Ray for our refusal to just up and agree with him and pronounce it a helix.

"A memorial service?" Ray asks, his eyes more confused than merry.

"Yes," I say. "I think we can agree that our calculations on the A form aren't dispositive of a helix, correct?"

"You are correct. At least not at this stage, and I feel as if we've been at this stage forever."

"This is utterly contradictory to our belief about the B form, which seems to be a perfect helix, am I right?"

"Absolutely."

"Are you feeling ready to lay the A form to rest, at least as far as the King's scientists are concerned? Or at least get the advocates for the A form helix off our backs for a time so we can make a determination unencumbered by their harassment?"

He tosses a handful of paperwork on the table and exclaims, "Am I ever!"

The poor fellow, I think. He works tirelessly and good-naturedly on this seemingly Sisyphean task. How fortunate I am that he's my assistant, in so many ways.

Across the lab tabletop—littered with formulas and scribbling and lines upon lines of calculations—I slide a little note I wrote on a three-by-six-inch notecard with my fountain pen. I had rimmed the edges in black to make a facsimile of a mourning card, and I'd penned a farewell note to the aspiration that the A form is anything but crystalline.

In the note, I announce the death of the "late helix," contritely, of course, after a long illness. I then invite everyone to a memorial service to mourn its passing.

"It's brilliant, Rosalind. Even though, of course, we know nothing of the sort. With certainty, anyway," Ray says with a whistle after he scans it, "but it's biting."

"That's the point, I think. To cut off all the ongoing idle speculation, not to mention the relentless, insidious bullying. And allow us to continue our analysis without interference, so we can make a thorough, informed study of *both* forms before we race off to model building or unsubstantiated conclusions. It's the only way science can honestly be conducted." This is the core of my scientific education—work tirelessly and proceed cautiously.

Ray nods very slowly. For one usually so ebullient, his face is strangely closed and somber. "You know that Wilkins will go mad?"

Have I gone too far? Will this put Ray in too much of a compromising position? The poor chap is already on a tightrope, teetering between me and Wilkins as it is. And he doesn't yet know about my impending departure, which may well leave him dependent on Wilkins.

I pull the card away from him. "Never mind. I was getting ahead of myself and acting every bit as foolish and immature as that damned Seeds."

Ray tugs the card back from me. "No, I think you're onto something here. This whole ceremony and notice is just a bit of an academic prank, far less insulting than what Seeds usually gets up to." His face lights up again. "And you've been the brunt of too many of his jokes and too much of Wilkins's gossip and pressure. Your work—"

I interrupt him. "*Our* work." Every paper we publish on our research will have Ray's name right alongside mine. I am a firm believer in giving full credit, no matter the rank.

"Our work," he concedes, even though he knows I'll get most of the credit because he doesn't yet have his doctorate, "has been maligned by Wilkins both internally and externally for long enough. We've got the proof"—he gestures to the mountains of calculations of the lab tables and my desk—"and it's high time he stops criticizing you and acting as if this project belongs to him."

I am taken aback by his strong emotions and the show of support. The affable Ray usually keeps the mood light, but he's shown himself to be capable of gallantry. *Who's King Arthur now?* I think ruefully. I'm so used to defending myself—alone among male scientists, alone among my family members—that this groundswell of feeling leaves me quite moved. Without thought, without taking that long beat to quell my impulses, I do something I've so rarely done before that I can count the times on my hands. I give Ray a quick embrace.

Then, embarrassed with cheeks aflame, I say, "Sorry, Ray. It's just, it's just—"

Witnessing my unease, Ray says, "None of that, now. I'm only speaking the truth, and we both know it." A broad smile forms on his face as he gestures to my flushed cheeks and says, "Not to mention that we can't give that Seeds any ammunition to call you Rosy."

CHAPTER THIRTY-FOUR

October 4, 1952
London, England

"I hear they've got a Pauling at the Cavendish now," Ray says as he returns to the laboratory with two steaming cups of coffee, one for me and one for him, to help get us through this long afternoon of numbers. Without Ray, I would be utterly cut off from the scuttlebutt both inside and outside King's, especially since my little memorial prank was poorly received by Wilkins, and his barricade has only grown higher and wider, with fiercer guards, ever since.

"I thought Linus Pauling was banned from leaving America. Some nonsense about his politics?" I say. Randall still hasn't forgiven Pauling's demand for our DNA images so he could build a model based upon them as he had with protein, and I still haven't forgiven Wilkins for telling Pauling that I had no plans to study my own images. *Oh my*, I think. How Randall will stew over this news, a coup for Cambridge. "How did the Cavendish manage to overcome that ban and lure him away from Caltech?"

"It's not Linus Pauling who's at the Cavendish but his son Peter."

I push back from the table, sliding my pencil behind my ear. This is an interesting development, and I can envision the Cavendish scientists—Crick and Watson in particular—clinking their pints in delight at getting the son. I bet Crick and Watson have designs on using the son to get information from the father, who they idolize for his success in model building. But I would never say aloud something so scurrilous. Not without proof anyway.

Instead, I say, "What sort of scientist is he?"

"Not sure, actually, not with all the lines between disciplines blurring these days. I did hear that he'll be studying under Kendrew. So molecular biology, I'm guessing?"

"How did you hear?"

Ray takes a long sip of his coffee and then answers, "The usual way."

"The pub?"

"Yes, but I plumb forgot about it until I overheard Wilkins and one of his chums nattering on about this new Pauling at the coffee stand. Thought you'd like to know."

"I'm very appreciative, Ray," I say quietly. Sometimes I feel like he's the only one truly in my corner. I have Freda, of course, but that friendship operates outside the perimeter of my feud with Wilkins since she runs the photographic lab, where he is rarely to be found.

He pauses in the middle of a sip. Is he debating about saying more? What else is there?

"You know that Wilkins spends many of his weekends at

Cambridge. He's grown very close to Crick and his wife, Odile, and he stays either with them or with Watson. They all spend many hours together at their favorite Cambridge pub, the Eagle."

"I'm not surprised," I say, wondering why he hesitated to tell me this. I had already surmised a relatively close relationship between Wilkins and Crick, although I hadn't envisioned it had progressed to weekend stays at their homes.

"It seems that Wilkins has gotten to know this Peter Pauling as well, because he often comes to Sunday lunch at the Cricks' home with Wilkins and Watson."

Ah, I think. *This interest in Pauling is precisely as I suspected.* They are trying to elicit information about the senior Pauling's work about molecular model building and his conclusions about helices. To what end though? Bragg, the head of the Cavendish, has barred them from working on DNA.

But I don't say this. There is a limit on what I'll speculate about aloud, even to Ray. Instead, I say, "What a motley crew. I pity Crick's wife."

Ray continues. "I overheard Wilkins say that the lot of them are hoping to convince Bragg to overturn his prohibition on DNA research."

I recline in my seat, pushed back by the weight of this information. I feel Wilkins and his compatriots breathing down my neck, and I can almost sense their hands on my back, forcing me into a race I never wanted to enter. Or pushing me out of the competition altogether and to the ground. I cannot wait to leave this poisonous place. If I was not so close to completion of my project and so near the end of my time at King's, I might just walk out the door today. But I am a scientist above all else.

Ray is staring at me. When I see his hangdog expression and his eager-to-please eyes, I realize that I've got to tell him about my plans. He has been a trusted assistant and loyal friend, and he deserves to know that I'm leaving so he can make arrangements. But my stomach flips at the thought of letting him down, as this news surely will.

"Ray, there's something I need to tell you."

"Yes?" His eyes widen and appear so innocent, I can hardly proceed.

I force myself to say the words. "I'm leaving King's. I am going to Birkbeck to work under Bernal."

Is that a gasp I hear from him? Oh my God, I'm usually stalwart when it comes to emotional matters, but this is heartbreaking. How can I let Ray down when he's stood up for me over and over?

A long moment passes when neither of us speaks. "Is it really so bad?" he asks, his voice quivering ever so slightly.

"I would have left a long time ago if it wasn't for you. Your support—as a scientist and as a friend—is the only reason I've lasted for nearly two years here. And I am sorry that I'll be abandoning you now."

"Oh, Rosalind." He lowers himself down into the nearest chair.

"I know that your efforts to defend me haven't made you the most popular fellow around here—"

"Please don't concern yourself about that. You're in the right, and I couldn't let you go about defenseless."

"Ray, you're really too kind." I shake my head. "I sometimes wonder how things devolved so badly with Wilkins."

"I sometimes wonder if it didn't start out with unrequited feelings on Wilkins's part," Ray says with a small smile.

I'm taken aback. Is Ray being serious? He cannot possibly mean it; I recall my interactions with Wilkins being fraught from the start. But is this yet another instance of my misapprehension? I decide that Ray must be joking.

"That's not funny, Ray," I say.

"I'm not trying to be humorous," he says. The dismay must be evident on my face, because Ray hurriedly adds, "That's all just speculation on my part, Rosalind. No proof in it."

"I'm certainly glad to hear that it's all just conjecture," I say with relief, and then add, "and I am terribly sorry to leave you behind, particularly when we are so close to finalizing our work and writing it up."

"Honestly, I'm just sad to see you go. You're the finest scientist I've ever worked with, and the most dedicated. I hate to let your DNA work go unfinished when you've suffered through so much to do it right."

I put the strange, errant comment about Wilkins aside and say, "There's no reason we can't write up a few papers on our research before I leave."

"Really?" He stands up again, and the spark returns to his eyes.

"Absolutely. I expect we can publish two or three papers in *Acta Crystallographica* or *Nature* on our results, and I'll do everything in my power to help you conclude your dissertation. Even after I leave. Given the timing—"

Interrupting, he asks, "When are you leaving?"

"Sometime between January and February. I know you'll still

need to find an advisor to see you through to the end of your doctorate, but I feel certain we can make headway on your dissertation. And who knows? Perhaps Randall will allow me to stay on as your advisor even when I'm at Birkbeck. I'd be happy to do so."

"That would mean the world, Rosalind."

"Ray, after all we've been through, I would not leave you to the wolves." I smile, but that disappears when I think about Ray's theories about Wilkins and his feelings. "And by wolves, I mean Wilkins and his pack."

CHAPTER THIRTY-FIVE

December 12, 1952
London, England

THE LAST GOLDEN REMNANTS OF THE WINTER SUN DISAPPEAR beneath the sliver of the horizon we can see from my parents' dining room window. Papa places his hands over the century-old, gleaming silver menorah, passed down through his family for generations, in a gesture of prayer. Before he lights the candle to signify the first evening of Hanukkah, he says the first two ritual blessings of thanksgiving, one for sanctifying God's followers with the commandments and another for providing miracles for our ancestors. Since I don't follow my father's faith and I think miracles are more miscalculation and misunderstanding than anything else, it is the final blessing, spoken only on the first day of Hanukkah, that I prefer: *Baruch atah Adonai, Elohenu Melech ha'olam, shehecheyanu, v'kiyimanu, v'higiyanu la'zman hazeh*. While I don't believe that it is God who has granted and sustained life, as the blessing says, I do believe in the sanctity of life. For me, faith is for this world—the belief in doing our best to comprehend and improve life, in my case through the lens of science—and for that, I close my eyes and pray, to whom or what I do not know.

My father lights the menorah candle on the far right, and I watch as the candlelight illuminates the many faces of my sprawling family. Tonight, we have not only my beloved brother Colin and his wife, Charlotte; my sister, Jenifer; and my brother Roland and his wife, but also my aunt Mamie and her husband, Norman, and my aunt Alice. Only David is absent, as he's required to visit his wife's family's home this Hanukkah. I gaze at each of them, thinking about how different and yet interconnected we are, like the disparate components of DNA. If only I could understand better the precise nature of both sets of ties, what insights I would have to help guide me through the world of my family and the invisible world of our genetics.

With the blessings over, Mama begins to fuss. Over the meal she's instructed the cook to prepare, over the manner in which the maids are beginning to lay out the meal on the table, over my father's approval and pleasure. As always, I cringe at the way in which Mama's relinquished her own opinions and beliefs for the opinions and beliefs of my father, not that she seems to mind it. Not for the first time, I wonder if this is why the solitude of the scientist's life appeals to me so strongly. I could never make such a surrender, nor would I ever want to do so. And it seems to be what marriage requires.

Unable to watch Mama's fretting, I wander over to the wide, beveled windows that display the treetops of Kensington Gardens a few blocks away, where my childhood governess, Nannie Griffiths, would take us to play. Although this dark and blustery evening hardly mirrors those merry, bright afternoons when I frolicked around the park's Round Pond and Peter Pan statue with my siblings. My parents' four-story town house, more comfortable than luxurious, somehow feels like both the welcoming embrace of my childhood and a too-small cage. And I suddenly feel the urge to leave. How soon, I wonder, can I do so without offending anyone?

I feel rather than see someone join me. Glancing over, I see the elegant profile of my favorite aunt, Mamie. While I've come to appreciate and enjoy my aunt Alice since I returned to London, as the proximity of our flats allows for easy visits, I admire the intellect and political work undertaken by my father's older sister, Mamie. The maternal support and encouragement Mamie offers means the world; it replaces the approval sometimes withheld by my mother, or the approval I imagine she holds back, in any event.

We smile at each other, and she says, "Everything all right, Rosalind?"

"Of course, Aunt Mamie," I answer. "Why do you ask?"

"You don't look entirely well. Perhaps overtired? Is King's College wearing you down?"

"The work is exciting, but I confess that the environment, well—" I hesitate. Do I really want to relive this tonight? With my parents so near? I give her a half smile and a shorthand version of my situation. "I think you know what it's like to be in a man's world."

Her warm hand rests on my forearm. "I certainly do, my dear niece. Serving on the county council can be a draining experience as one of the few women, and I imagine it's the same for you in science. But it's a sacrifice we must make to do good and set an example."

"Of course, Aunt Mamie. That's precisely what I remind myself when the obstacles mount."

"Good girl," she says, this time patting my arm. Somehow, when Aunt Mamie says this phrase, I find it heartening. But when Watson uttered it, I could barely keep my rage at bay. "I suppose you have some grand winter adventure to help restore your spirits. Each year seems to top the next."

I am reluctant to reply. This year, I simply cannot muster the energy to plan and undertake a journey. Is the exhaustion due to the stress of Wilkins or the guilt I feel at leaving Ray behind? All I can manage is finishing this sprint while keeping my detractors at arm's length and my competitors far behind me. I concoct a palatable response for my aunt, one that hints at the truth without revealing the awfulness of my struggles. "Just between us? I don't think I could bear one more lecture from my father on my decisions."

"Just between us. Although your father believes that he will protect you with his traditions."

I ignore her explanation of Papa's motives—I know he's well-intentioned—and say, "This fellowship at King's has presented tremendous scientific opportunities, but the toll of being a female scientist at that particular institution is too much. I've been offered a better role at Birkbeck in a more pleasant environment. But for the moment, I've got to complete a mountain of research before I leave in the next month or two. Sadly, that leaves little time for a holiday."

From her stare, it is clear Aunt Mamie perceives more of my situation than I'd hoped she would. Questions begin to form on her lips, but for once, I am saved by Mama's summoning. "Rosalind? Mamie? It's time to begin the meal."

A chair has been reserved for me at the end of the long dining room table opposite my father. There, among my sister, my aunts, and my sisters-in-law, I take inventory of the repast. All the usual Hanukkah dishes—from the aromatic brisket to the perfectly crisp latkes—are spread out on the table, alongside a traditional English supper should we tire of the holiday fare. The candle-light flickers and the china gleams, and everyone seems lit from within by the warmth of the holiday. It is in these moments that I wonder—despite my love of and commitment to science—if I have chosen the right track. Should I be following the long-established path carved out for me by my family, a path stolen from so many Jewish women and men by the Nazis during this past, horrible war? Do I owe it to all of them to carry on the Franklin traditions in their name?

But then, I watch as these women ensure that their husbands and brothers are well served before they fill their own plates with food and keep constant watch on their needs as the dinner progresses. Even Mamie, who is a force in her political realm, seems to make herself small in the presence of these men—her voice, her opinions, her very being. I cannot lead this life of diminution, even if it is a noble, traditional existence in its way. I am a scientist, first and always, and I must carry on in its name for all of humankind.

CHAPTER THIRTY-SIX

December 15, 1952
London, England

ADMIT IT, I THINK. *YOU'VE NOW WILLINGLY ENTERED A RACE.* Not the contest I unwittingly signed up for when I joined King's College but a dash to complete my work before my departure. And a competition to pull Ray alongside me to the finish line.

To do so, I will have to put blinders on and spend most of my time in the laboratory and my office, risking Papa's wrath. I'll have to decline family dinners, tea with my aunts, the mandatory social events for Papa's pet charity, the Working Men's College, and even outings with Ursula, with whom I usually never cancel. I have to be single-minded. Only requests from Randall can take me off task, as I don't want any lingering obligations to him and King's to keep me tethered to this place.

Ray and I stand around like animals in a zoo awaiting visitors. The annual meeting of the Medical Research Council's biophysics committee is being held today at King's, and the scientists are meant to make themselves available after lunch—for the two-hour stretch from two o'clock to four o'clock—to take questions from committee members and show them around our labs. We are meant to be charming, brilliant, and exceptionally on top of the projects described in the report disseminated to the committee members this morning. Preparing those materials at Randall's behest has caused me undue agitation; I loathe releasing any data in the lead-up to my publications. But what choice do I have? It's all part of the process of securing the necessary funding to keep the unit afloat.

I cannot wait to put the day behind me. Glancing over at Ray, I see that he looks as uncomfortable in his starched lab coat reenacting experiments as I feel. A wave of laughter overtakes me at the ridiculousness of this playacting, and it becomes infectious. Ray and I are practically doubled over with belly laughs when I hear someone walk into the laboratory.

"My, my, my. I don't usually see *my* scientists having so much fun. I must ask Professor Randall for his secret." A deep voice with a German accent resonates in the chamber. I look at the doorway to see Max Perutz of the Cavendish entering the lab. What is he doing here? Could he possibly be on the Medical Research Council or its biophysics committee?

"We do get excited about our discoveries over here," I say, the smile still on my face.

"That's why I made a beeline after the luncheon. I read about the report this morning and am very curious about your research," Perutz says. And then, as if answering my unspoken question, he adds, "I am a member of the committee."

Immediately, I tense. Perutz wasn't terribly interested in my research during the Cavendish conference a year and a half ago. What has changed? Is it that my work has grown more appealing to him somehow, or is he here in his official committee capacity? Or is something else afoot, as Ray suggested?

Ray, ever cognizant of my moods, chimes in, "That's why we are here. To answer your questions."

"And you are?" Perutz asks in an arch tone.

Very few things can shake Ray's affability, and a patronizing inflection isn't one of them. This quality is one I've grown to admire, and I wish I could be so impervious to slights.

With a winning smile, he answers, "My name is Raymond Gosling, and it's my honor to be Dr. Franklin's assistant."

Perutz nods absently, as if he didn't really care who Ray was, and turns his intense gaze upon me. "From the description in the report, it sounds as if you're on the brink of a major discovery, Miss Franklin. If you haven't already teetered over the edge."

"To what in particular are you referring, Dr. Perutz?" I emphasize the "Doctor" to highlight the fact he called me "Miss" instead of using the proper moniker: "Doctor." I can guess that he'd like to hear minute details about the structure of DNA, but I don't want to open discussion to his full inquiry. This is the precise reason I'd felt uncomfortable writing up my work for Randall's report; I prefer to share it with the larger scientific and public realm only when it's utterly final and published in a journal. Period.

"I would welcome a discussion about the events that led up to your discovery of the A and B forms of DNA, the processes by which you studied the two forms, including your crystallographic as well as mathematical and scientific analysis of the images, and more information about the unit cell beyond the data you included in your report. Perhaps you could share the length, width, and angles of the unit cell?"

Why on earth would Perutz want these sorts of minute details? The only possible reason a scientist would want this level of description is that they have some use for the data, and yet, the head of Perutz's unit, the famous Lawrence Bragg, has a gentleman's agreement with Randall not to work on DNA. *What a conundrum*, I think. I cannot ask for an explanation without insulting Perutz, and yet I'm extremely uncomfortable providing more information. Ray is watching my reaction, and I see his mouth open to answer for me. But I know I must formulate a reply.

"I wish I could be more accommodating, Dr. Perutz. Unfortunately, we are still proceeding with our work on those elements. It would be premature—and dare I say even unprofessional—to share them now." I venture a smile that I hope doesn't resemble a grimace. "That said, I'd be more than happy to talk to you generally about the topics covered in the report and show you our equipment."

From the way he raises his eyebrows and shrinks away from me, Perutz is clearly taken aback. As the head of a major laboratory at Cambridge University, I suppose he's unaccustomed to people declining his requests. Especially women.

"So we can expect you to expand upon this report with a paper in a scientific journal quite soon then?"

"As soon as is scientifically appropriate."

He nods, then turns to leave the laboratory. Just I am about to sigh in relief, he spins back toward me, as if an idea occurred to him this very moment. As if his next request isn't the reason he came into my laboratory in the first place.

"Might I see a few of your crystallographic images? I'm told they're outstanding."

I shoot a quick glance at Ray, and I see we are of like mind. So few people have seen our X-ray crystallographic pictures, the number of candidates who could have told Perutz about the quality of the images is miniscule.

"What a lovely compliment, Dr. Perutz. Who told you about them?"

Perutz's cheeks unexpectedly flush, and rather than identify Randall as the braggart who disseminated information about my photographs as I suspected, he stammers, "I-I can't remember."

Is it possible that Randall isn't the one who told him about Photo 51 and the others like it?

"Strange, that. Well, when it's scientifically appropriate to share our"—I look over at Ray—"images with the larger community, I'll make certain you are one of the first to have access."

CHAPTER THIRTY-SEVEN

January 28, 1953
London, England

Afternoon tea is not the usual cheerful affair this afternoon. Randall's mood doesn't strike me as odd or different when I first enter the conference room, but then I'm distracted by the designs in my mind for my model building; I finally feel that the research is ready for this next step. But Ray certainly notices Randall's state of mind, and he leans over to me and whispers, "King John is certainly miffed about something."

Glancing over at Randall, I agree that he does seem off. He's pacing around the tea station instead of his typical jolly chin-wagging. Freda, who's been standing alongside us, adds, "Definitely. He looks restless or even upset." How I wish my paths had crossed more with Freda and less with Wilkins and his cronies. My experience at King's might have been entirely different.

"Let's gather round, people," Randall calls out.

The low hum of conversation ceases, and scientists and

assistants alike drift toward the tea table, where Randall is holding court. I peek around the room to ascertain Wilkins's whereabouts, and I spot him on the periphery, flanked by his usual chaps.

"I've received some rather disturbing news today from our cohorts at the Cavendish."

Ray and I glance at each other, and I wonder if he's making the same sort of guesses as me. Will this "disturbing news" explain Perutz's strange visit to my lab?

"Rumors have been circulating for some weeks that Linus Pauling"—Randall says the name like a curse, leaving no doubt about our supervisor's view of the man—"has turned his sights on DNA and away from proteins. I did not give this gossip much credence until today when I heard from Sir Lawrence Bragg of the Cavendish. He told me, in no uncertain terms, that Pauling will be publishing a paper on the structure of DNA in the coming weeks in the *Proceedings of the National Academy of Sciences*."

No, I think. How could Pauling have solved this puzzle before us? By all accounts, he has been working exclusively on protein until recently, and his lack of X-ray crystallographic evidence of the DNA structure is apparent from his request for *my* images. Why is the esteemed scientist rushing to answer this huge mystery when it hasn't even been long in his sights? Upon what data is he relying to build one of his famous models? To my knowledge, I am the only one with such data.

"How does Bragg know what Pauling is up to?" someone yells out. "It's not like they are fast friends." This allusion to the rivalry that has long existed between Bragg and Pauling is a fair point. Why would Bragg get advance word about Pauling's paper?

Then I remember.

"Pauling's son Peter works for Perutz at the Cavendish, under Bragg. Sir Lawrence heard it directly from the horse's mouth via the horse's son. So I think there can be no doubt," Randall says.

The respectful silence of the conference room gives way to chatter as the news makes its way across the unit. Randall holds up his hand. "Quiet down, people. I'm not finished."

"It's upsetting news, to say the least, not to mention curious. Before I talk further about the ramifications for our own unit, I want to share my understanding of what will be in his paper. We need to understand what we are dealing with here."

Randall clears his throat, and I find that my stomach is churning. What has Pauling surmised about DNA? I've made many a bold statement about science not being a race, and yet I don't want Pauling to win this sprint without having labored as Ray and I have. It goes against my sense of justice and fair play, especially since I am almost out of time here. I've already asked Bernal for extra weeks beyond my original January 1 start date to complete my DNA work before starting at Birkbeck and I doubt I can wrangle much more.

"Apparently, Pauling believes that the structure of DNA is a triple-stranded helix with the phosphates at the center. He has built one of his famous models to that effect." The sneer is evident is Randall's tone.

A helix, yes, he's got that right, even though I'm not sure how without my images. But triple strands? Phosphates at the center? Those are the precise mistakes that Crick and Watson made when they built their ill-fated model. I want to cry huzzah, but instead, I shoot Ray a small smile.

My loyal assistant doesn't return the smile but calls out a question to Randall. "Are they ionized phosphates or not?"

Only he and I would really understand the implications of the answer to this question. If the phosphates haven't been ionized by adding the electrical charge that phosphates get from water, then it is yet another reason why Pauling's model is wrong.

Distractedly, Randall looks down at his notes, saying, "No, I don't believe so. But I will check."

Ray and I glance at each other, ebullient at Pauling's mistakes. He will not come first in revealing the *real* structure of DNA, regardless of his reputation. Although we may have to leave it to the scientific community to bring down the great man on his model, we know that Pauling has it all wrong and that we still have a chance. And we are so very close.

Even Randall doesn't realize the magnitude of what he just said. "Pauling does make some compelling arguments about the importance of DNA—comparable to proteins, he says—and the role it plays in the transmission of hereditary characteristics, the very stuff of life." He then takes a deep breath and goes on. "Obviously, this news about Pauling's paper is disheartening in and of itself. But there's more. There is an additional, unpleasant effect of its pending publication."

Oh no, I think. I hope it's not what I'm imagining. Because the consequence I'm envisioning is far, far worse than Pauling publishing a severely flawed paper about the structure of DNA.

Rage mounts in Randall's voice with each word that follows. "It seems that Lawrence Bragg has determined that having lost part of the protein race to Linus Pauling some time ago, he has no intention of losing again, this time with the DNA race. So Bragg has now decided to break the gentleman's agreement he entered into with me, between King's and the Cavendish. He has lifted the ban at the Cavendish that prevents its scientists from working on DNA, never mind that we've been laboring on it for years and are very nearly there."

Someone lets out a gasp. Honestly, I'm surprised that it's not a collective gasp. Because breaking a gentleman's agreement between scientists to claim an investigation that's already underway at another lab is simply *not done.*

Randall continues, "From this point forward, *both* our laboratories will be engaged in the race to ascertain the structure of DNA—in part against each other."

CHAPTER THIRTY-EIGHT

January 30, 1953
London, England

My laboratory is dark. I've closed the blinds and the doors to ensure that nothing will interfere with the clarity of my examination. I want the dots and flecks on the film to speak to me in their language, to confide in me the secrets of their structure. *We must make haste*, I whisper to them. *My time is running short.*

I position a photograph over the light box. Focusing on the patterns, I see the spirals unfolding before me and the chains that link and bind them. And then suddenly, I can see nothing at all. My lab is blindingly bright, and my epiphany has gone black.

Squinting as my eyes adjust to the brightness, I look toward the lab door. I see a figure, lanky with a high crown of curly hair. When my vision clears, I realize who has ventured into my laboratory, uninvited without even the courtesy of a knock. James Watson.

"What are you doing here?" I blurt out, and for once, I don't chastise myself for failing to moderate my language. Watson deserves every curt remark I can throw his way—for his rudeness at this moment and for his long-standing use of a patronizing tone in my presence.

"Hello to you too," he replies in his nasal American accent.

I decide to ignore his coarse retort. "Can I help you?"

"Rosy, I haven't exactly stumbled in here by accident, you know."

"My name is not Rosy."

His brows furrow in confusion. "I do apologize, but I honestly thought that was your nickname."

I don't sense mockery in his tone, but that doesn't mean I should give him the benefit of the doubt. After all, I know from whence the name "Rosy" stems, and I can imagine many derogatory discussions about me over pints at a Cambridge pub. "My name is Rosalind Franklin, and we are hardly on a nickname basis, in any event. You may call me Dr. Franklin." I rarely insist on this formal appellation, but somehow, with him, right now, it seems absolutely necessary.

"All righty then, Dr. Franklin, I'm not in your office today by accident."

"Although you are here unannounced."

"I'm sorry for barging in, but the lights were off and the door ajar."

"I'm quite certain that the door wasn't ajar. I very intentionally closed every aperture so I could better use my light box. In reality, you opened my door without knocking, and then you walked inside when you saw the lab was dark and believed no one to be present."

Watson is frozen, and I take advantage of the lull.

"It seems a simple deduction that you were not in fact looking for me but rather for something in my lab," I say, guessing at what lured him into my laboratory. My notes and my pictures. The sort of data that will help him along in this race now that the Cavendish has officially entered it, even though I suspect they've secretly been competing all along. But I dare not go that far, even with Watson. My incendiary accusations are without proof.

"You have it all wrong." He reaches into his bag, pulling out a curled packet of papers. "I came to see if you'd like to read Pauling's manuscript. An olive branch, if you will."

While I would indeed like to read the paper before publication, I will not give Watson the satisfaction. This proffer of Pauling's manuscript is nothing but a ruse, a simple cover-up to explain his illicit presence in my laboratory. Does he take me for a fool?

"I don't need to read Pauling's paper to know that it's all wrong."

"No?" He seems surprised. I'm certain that he lunged at the first opportunity to read Pauling's words and only now is beginning to comprehend them. His knowledge of and experience with DNA is shallow.

"No." I allow myself a chuckle. "His model looks just like yours. And that was as wrong as it could be."

His otherwise boyish face contorts with anger. "You don't know anything. You are hopeless at interpreting crystallographic images. If you had any sense, you'd learn theory and come to the ready conclusion that the A and B forms of DNA are helices and that any deviations from the images have to do with the structure of helices inserted into crystallized ladders. Never mind your damnable incessant X-rays and your obsession with hard facts."

I am gobsmacked by his words. Where is this fury and stream of insults coming from? Does it emanate from some rant by Wilkins that Watson has adopted as his own, or does it stem from Watson's own insecurities? It is beyond unprofessional; it is rude and insulting in the extreme. Anger surges within me, but then the hilarity of this situation—this novice with no experience accusing me of uselessness—takes hold and I begin laughing.

"That's rich coming from you, who must be the only scientist out there who doesn't hold hard facts in high regard. Not to mention you're hardly a world-class crystallographer yourself. And you've labored long and hard to investigate and experiment with DNA, haven't you?" I say, but once the laughter subsides, I decide I'm done pretending that I'm oblivious to what is happening right here, right now. "How dare you," I utter, walking toward him. "How dare you sneak into my office and, when caught out, pretend to offer me a gift, only to slander me instead. This is my lab, in my biophysics unit, and you have trespassed upon it and me."

I take one step closer to him, but he doesn't move. He is over six feet tall, towering over me, and I begin to wonder if I'm making a horrible mistake. Ray will not be back until later this afternoon, and as Randall pointed out, this room is isolated. Would anyone hear me if I were to scream? Would Watson do something to make me scream?

I cannot think about that now. I must proceed full bore.

"I think we both know why you are here. Bragg lifted the ban on DNA research, and suddenly you're omnipresent at King's, the center of DNA investigation. That cannot be a coincidence. I saw you here yesterday and two days before that. In fact, Professor Randall has become so tired of your loitering around our unit"—I pause, allowing that little tidbit to sink in, his alienation of the famous Randall—"that he ordered Wilkins not to let you in his sight again."

His eyes widen at this news, but he presses ahead. "What are you accusing me of, Rosy?"

"What are you guilty of, Jimmy?"

A male voice echoes down the empty corridor outside my office. I would love nothing more than to see Randall appear in my doorway at this very moment. Particularly since he and I had a very interesting discussion where I explained why Pauling's model and manuscript were wrong. When I did so, Randall's foul mood disappeared, and he unleashed me to finish my work with haste. He now sees victory as a possibility again in a race I still don't want to run.

But I suspect that Randall's presence in the lab is precisely what Watson fears, particularly since Randall would likely reach the same conclusions I am right now. Because on the sound of that male voice, Watson strides through the laboratory and out my door without another word.

CHAPTER THIRTY-NINE

January 31, 1953
London, England

THE SUN HAS NOT FULLY RISEN WHEN I UNLOCK MY OFFICE door the next morning, a Saturday, a day on which I've increasingly found it harder and harder to rouse myself early. I normally do not lock my office and laboratory, but my altercation with Watson yesterday left me unsettled. How determined is he to win the DNA race now that Bragg has given him license to do the work and Pauling's theory is wrong? Would he actually look at my research without my permission? How far would he go? Watson sees himself crossing that finish line first, with Crick and who knows what else at his side. I know it, but he needs data, and I'm the only one who has it.

I scan my office and the lab to ensure order prevails, and all seems undisturbed. After brewing myself a coffee *labo*-style, I settle into a long day's work. Bernal agreed to push back my start date at Birkbeck to mid-March—but no later—and I need to complete the models of the A and B forms, not to mention finish the three papers covering my work at King's that will be published jointly with Ray in April. The first paper announces my discovery of the two forms of DNA and the conditions for the change from the dry to the crystalline form and attaches the clearest images that Ray and I took of both forms. The second paper shares all the X-ray crystallography data and measurements of the A form Ray and I procured over the past six months, and the final paper generally recaps our research on the B form. Each is singular and important in its own right and may well beat Watson and Crick and whoever else at the Cavendish to the punch.

As I sort piles of data for the different papers, I hear a door slam in the hallway. I freeze, suddenly terrified that it could be Watson returning. My tension lessens when I recall that access to the building requires a key and that oodles of scientists come in on Saturdays.

Only when Ray pokes his head in my office a few seconds later do I fully relax. "Thank goodness, it's you. I was wondering who that was bungling about in the corridor," I say by way of greeting.

"I'm so glad you're here."

I laugh, but the humor in his remark is lost on him. "I'm always here on the weekends, Ray."

"Right. I should've known," he says with a ghost of his usual smile.

"Yes, you should have. What prompted you to come in this morning?" I ask while continuing to sort data.

He sits in the chair across from me and my piles, his head in his hands. He does not answer me.

I stop organizing the research material and study Ray. His eyes are bloodshot, whether from the early hour or perhaps from too many pints last night, I cannot say. Beyond that, there is a heaviness about him, discordant with the lightness he usually brings into every room he enters. Something is terribly wrong.

"What is it, Ray? All you all right?"

"I'm not sure." His voice is shaky.

"You can tell me."

He takes a deep breath. "It's a story with two parts, but I didn't understand how the puzzle pieces fit together until last night."

"Tell me. I'm certain it's not as bad you think."

"No, I'm quite certain it is. Last evening, I went to the pub with Wilkins and his chums, as I often do. But someone new joined us—that chap Watson."

"Oh no," I say, wishing that I'd told him about my run-in with Watson yesterday afternoon. I hadn't because I thought the ever-valiant Ray might have slugged the fellow, should he run into him in the King's hallways. I would have never believed Wilkins would bring Watson out to the pub, not after Randall's reaction anyway.

"Oh yes. After a few pints, Watson's lips became loose. And he started to brag about how *his* team at the Cavendish—mostly just him and Crick—were going to build the perfect model of DNA, the B form first, then a helical A form. I goaded him on and mocked him a bit based on the lethal flaws in his first model. But that incited him—that and the pints, of course—and he began to talk about how and why this model would be different."

I lean forward in my chair, eager to hear where this is going. Why is he feeling badly about sharing this news? Is it that he strayed from his normal good-natured character to goad Watson? This sort of inside information is the only reason I like his trips to the pub with Wilkins.

"Watson then mentioned the Medical Research Council report on our unit that we prepared. He spouted off all sorts of data from it that he planned on using for his model—*our* data."

I feel queasy. "How did he get the report? It's meant to be private, for committee members only."

At the same time, we say, "Perutz." Obviously, the head of the biophysics unit Watson and Crick work for would make that report available to his key scientists once Bragg lifted the ban on DNA work. Even though it wasn't appropriate to do so. Watson and Crick are definitely not on the Medical Research Council biophysics unit committee after all.

An image of Perutz appears in my mind, and I think better of my supposition. "But Perutz seems upstanding. I find it hard to believe that he'd cross the boundaries and give it to Crick and Watson. Could Wilkins have gotten his hands on the report and given it to them?"

"I thought of that as well, but first of all, I'm not certain Wilkins had the final report. Not to mention he was standing right there during this exchange, and I didn't see a flash of guilt on his face or any strange glances between Watson and Wilkins."

I trust Ray's assessment; he's an excellent judge of character. Standing up, I begin to pace the room. "However Watson got it, it gives him and Crick a leg up they don't deserve. But what can we do? Ask Crick and Watson to relinquish it? I imagine they'd deny having it. Should we complain to Randall?"

"Randall hates whinging."

"True enough. But does illicit sharing of scientific information really count as whinging?"

"I suppose you're right."

"While I hope that Crick and Watson don't have the Medical Research Council report, it's important to remember that even if they do, it only contains very high level data. I'm not sure it will provide the details they need." Am I saying this to make myself feel better or to assuage Ray? Because something then occurs to me. "But it does contain some preliminary measurements on the outer backbone of the helix, into which the bases would presumably fit. That information might prove helpful to them if they actually do venture another model."

"Oh no," Ray mutters, almost to himself, and then looks down at the floor. "But I'm sorry to say there's more, Rosalind. That was only the first part of this awful story."

"No." I sit back down. What could be more dreadful than the news he's already shared?

"You remember that Randall denied your request to oversee my dissertation after you leave?"

"Of course," I answer. Although I knew it was unorthodox for a scientist to oversee a doctoral candidate's dissertation once he or she has left the university awarding the candidate's degree, I had thought that Randall might make an exception for Ray and me since our research and his thesis are so far along. That said, Randall's rejection did not surprise me.

"Well, I'll need to get another supervisor, and the only possible candidate is Wilkins." He grimaces at this necessary evil. "Last week, I met with him, and he asked to review my progress, to see if he could manage the workload of overseeing me."

"That's normal enough."

"Yes." He nods, my reassurance not lightening his mood. "We looked through my notebooks and our images. He spent a long, long time studying Photo 51, and I began to regret showing it to him."

"You had to give him access, Ray. Otherwise, he might not have agreed to take you on."

"True enough." He pauses, takes another deep breath, and then continues. "But I'm afraid Wilkins's familiarity with our images might have taken an unpleasant turn last night."

"What do you mean?"

"After Watson claimed that he had access to the Medical Research Council report, he and Wilkins got another pint and started talking quietly. They stepped away from the group, such that I couldn't make out what they were saying. But a few minutes later, they said good night, and I heard Wilkins mutter to one of the lads that he needed to stop by the lab because he'd forgotten something. Then Watson and Wilkins left together."

Ray grows quiet, and I'm guessing that this is the revelation to which he'd been building. But it's not having the bombshell impact that he anticipated. "So?" I ask.

"This is the second part of the story. I have no proof, but I suspect that Wilkins showed Watson some of our research. Whether it was our notebooks or our images, I don't know."

Now I see, and my earlier queasiness turns into nausea. Does Watson now have not only the Medical Research Council report but also the fruits of our labors as well? But then, I remember something marvelous.

"Not to worry, Ray. I locked the doors to the lab and my

office last night," I say and then tell him about my incident with Watson. "You needn't worry about Wilkins showing Watson our research after all."

Ray's expression doesn't change. If anything, he appears more dejected.

"Rosalind, you're not the only one with a key."

CHAPTER FORTY

February 23, 1953
London, England

THREE WEEKS PASS WITH NOTHING BUT FRANTIC, CONSTANT work, with the phantomlike hounds of the Cavendish hard on our heels as if we were in some Arthur Conan Doyle Baskerville story. What else can Ray and I do? We have no path except forward. Without any clear proof of wrongdoing, we cannot act on our suspicions. No true scientist ever makes assertions without proof, and we are scientists above all else.

With my departure fixed for a firm Friday, March 13—I am unable to put off Birkbeck a day past Monday, March 16—Ray and I manage to finish our two papers for *Acta Crystallographica* as well as the third for *Nature* and submit them for publication in April. I'd made the request for an earlier release date, but the journal told us that was impossible due to prior commitments. We hope our papers revealing several new discoveries about the structure of DNA are published before the Cavendish submits something they've cobbled together on the back of our research. With Pauling's *Nature* paper receiving the sort of scientific criticism we expected, the race for the structure of DNA has narrowed to us and the Cavendish.

In the meantime, Ray and I begin to build models. With our wealth of data on both forms and a final review of the entirety of the scientific landscape from a bird's-eye view, I see that both A and B forms are indeed two-chain helices. With this hard-won conclusion, we begin to the final stage—constructing the pairings of DNA's component parts, adenine, cytosine, guanine, and thymine, and seeing which pairings fit within the diameters I'd determined. By placing the phosphate backbone on the outside and the bases in the center, I hope to see the pattern emerge, to unveil the secret of traits replicating and passing along. I know that I am almost there; I can nearly see the solution in the periphery of my vision. I need only to proceed with my work, to allot the time necessary, and the answers of the operation of the pairings will reveal themselves to me. I am buoyant with the knowledge that the secret of life is nearly at hand.

Much to the dismay of Mama and Papa, who have been begging to see me, the only break in work I allow myself is a visit with Adrienne, who is in London for a brief stint to give a presentation. I leave work unconscionably early to have tea with her at her hotel, the St. Ermin's, and I stop home briefly to put on one of my little-worn fashionable dresses. Opening my closet, I stare at the four brightly hued garments, thinking how forlorn they appear. When did I last wear anything but my white blouses, dark skirts, and lab coats? Was it the Hanukkah dinner in December? It's been so long I cannot clearly remember.

Smart dress donned, hair brushed with the sides tucked into combs, powder puffed on the nose, and a deep-red lipstick drawn on the usually naked lips, I stare at myself in the mirror. How gaunt I am. When did I become so thin and tired-looking? And the dark circles under my eyes appear as though they're etched in charcoal. I'll have to ring Ursula to see if she has any cosmetic recommendations to help with this.

Even still, I am as ready to meet my mentor as I'll ever be. How I wish she lived in London. Could her sage and calm advice have helped prevent the terrible situation in which I find myself at King's? While Anne, Vittorio, and Ursula—and even Colin and his wife—have all listened and sympathized with my plight, the strong, guiding hand of my mentor, who knows the players and institutions as well as my impossible position, would have been invaluable.

Hopping out of the cab and passing by the doorman, I walk into the lobby of St. Ermin's Hotel. While not as luxurious as the Savoy, where I've had countless Franklin family high teas, it is an attractive place with a storied history. I spy Adrienne across the lobby at a cozy table for two near the marble fireplace.

We squeal and embrace at our reunion, long overdue. As we settle in our seats, I suddenly feel shy about divulging the latest developments in the competition for DNA. What will Adrienne think? Hasn't she managed to avoid the sort of ill-treatment I'm experiencing during the many decades of her career? Is it possible that I've done something wrong, taken some misstep that has yielded this insurmountable animosity with Wilkins and the Cavendish scientists? I do fear that somehow I, too, have contributed to the tenor of this race for DNA.

Instead, in my neglected French, I focus our conversation on her job and her daughter. When the discussion about Adrienne dries up, I steer the talk with unusual deftness to Paris and politics and art and opera and anything but King's and DNA.

"You think I haven't noticed that you will speak about everything except yourself?" she asks. "Let's begin with your family."

"They are fine. I mean, they are the same."

"With respect to you, you mean?"

"Yes. They remain perplexed about my dedication to science and concerned about the number of hours that I work."

She chuckles. "How *is* your scientific work?"

I sigh and allow my erect posture to sag. All my energy has been poured into the facade I'm maintaining for Adrienne, and now that I've been called out, I deflate like a balloon. "Where to begin?"

"How about where you last left off? When you were last in Paris, a year ago December? The letters you send are brief and cannot give the full picture."

Paris. The very mention of the place causes a confusing blend of joy and despair to course through me. The collegial *labo*, the respectfulness of my female *and* male peers, the acceptance—dare I say celebration—of my strange, blunt personality, and, of course, the city itself. How will I ever find another situation so well-suited for me? Damn Jacques Mering. Damn me for being so gullible as to fall for him and then sacrifice my circumstances when he tired of me and I became uncomfortable in his presence.

Tears well up in my eyes, but I force them back with a surge of anger as I begin to talk about Wilkins and Watson and Crick and the injustice of this stupid race. When I finish, Adrienne asks, "I can see how this quest has consumed you, never mind that you are dealing with a *situation terrible*—the worst I have ever heard. But you are hunting for the answer to one of the central scientific mysteries. It's the Holy Grail for many."

I am surprised to hear her reference a Christian legend, although I suppose that the tales of King Arthur have literary significance beyond Christianity. "But it's not *my* Holy Grail, Adrienne. Yes, there have been moments when the importance of this research has swept me up. Yes, there have been flashes when I envisioned myself unlocking DNA's secrets and receiving accolades for this project, especially when I am so very close. I am weeks, at most two or three months, away from solving the puzzle of DNA. And yet—"

Adrienne, in the most elegant, French way possible, interrupts me. "Yet you must leave."

"Yes," I say. "I have spent two years toiling, largely alone save for one wonderful, loyal assistant, while certain fellow scientists malign me privately and publicly. And now my research is under siege by my self-proclaimed enemies who want to shortcut the discovery process by building a model using no independent research but my hard-won data—my X-ray crystallographic images as well as all the measurements I amassed and put into the Medical Research Council report. I cannot sit by and participate in this madness any longer, even if it means I leave without fully finishing. Without completing my model of DNA."

"I can see the toll it is taking on you, my dear Rosalind—in your eyes, your weight, your spirit." She reaches out and lightly rubs the top of my hand. "But I do not like your sacrifice to be for naught. You have put *all* of yourself into this work. Must you leave before the race is called?"

"I have been offered another position, researching viruses at Birkbeck under Bernal. I dare not hope that it's the *labo,* and I have no illusions that London is Paris. I'll also be leaving behind my fresh, gleaming, state-of-the-art laboratory at King's for a hodgepodge of a lab in a town house. But it does seem to be a place where I might do good, noble work with scientists who don't find me loathsome, and I admire Bernal's vision of science as serving the primary needs of humanity, such as health and justice, even if his views are motivated by his Marxist and communist leanings. And because I've already pushed back my starting date by three months, I cannot risk losing the opportunity by delaying any longer."

"It seems inevitable, *ma chère,*" Adrienne coos and then wraps me in an embrace.

From within the fold of her arms, I whisper, "It is perhaps my last, best chance to capture some of what I had in Paris."

CHAPTER FORTY-ONE

March 13, 1953
London, England

"WHAT ARE YOU SO DAMN TRIUMPHANT ABOUT? IT'S NOT AS if *our* lab got the golden goose!" Randall's voice booms throughout the corridor, and I watch our group flinch almost in unison at this unexpectedly harsh outburst. Randall does his level best to appear even and affable most days. Marianne, Freda, and Alec manage to mask their discomfort immediately, but Ray has a harder time hiding his reaction. And we are all justifiably worried. What has happened?

We are gathered outside Randall's office for my farewell lunch. Instead of the usual visit to the students' union, our supervisor has arranged for a capital lunch at Simpson's in the Strand, one of London's oldest restaurants and still capable of serving a tremendous roast despite the rationing rules. It is an unexpectedly kind gesture for my final day at King's.

Footsteps sound in Randall's office, and we busy ourselves

by pretending to be deep in conversation over the unseasonably warm weather. To my surprise and, from the looks on their faces, everyone else's, Wilkins exits from Randall's office. *He* was the target of the tongue-lashing. I would expect his face to have a hangdog expression, but Wilkins is smiling.

"Ah, delighted to see you all. Saves me heaps of time getting the word out. One bird, one stone and all that," Wilkins says with a smile that's a shade too bright.

Somehow Ray puts aside the strangeness of this situation and musters up a return smile. Perhaps all those evenings in the pub—pretending and listening—have been good practice for this moment. "Good to see you as well, Maurice. What's this 'word' then?"

"I spent the afternoon at the Cavendish yesterday. Kendrew called me up and said I must rush down on the next train to see what Crick and Watson had gotten up to."

Kendrew summoned *only* Wilkins to inspect Crick and Watson's work? The last time an urgent request for our presence had been issued by Kendrew, it had been for me as well.

My stomach lurches thinking about the last time we went to the Cavendish, and I feel as though the room is swaying. Is he going to say the words that I've been dreading? Words that will enrage and disappoint me? I cannot imagine what else would prompt Randall to such fury, but nor can I really believe it could be true.

His hair flopping onto his forehead, Wilkins cries out excitedly, "They've solved it! Watson and Crick have discovered the final pieces of the structure of DNA. We already knew that the phosphates form the outside rails of the spiral staircase with the bases facing in like treads in the staircase, but Crick and Watson have learned that the two paired bases of adenine and thymine along with guanine and cytosine form the steps connecting the rails. And they unearthed more—when the rails come apart, each of the bases seeks out its complement base, forming new steps identical to the old." He turns and pointedly looks at me, the venom in his eyes undisguised. "And all they needed to do was build a model, as I've been pushing for all along."

I pause, processing what Wilkins has just said about the structure of DNA while allowing the fact to register that he failed to give me credit for discovering that phosphates are on the outside. Crick and Watson's proposal makes sense, and for a split second—before I really allow the inequity of this situation to register and before I even contemplate how unimportant who made the discovery first *should* be—the simple beauty of the interior structure of DNA washes over me in waves. How brilliant and graceful nature is. This is the solution that has been niggling at me around the periphery of my thoughts; while I'd long since uncovered the structure and measurements of the helix and I'd already formed a theory about the interchangeability of the bases, it was only a small step from there to the specific pairings and re-pairings of adenine, thymine, guanine, and cytosine. If I had just a little bit more time, I feel quite sure I would have been able to glimpse it in full and claim the entirety of the solution as my own. But time is one of many things Wilkins has stolen from me.

But how dare the upstarts claim this solution as their own. After two years of research, *I* am the one who's definitively proven that DNA has two helical forms, each with two specific chains with the phosphate groups on the outside, and *I* am the one who's uncovered all the necessary measurements for model building. In fact, I am standing on the precipice of solving the puzzle of the interior placement of DNA's bases myself and I'm about to build my own model reflecting my discoveries. But as I think about the deceit inherent in Crick and Watson's model—the steps they must have taken to make this leap without any investigation of their own—Wilkins and Ray and all the others suddenly seem very far away. I can make out their voices and see their faces, but my vision and hearing function as if I'm underwater and swaying in the waves.

"Good God, how did they manage that?" Ray asks, all feigned innocence. He and I are of like mind, if not disposition. "Bragg lifted the ban on DNA research less than six weeks ago."

"Must be quick studies," Wilkins replies, the smug smirk never leaving his face.

"But how could they possibly have amassed enough research on the structure of DNA in six weeks? You can't make a model on ideas alone." Ray is baiting Wilkins, but his tone is convincingly confused. Only I see where he's leading Wilkins.

I surface. The gravity and horror of Wilkins's announcement becomes immediate and clear. I cannot play Ray's long game, and there will be no pause so I can hold my tongue. Wilkins doesn't deserve it. The man couldn't make sense of a model or create a proper X-ray diffraction image if he tried, and I don't think he's attempted either.

"I can think of one way that they got enough research to make a model," I say, enunciating each word very carefully, making abundantly clear my meaning. Then I pointedly stare at Wilkins. "Watson has been sniffing around King's for weeks."

Wilkins's face flushes, and I'm certain I've hit the mark. "Well, um—"

Just then, Randall storms out of his office. "Oh, I see Maurice has divulged his *good* news to you. Why he's so elated to share this development is beyond me. I, for one, am furious."

Almost as one, we avert our eyes. None of us wants to get caught in the cross fire of Randall's rare anger. Although I am delighted to see Wilkins in Randall's line of sight.

"Fine mess we're in now. Two years in, and Rosalind is so close. She's got papers lined up for publication next month that demonstrate her revolutionary findings. And because Bragg broke his promise and Rosalind has to leave—" Randall looks at Wilkins, and I swear I see blame in his eyes.

"But, sir," Wilkins rushes in. "As I told you, I made a deal with the Cavendish."

I note that Wilkins does not say he made a deal with Crick or Watson. He is very careful to avoid mentioning their names now that Randall is here. I'm certain Wilkins doesn't want to remind Randall how often Watson was at King's recently and how friendly he's become with Crick, Watson, and Pauling the younger. The logical extrapolation of this information is damning.

"The Cavendish will write a letter for *Nature* reporting on their model and hypothesis, and we—I mean King's—will publish one in that same edition of *Nature*. That way, King's contributions will be known," Wilkins says.

"I am the head of this unit, Maurice, not you. I am the one who should be striking deals. Having broken our gentleman's agreement to keep out of DNA, the Cavendish has proven to be untrustworthy. I wish you'd never made an agreement with them on publications. You had no right to do so, in fact." Randall's face is practically purple, and his trademark tie is askew. He turns to me. "Rosalind, I know this is your last day, but I have a favor to ask of you. Can you write an addendum to one of your papers about your own findings? I'll make certain it is published in the same edition of *Nature* as Crick and Watson's paper."

Fury has built to a near crescendo within me, but I must push it away, for now at least. "Of course, sir. I'd be happy to make sure our two years' worth of research here at King's gets at least *some* of the recognition it deserves. But please understand that we would be receiving *all* the accolades if only we'd been allowed a bit more time."

CHAPTER FORTY-TWO

March 14, 1953
London, England

"Aren't we meant to be celebrating, Miss Rosalind? We're supposed to be marking your departure from King's College with champagne and a decadent meal. And toasting to your new role at Birkbeck." Ursula pouts over her flute of sparkling Moët & Chandon, which glistens even more than her cinched, full-skirted cobalt dress with its crystal trim in a matching shade of blue. She looks picture-perfect against the vivid crimson banquettes for which Rules restaurant, a London institution for a century and a half, is known.

"I'm sorry, Miss Ursula. There's nowhere I'd rather be than here with you. It's just that something unexpected occurred right as I was departing from King's yesterday, and I'm having some mixed feelings at the moment." I smooth my decidedly less fashionable violet patterned dress, purchased in Paris over five years ago. My stomach is unsettled and has been for some weeks, and

I'm trying to delay sipping my champagne. Just as I've tried to delay the unavoidable conversation to come by discussing the big events of the day—the recent death of Stalin and the crowning of Queen Elizabeth this summer.

"Can you tell me what happened? You're always so reticent to talk about work." She takes a sip from her flute and then adds, "As long as it doesn't involve detailed scientific data that I'll *never* be able to understand."

I laugh. Ursula always pretends that she cannot make heads or tails of my work, but in truth, she's extremely bright and soared through St. Paul's at my side. She simply wasn't swayed by the academic world and yielded to family pressure to marry. Either that or her delightful husband, Frank, simply captured her fancy.

"If you insist," I say and launch into the contretemps at King's, supposing that I should be thankful that Mama and Papa have not weighed in on this job change and situation due to their distraction at the arrival of three new grandchildren from my three brothers. "So now Crick and Watson are receiving the lion's share of credit—on the back of my research, of course, thanks to Wilkins—while I and my King's College colleagues are in a mad scramble to put pen to paper and get some crumbs of recognition."

"Do you mean to tell me that you haven't told your superiors about their behavior? What they've done is criminal."

"Miss Ursula, I haven't got any proof that Wilkins shared my data with Crick and Watson or that the three men were in cahoots. As a scientist, I'd be acting against my own maxim if I accused any one of them without evidence. Without it, no one would believe me, especially since I'm a woman; they'd just chalk it up to sour grapes. They already think I'm a hysterical shrew."

"I met that awful Crick. If Wilkins and Watson are cut from the same cloth, I am not surprised that they helped themselves to your research. How perfectly ungentlemanly and reprehensible."

"Unfortunately, it's not a crime to be ungentlemanly." A rueful laugh escapes from my lips. "Imagine, Ray has the ridiculous notion that Wilkins's animosity stems from some unrequited feelings he had for me when I started. Emotions Wilkins kept so well-hidden behind a veneer of condescension that I couldn't detect them at all."

"Why is that so hard to believe? You're a beautiful, brilliant woman, and if he's as insecure as you've described, he could be motivated by a perceived rejection—in addition to his own failure to solve this scientific riddle." She reaches for my hand. "Either way, dear cousin, you had to leave that awful place. I witnessed only a slice of the deprecatory treatment you received regularly, and it was unbearable and unacceptable. You *had* to leave. I need only look into your face and see the terrible tax that environment has levied upon you."

I try to make light of her solemn words. "I suppose I should be a bigger fan of cosmetics."

"Don't try to push me away with a joke. Miss Rosalind, I'm deadly serious. No job is worth the toll King's has taken on you."

Although Ursula and I are so very close, the one area that she doesn't understand is the depth of my commitment. I explain, "But I would not erase those years to spare myself the torment, Miss Ursula. Science *is* life, dear cousin. It is the lens through which I see and experience and make sense of the world around me, and it is my way of giving back. In solving crucial scientific mysteries at King's, I became closer and closer to the understanding of life itself. And I wouldn't undo that for anything. That *is* my faith."

"So you'll just let them get away with stealing? The data and the research and the photographs you have worked on for years?" Ursula has an indignant expression on her face, and I know, diminutive as she is, she'd act as my champion and excoriate those men if she could.

I am quiet for a long moment. What should I do? This question has circled around and around in my mind since yesterday—and, to a lesser extent, for the past several weeks—and the path forward has not materialized before me until now.

"I think I have a choice. I can either wallow in my anger and outrage at the injustice of the way in which my hard-won research was possibly stolen and used, or I can move forward with my life, engaging in the satisfying, important scientific work I love."

"You are more noble than I would be." She sighs. "What path will you choose? Need I even ask?"

"My future—and my legacy, I hope—lie ahead of me. I must put the misfortune of King's in my past."

PART THREE

CHAPTER FORTY-THREE

December 8, 1953
London, England

I HEAR A THUD OF FOOTSTEPS APPROACHING UP THE STEEP SET of stairs leading to my office and lab. The fifth floor of the ramshackle town house that Birkbeck calls home is empty save for me, and given the rather arduous climb to the former maid's quarters, I don't receive many unscheduled visitors. Who on earth is popping in on this frigid December day, even colder and draftier up here on the top floor of this eighteenth-century building, the redbrick exterior of which still bears the scars of bomb damage from the war?

"Knock, knock," a voice calls out rather than actually knocking on my half-open door. "How's my Turner and Newall Fellow?" The title—and funding—has followed me here from King's.

I recognize the voice. It's my boss, the famous John Desmond Bernal, whose renown extends so far and wide that his colleagues call him by the nickname "Sage" when they're not using his initials, JD. Not only is he expert in crystallography—he taught Perutz, for goodness' sake—but he seems to be knowledgeable about every other subject, from architecture to politics. Although his brilliance and deep understanding of X-ray crystallography attracted me to his unit, in some ways, it is also the absence of certain qualities that I grew to dislike about Randall—the constant angling for something, whether it was funds, recognition, or accolades—that draws me to Bernal. Like me, Bernal cares mostly about knowledge, even in the way it represents a kind of faith, in that we both believe doing our utmost scientifically to improve the lot of mankind reflects our faith in the future of ourselves as individuals and our successors. To me, it is a more palpable, understandable faith than the sort of belief Papa has about the afterlife. Perhaps it is this purer pursuit that makes me feel more at ease at Birkbeck than King's. That and the nonsectarian nature of the place—no more religious clerics wandering about the corridors.

How my criteria have changed since my salad days at the *labo.*

Jumping up from my desk chair, I rush to greet him. "To what do I owe the unexpected pleasure, sir?"

"How many times have I told you, Rosalind, I don't believe in all that hierarchical 'sir' business." He pretends to scold me, and I shouldn't be surprised at his stance. Bernal makes no secret of his fascination and allegiance with the Soviet Union and its politics, as had one of my previous superiors, Monsieur Marcel Mathieu. But like Monsieur Mathieu, Bernal knows not to raise such topics with me, as I've made clear my loathing of the Cold War race to stockpile arms. Consequently, I only learn about his Marxist endeavors—such as his meetings with Nikita Khrushchev and

Mao Tse-tung—from overheard conversations when he's actually in London and assembles a group lunch. Is it his communist and Marxist leanings that make Anne dislike him so? Or could it be some of his more personal choices? I must ask her this weekend when I visit her and David in Oxford, a sort of send-off before they return to America.

"Call me JD, and I'll call you Rosalind," he says.

"All right." My old habit nearly kicks in, and I have to stop myself from using the word "sir." Will I ever feel comfortable referring to the esteemed, fifty-two-year-old scientist by the youthful sounding JD?

"I hate that you're forced to use our old equipment in the basement, using an umbrella, for heaven's sake, to keep yourself and the specimens dry thanks to the leaks down there. It's a far cry from your spanking-new digs at King's."

"Please don't apologize—" I hesitate, finding it easier not to call him any name at all than to use JD. "I'm loads happier here than I was at King's, and I'm thrilled about the assignment you've given me."

What I'm saying is true. The only thing I miss from my time at King's is Ray. His optimism, his insights, his friendship, all made King's palatable for a time. If I could have him working with me here, it would be "dreamy," a new word Ursula likes to bandy about. I don't care about the state of the laboratory and unit offices, but I would like to have a trusted colleague and friend here. I'm fairly isolated up here in the peak of the town house.

But Ray cannot leave King's, of course, until he has his doctorate, a goal that is requiring finesse on his part. Although aligning with me during my tenure made him somewhat ostracized—for which I continue to apologize—he's managed to bridge the gap with Wilkins, who agreed to oversee his dissertation, ostensibly. All those nights in the pub paid off, I guess. This "oversight" is in name only, however, as Ray and I continue to work together on the sly, on both his thesis and a few final papers on our research; Wilkins doesn't have the skill set or scientific knowledge to oversee Ray, no matter what he claims. After a parting missive sent to me from Randall in which he drew a line in the sand around Ray and all things DNA, subterfuge is our only option. Randall has proven himself to be different from the man I imagined him to be, as evidenced by how far he went to exclude me from the King's party celebrating our triumvirate of *Nature* papers on DNA. He knows more than most how central I am to those discoveries.

"I'm glad to hear it, but I do hope that the new year brings with it some new equipment. We've placed the order with the manufacturers and done the requisite begging with the governmental entities funding the purchases, but you know how unpopular I am. My requests always end up on the bottom of the list," he says with an apologetic smile, and I realize that despite Bernal's brilliance and reputation for his scientific acumen, I will have to contend with the general loathing of his communist politics. "You've got such a nimble mind, and you're such a brilliant experimenter, I don't want to waste a second of your time here." He takes another step closer to me.

Even though he's uncomfortably near, I don't worry, although I am well aware of his terrible reputation as a lothario, one of the reasons I suspect Anne doesn't like him. Even when I was in Paris, my *labo* colleagues used to speak about his legendary prowess as a ladies' man, which I find hard to fathom given his appalling teeth, droopy jowls, and unkempt flops of thick hair. My opinion of his attractiveness notwithstanding, he seems to keep a veritable harem: not only a wife and a couple of mistresses and children with them all but also a steady stream of short-term liaisons, as various members of our unit have often observed random women exiting from the apartment he keeps in the town house next door, which is rumored to have a mural drawn on the wall by his friend and fellow communist, Pablo Picasso. But I've made my lack of interest apparent from my first day when he asked me to drinks—just us two—and I declined on the grounds that I only socialize with my peers in groups. A necessary untruth.

Ever since I drew that line, I have found my dealings with Bernal to be supportive and unobtrusive. He gave me my mission, and he left me to it; I enjoy the trust he grants me and all his scientists, even in areas of safety protocols, which are largely left to our discretion except for the mandatory physical exams by the university physician. When it became clear that the specialized crystallographic equipment I ordered might not be ready for some months, he encouraged me to finalize my DNA work even though Randall told me not to do so, and after I completed that, he supported travel to conferences in Germany and France as well as a long journey to Israel, where I managed to unwind a bit but did not reverse my skepticism about the idyllic Zionist idea of a country for the Jewish people.

"Even though I'd love to be working with the new equipment, the time has hardly been wasted. I found the time in Israel to be particularly insightful for my work." I know he values confidence, so I meet his gaze head-on. "It helped inspire an idea for tackling this new acid you'd like me to unpuzzle."

Bernal smiles. "I cannot wait to see what you'll uncover. Thank you for your patience as we head into the new year."

As I return the smile, I think about my new subject—ribonucleic acid, the important cousin to DNA that is found in every cell, including the tobacco mosaic virus that I'll be using to study the acid. The tobacco mosaic virus was the very first virus to be discovered and is the prototype for nearly all investigation into the structure of viruses and the consequent structure of ribonucleic acid, or RNA. Working out this architecture and the relevance of RNA to the reproduction of viruses is not only an important new puzzle but is directly related to my work on DNA. And I believe the broad implications of this research—particularly to devastating and sweeping viruses like polio—cannot be overstated.

The notion of turning my talents to this new target is exhilarating, and I know I've made the right decision to put the poison of the past behind me. The fact that Crick and Watson's model failed to receive the immediate recognition and waves of acceptance by the scientific community they anticipated certainly helps, although the tide does seem to be turning. Travel, new horizons, a more respectful superior: all these things have made this past year at Birkbeck a little like heaven on earth. If I believed in all that.

CHAPTER FORTY-FOUR

December 14, 1954
London, England

Umbrella in hand, I leave my office, intending to descend the six flights of stairs to the basement to set up a couple of experiments. The sound of rain tipping down on the roof is my signal to arrive prepared for the constant drizzle that will be present not only outside on the streets but inside the subterranean laboratory. Normally, I'd hold off to avoid getting drenched, but I'm halfway through capturing a new image, and I want to make certain I calculated the right angle with my North American Philips camera.

Just as I'm about midway down the staircase from the attic, I bump into a sprightly chap with large glasses and curly, dark hair coming up the stairs. "Hello there. May I help you?" I offer, assuming he's lost, because I have no appointments today and no reason to expect visitors up here.

"As a matter of fact, you can. I'm hoping to find Dr. Rosalind

Franklin." He has a melodic accent, somewhere between English and Australian with a lilt all its own.

"That's me."

"Lovely, lovely." He stretches out his hand to greet me with a shake, balancing a box in his other. "Such a pleasure to meet you. I'm Aaron Klug, and we're meant to be floor mates."

Did I hear him correctly? He's going to be my neighbor up here on the former maid's floor? I would have assumed that a Birkbeck administrator would have sent a formal notice, but then, this isn't exactly a formal institution. And since Bernal has been on the road in continental Europe for the past several weeks, the finer details seem to have been left to chance and whim.

"Welcome," I say with a smile, as if I've been expecting him. What else can I do but offer him my hospitality? Anyway, it will be pleasant to have another person in this drafty, empty space. As long as he's not another Wilkins.

I notice another box on the step behind him. He must have put it down when he heard me approach so there would be room for me to pass. *A sign of thoughtfulness*, I think. Reaching down for the battered crate, I say, "Let me help you with that. I'll show you your new digs."

"That would be much appreciated," he says.

As I start back up the stairs, I can't help but ask, "Are you South African?"

"I am." He sounds surprised. "Not many people guess my accent correctly, although I'm not a native South African. My parents moved there from Lithuania when I was two, which turned out to be wise in hindsight."

I turn back toward him. "Why is that?"

"It saved us from the concentration camps."

I almost drop the box I'm carrying. Most English people don't talk so openly about being Jewish, particularly with those they don't know well; I found the French to be more casual about discussing it. Even my own family, who are firmly ensconced in the upper-class Jewish "cousinhood" of London and well established in society, can be remarkably closemouthed. Aaron's frankness prompts to me to an unexpected candor of my own. "Living here in England spared my family." We share a look of recognition, and I feel an unspoken kinship with this young man. We reach the landing, and I walk him over to the section apportioned for another office and lab. It's been empty since I arrived, and I realize that a stack of my own books sits in the corner. "Oh, I'm sorry. I just returned from America, and if I had known you were coming, I would have made tidying this space a priority."

"Please don't fuss over something so unimportant, Dr. Franklin," he insists.

"Call me Rosalind, please."

"Only if you call me Aaron."

As we set the boxes down, he asks, "Where did you go in America?"

"I had the opportunity to tour their vast northern states, which they call New England."

We laugh at the idea of the new, expansive America comparing itself to its old, cramped mother country.

"Then I made my way across the interior, stopping at Chicago and St. Louis and Madison, Wisconsin, along the way, before I landed in California for a stint and then made my way to Arizona. What a shock all that sun was, especially in the desert and Grand Canyon."

"It sounds wonderful. My wife and I long to go one day. We miss the climate of South Africa, and I hear parts of America mirror it."

Wonderful cannot even begin to capture the marvels of America. Quite possibly the most surprising experience, however, wasn't a place but a person. On the first leg of my journey, which was part of the Gordon Conference on coal in New Hampshire, I had been invited to visit the Marine Biological Laboratory at Woods Hole, Massachusetts, a biological research center located at the very tip of Cape Cod, a narrow peninsula south of Boston that extends into the Atlantic Ocean. Important work by Thomas Hunt Morgan of Columbia University had been conducted there on genetics, specifically the role of chromosomes in heredity, which led me to accept the offer.

A kindly Woods Hole scientist was guiding me around the sprawling seaside property when I quite literally bumped into James Watson, of all people. Startled to see him, I'd blurted out, "What on earth are *you* doing here?"

I hadn't seen Watson since the explosive encounter in my King's College lab, so I expected him to reply in kind. I even braced myself for another showdown.

"Dr. Franklin!" he exclaimed, as if we were friendly acquaintances, although I noted that he was careful to call me by my formal name instead of the reprehensible Rosy. "How lovely to see you in America!"

"You as well," I answered warily, very cognizant of my guide's eyes upon me. "I thought you had left Cambridge for Caltech, but here you are in Massachusetts. Is my information wrong?"

I hadn't exactly kept tabs on Watson since I left King's—I'd tried to put the entire debacle behind me, aside from the science—but public mentions of him and Crick kept surfacing as the double helix theory began to gain acceptance and Crick and Watson started to gain in popularity. Last I'd read, he was in California.

"As usual, your information is 'spot-on,' as you British say," he said with a smile. "I'm touring the Woods Hole facility and hearing about their research. Are you doing the same?"

Why was he being so friendly and solicitous, I wondered. I would know how to react if he'd been the condescending scientist I'd met in England. But what was I meant to do with this strange congeniality?

"I am indeed." I decided to match his tenor, no matter how I actually felt about Watson and his behavior over my DNA research. After all, I needed to maintain a good impression on my hosts at Woods Hole.

"It's an impressive place."

"It is," I answer, unsure what to say next. Just then, my guide chimed in and asked if Watson would like to join our tour.

I wanted to cry out "No!" but how could I? So I found myself walking side by side with a man I abhorred across the Woods Hole campus.

"I understand you're working on the tobacco mosaic virus," he said as we skirted the seaside portion of the facility.

"Are you keeping tabs on me?" I accused him quietly.

"No, no, Dr. Franklin." He held up his hand in protest. "I ran into Bernal before I left England, and he told me. How is your research going?"

"Well," I said, trying to calm my racing heart. I had no intention of giving him any details; I knew all too well what he did with other scientists' research.

"I'm not certain about the parameters of your study, but I'd be happy to share with you all the research I gathered when I studied the tobacco mosaic virus myself." He paused, and I was glad that he didn't mention he'd studied the tobacco mosaic virus at the Cavendish during the period when Bragg prohibited him and Watson from investigating DNA. I wasn't entirely certain I could continue this conversation if he had. "I'd determined that the protein subunits of the tobacco mosaic virus take a helix form. But you'll want to reach your own conclusions, of course." He stared at me with an apologetic expression.

Was it possible he felt badly for his actions? I softened toward him for a moment but then reminded myself of what he'd done. And how he'd had plenty of opportunities to give me proper credit since the publication of his and Crick's paper, and he'd done nothing. Other than "allow" me to submit a paper to be published alongside the famous article penned by him and Crick, a paper that was all but ignored.

"Thank you," I replied. It was the only thing I could say in the presence of our Woods Hole guide.

The terrain grew narrow, and we had to organize into a single-file line for the next stretch. Our guide took the lead with me and then Watson following. Over my shoulder, I felt rather than saw Watson grow closer to me. Then I heard his voice, although his volume was low. "I feel as though we judged you unfairly when we were working on DNA."

Was this his way of apologizing? These paltry words, empty of any real remorse, weren't enough. But I thought about what I'd said to Ursula about moving forward, putting the ugliness and disappointment of King's and DNA and these men behind me.

I decided that I would accept his bare olive branch of words and research, but I would not forgive. And I would *never* forget.

I would never broach the topic of Wilkins, Watson, or Crick with Aaron. Not yet anyway. Instead, I say, "Oh, I hope you have the opportunity. Boston in particular is wonderful, similar to London but with a freshness that's very American. Not only is the country so vast and wide and diverse in its landscapes and plentiful in its meals, but it is home to many first-class scientists and laboratories. I met Erwin Chargaff, George Gamow, Vladimir Vand, and Isidor Fankuchen—I could go on and on."

His eyes widen. "What renowned experts you've met! Not that we aren't working in the midst of some famous ones here as well. What is your specialty, Rosalind? I heard someone mention that you are a physical chemist, but beyond that, I don't know."

"Would you like to see what I'm working in?" I ask. It has been ages since I had anyone with whom I could discuss my ongoing work; while the Birkbeck folks are kinder than the King's, they aren't exactly friendly, which, I believe, stems from the fact that I'm not a fan of the Communist Party as many of them are. And anyway, I'd grown accustomed to having a daily rapport with Ray and, before that, with my *labo* colleagues and Jacques. The thought of Jacques makes me long for his intellect and humor, just when I'd believed I'd successfully banished him from my mind.

"Would I? Lead the way."

I direct him into my office, where I happen to have several images spread across a light box. They aren't yet of the quality that I'd like, but I am getting closer. "Are you familiar with the tobacco mosaic virus?"

"Can't say that I am."

I hand him a normal photograph comparing two tobacco leaves. "As you can see in this photo, the virus causes curling and a mottled, mosaiclike pattern of various shades of green to appear on a tobacco leaf. I'm sure you know that viruses are inert molecules made up of RNA and DNA and proteins, lifeless until they enter a cell, take it over, and begin their process of duplication. The tobacco mosaic virus, or TMV as we call it, injects itself into a living cell in a manner similar to a needle and syringe. This particular virus is uniquely situated to help us determine where in the cell the RNA is located—in the center or hidden away in a corner? A Yale biophysicist and crystallographer, Don Caspar, recently discovered that the center of TMV is hollow, which—if we can verify that—answers part of the question and challenges us to find the RNA in the corners. Once we definitively identify the location, we can get down to the hard business of discovering its structure and then, of course, the way in which it functions."

We pour through several of my crystallographic images on the light box, and Aaron asks probing questions. His queries make me think differently about the material before me, but he does so in such a genuine, curious fashion that I cannot possibly be insulted. He has a quick, theoretical mind.

As he studies one particular picture, I notice that his bushy eyebrows, otherwise hidden behind the thick rim of his glasses, slant upward excitedly. He turns to me and asks, "I know we've just met, and even though I'm a physical chemist like you and a crystallographer, I don't have any experience with viruses whatsoever, but—" He pauses.

"Yes?" I prompt him to continue.

"Would you care for a partner in your work?"

CHAPTER FORTY-FIVE

August 4, 1955
London, England

WE STAND IN A CIRCLE IN MY OFFICE. AARON AND I, ALONG-side our new assistants, John Finch and Kenneth Holmes, are in a fierce debate. Never mind that I am in charge of this little family; we speak to one another with bluntness and honesty and respect, and I adore it.

X-ray images litter the floor in what to anyone but us would appear to be a haphazard manner. We've been laboring for over a year to achieve the crispest images of the virus we can, and the scattered photos are the fruits of those labors. Only then, we had all agreed, could we begin to assemble a model of its infrastructure and get to the crux of inquiry, the nature of RNA. How heartening it is to work with a team of scientists who don't challenge this basic tenet the way that Wilkins did.

Today, we start the model building of this strangely designed virus, which is made up of protein subunits arranged in circles around a core with the RNA woven in between the protein. Or so we think. A bin of bits and pieces—stand-ins for our X-rayed biological materials—sits at the center of our circle. Each of us holds a different opinion as to how to begin.

"What if we just start making circles of the protein subunits?" Ken says.

"That's one approach. But when I discussed this with Crick—at a very high level of course, as we are still very hush-hush about our findings—he suggested first building the inner core around which the architecture of the virus might hang." I speak into the silence following Ken's idea.

In another unexpected turn of events—unsurprising in some ways given the smallness of my scientific circles—I'd run into Crick at a conference, and he was every bit as avuncular and attentive as Watson had been in America. Neither one of us spoke about what had transpired with DNA, King's, the Cavendish, and *us*, but when another colleague interjected a question about Watson, I was heartened to hear a tinge of coldness in Crick's voice; I'd always disliked Watson more and attributed the bulk of the misconduct to him, whether or not that was true. Like his compatriot, I assume guilt motivated Crick to kindness, especially since scientists and even the public were starting to acknowledge the importance of their DNA model. I have no compunction about taking Crick up on his offer to assist and advise me whenever possible; I think it is the least he can do for me. He and Watson used me, and now I have every intention of doing the same, although I've always been more suspicious of Watson than Crick. In the name of science, of course, not personal glory and accolades, like them.

Aaron is quiet for a long moment, then says, "I don't care what Crick says. I care what you say."

"All right." I step back and study the images on the floor, trying to envision the three-dimensional shape in my mind's eye. "I'm struggling a bit because I cannot actually *see* the central core. We all know that Caspar has theorized it is empty, just a hole, and I tend to agree. But even X-ray photographs have their limits; they can't show the absence of something."

"Rosalind, sometimes you are just too literal and stubborn, clinging to your data and your photographs. You need to let go of images for a second and envision what might be, based on what you sense about the structure." Aaron's eyes are blazing, and he appears every bit as stubborn as he accuses me of being.

"I'm stubborn?" I am not asking him, I'm challenging him. My initial inclination is to defend myself, as I've had to do often over the years.

"Yes. Just because you're the finest, most systematic physical chemist and experimental crystallographer I've come across doesn't mean you aren't stubborn in the face of a little theory." Aaron enjoys highlighting the difference between us—he'd tell anyone who'd listen that we personify the dichotomy between theory and practice.

I look at his face and break out into laughter. Because he's right. I am bloody stubborn and overly literal, and I do need to step back from the data and envision what could be. What a relief it is to be myself in the company of another person and be understood, as I'd been in Paris. I know Aaron's intentions are kindly and his respect true; I had worried I'd never find that level of understanding again. And here, in this fifth-floor former maid's quarters at Birkbeck, I have it, as I did with Vittorio and, to a lesser extent, with Ray but without the tricky layer of the romantic relationship I had with Jacques.

"Okay, let's get to work using Ken's suggestion." I start pawing through the bin. "Can we use any of these objects for the shape of the protein subunits?"

We take turns holding up various and sundry objects—table tennis balls and erasers of different sizes and shapes among them—but none of them seem to fit. Returning to the images, we hope they prompt a brainstorm about the sort of object we might use to represent the protein.

Ken points to a particular photograph on the floor. "Look at that clear image there. Does that prompt any ideas?" A half smile appears on his face. "I'm rather proud of that one. It was taken just after I fixed the problems we had cleaning the Beaudouin X-ray camera by affixing a vacuum gauge to the X-ray tube."

"You did what?" I snap. "How does measuring vacuum have anything to do with cleaning the camera or taking crisp pictures?"

Ken, who'd been beaming a few minutes earlier because we followed his suggestion, stares down at the floor, and I realize I've gone too far.

"You're bullying him, Rosalind," Aaron says, as if I do not already know.

This criticism—unlike the earlier chastisement—I take seriously. Having suffered at the hands of patronizing superiors myself, I don't want to exact that sort of treatment on my assistants. But because I'm not always aware of this behavior while I'm doing it, Aaron has agreed to be my conscience and gatekeeper on this score.

"Apologies, Ken. You know I get carried away. And I'm not always terribly—" I drift off, unsure how to finish this sentence.

"Self-aware?" He supplies the word.

"That's the ticket. Are we good?" I ask solicitously.

"All good, Rosalind."

"Back to work everyone," Aaron barks now that the personal drama is over.

"Now who's doing the bullying?" I ask in jest, and everyone laughs.

"I have it!" Ken suddenly calls out. "What about a bicycle handlebar grip? It's almost the exact shape of the protein subunit."

"I think you might be right," I say slowly. "How did you ever think of such a thing?"

"I ride my bike to work most days, so I'm all too familiar with the shape."

"Brilliant," Aaron says, then turns to Ken and John. "How about you two head over to the Woolworth's on Oxford Street to see if they've got any?"

"Will do," John says, but before he and Ken head down the stairs, he asks, "How many do we need?"

Aaron looks over at me. He knows that I'll know the precise number without even checking my data; in that way, the big-picture theoretician and the detail-oriented experimenter complement each other perfectly. "Two hundred and eighty-eight," I say without a beat.

Ken and John break into hysterical laughter thinking of the conversation they'll be having with the Woolworth's salesclerk, and their cackles reverberate throughout my office as they leave. Just then, the internal mailman for Birkbeck drops a few letters on my desk, and Aaron announces, "I suppose I'll head down to the basement to check on a few experiments."

"Don't forget your umbrella. The forecast calls for rain," I call out as he exits my room.

"Outdoors and in," he adds.

As he leaves, I notice an envelope on the top of my mail pile from the British virologist and head of the Biochemical Department at the Rothamsted Experimental Station, Norman Pirie, and my stomach churns. Pirie, a member of the Agricultural Research Council who greatly disagrees with the findings I published in *Nature* that TMV rods are all the same length, has become an enemy of sorts, even refusing to send virus samples to our lab for study. What could he be writing about now? He's already made his feelings clear, and we have started growing our own viruses because of his retaliatory actions.

I slice open the letter. In its terse and unpleasant paragraphs, Pirie makes clear that he's filed an objection to the funds my group receives from the Agricultural Research Council with his "close friend," the head of the council, Sir William Slater. The council grant is the only financing my group receives, and without it, we will have to shut down. How will I keep my little family together?

CHAPTER FORTY-SIX

October 14, 1955, and March 2, 1956
London, England

The midday sun beats down on my face, and I lean back and close my eyes, savoring the warmth on my cheeks. Aaron, Ken, and John sit on either side of me on a bench in the grassy area near the entrance to our Birkbeck town house. They are chatting about some gossip to which I'm only half listening as I bask in this lovely day and the company of my trusted band of scientists. *How fortunate I am to have landed here after King's*, I think.

One by one, the men grow quiet. This silence is uncharacteristic, and I open my eyes to see what's wrong. I stare directly into the face of a dark-haired, mustached man who waits patiently before me.

"Are you Dr. Franklin?" he asks hesitantly.

"I am. And you are?"

"My name is Don Caspar. I'm a biophysicist from Yale, here for postdoctoral work and—"

Sitting up straight on the bench, I interrupt him. "Are you the same Don Caspar who theorized that the center of the tobacco mosaic virus is hollow?"

A wide grin appears under his bushy mustache, and his eyes widen in surprise. "That's me."

I stand up, and Aaron, Ken, and John follow suit. Stretching out my hand in greeting, I say, "Marvelous to meet you. We know your work, and I'm sure we all have questions for you. What brings you to Birkbeck?"

"Well, you do, Dr. Franklin."

"Me?"

"Yes. I heard about the research you were doing on tobacco mosaic viruses, and I thought—if you are interested—while I'm in England for my postdoctoral work in molecular biology at Cambridge, I might assist you in your tobacco mosaic virus investigation."

I don't reply, because I don't know what to say, and my Birkbeck team doesn't say anything either. To have a scientist whose work I've admired appear out of nowhere to offer his services seems almost too good to be true. And certainly more generous than I'd ever imagined. Is there a catch? How does this American scientist know what we are doing here?

Don pauses, staring at the three silent men, and then adds, "But if you've already got enough helping hands—"

I'm still wary, but I don't want to lose him just the same. "No, no, we could always use a few more, especially experienced and knowledgeable hands such as yours," I hasten to respond. "Pardon the slow reply. It's just that I'm surprised. We've only just begun to publish our work on the tobacco mosaic virus, so I'm not certain how you became familiar with what we are doing."

"That's easy enough to answer. Before coming here, I spent some time at Caltech, where Jim Watson told me very generally about your research and sang your praises. He said I should beg you for the opportunity to assist in your lab to work with tobacco mosaic viruses, because I'll never again work with an experimental scientist of your caliber and genius."

At the mention of Watson's name, I recoil ever so slightly, even though it seems he's complimenting from afar. The last time we met and in his letters since, Watson has been solicitous and laudatory. In fact, to my surprise, Watson had written that he'd heard of my financial plight and had advocated on my behalf with a scientist friend of Slater, but we shall see what comes of it. I hope this Don fellow doesn't notice my reaction. "Ah, it's becoming clear," I respond.

"If you'll have me."

Only because Don Caspar came with his own funding—and his own wealth of experience on the tobacco mosaic virus—were we able to welcome him during such uncertain financial times. Now that we've had the benefit of Don's intellect and passion for five months, I sometimes can't believe that I was skeptical about pursuing his interest in working with me only because it was Watson who suggested him for the role. What a loss it would have been if we had not brought Don Caspar on board. For the work and for me.

Now the five of us—Aaron, Ken, John, Don, and I—gather over a long rectangular table in the student union. We have a lot to review, but interruptions abound as our newest scientist garners lots of friendly backslaps and chatter.

"How do you know so many people at Birkbeck?" I ask Don, a wiry, affable man whose smile transforms his whole face. "You haven't been here a year."

"Unlike you, Rosalind, he's friendly," Aaron says with a broad smile.

I pretend to slap his arm. "I'm not *un*friendly. It's just that I'm often lost in my thoughts."

Ken chimes in, "Our colleagues don't know that. They think that you're judging them for being sympathetic to the Communist Party."

"They do?" I ask, alarmed. My views on the Soviet Union aren't secret—I still abhor the dangerous race to amass arms and develop ever-more deadly weapons—but I shudder at the thought that my fellow scientists think I am judging them. Having borne the brunt of unfair judgment in the past, I would not want others to think of me that way.

They chuckle, and I know they enjoy teasing me in a good-natured way. But I can see this isn't entirely a joke. "This isn't a put-on, is it?"

Still smiling, Aaron explains. "This place is populated by communists. No surprise given that Bernal is our fearless leader. And well, Rosalind, you have a posh accent, went to St. Paul's, and live in Kensington—"

John interrupts him, "Don't forget about the evening a Rolls Royce pulled up to the town house for you and you left in an evening gown! You should have seen the jaws dropping."

"What does that have to do with anything?" I ask.

"They think you're upper-class, even aristocratic. That's the very antithesis of their beliefs and one of the reasons they keep their distance," Aaron says.

This explanation surprises me. The notion that my dislike of the Soviet Union alienates my politically minded coworkers would not have been news to me, but the idea that my social standing upsets them does astonish.

"Well, I suppose I should be glad that they find my background unpalatable. At least I haven't actually done anything to offend them by my behavior," I announce.

The four men glance at one another, and I can tell they're not certain how to respond. And then Don says, "That's just extra," and they burst into another round of laughter.

Even I have to chortle at the little joke at my expense, in part because Don usually shies away from this sort of repartee. He always maintains that he's too new for such jibes, even though he's been with us almost five months now and can be quite gregarious. With everyone but me. With me, he's careful and smart and gentlemanly, but not in a patronizing way. And when I think no one is looking, I find myself sneaking glances at this brilliant man.

I'd had five months of magnificent collaboration with the mustached American, who shares my almost obsessive determination to unearth the structure of the virus and map RNA. We have been using isomorphic replacement—a brand new technique only tried by its developer, Max Perutz—in which we introduce a few heavy atoms into the virus protein. This approach is yielding unparalleled X-ray patterns of two different types, and the graphs of these images' measurements reveal the distance between the RNA and the virus's center and the location of the RNA itself. This helps us understand how the protein isolates the RNA until the RNA gets inside the cell and begins the process of replicating the virus. This exact information is vital, because it explains how the virus works and how it might be stopped.

Working with Don is intoxicating, and I often fantasize about the good our discoveries might do in the world. Could we come to understand the way in which viruses proliferate and then halt them with that knowledge? But I don't have those thoughts only about my projects with Don. Our Birkbeck research overall and my new team often make my work at King's seem small and petty in comparison; the real-life good our research might do in the near term thrills me. It helps heal the anger and disappointment that still creep up on me over what Wilkins, Watson, and Crick did to me, especially now that Crick and Watson are almost famous for "their" discovery.

My thoughts are suddenly beset by a pang of worry. I cannot lose this little family and all the secrets we might uncover together. But how can I keep us together without funding?

This nagging worry is one I've kept secret for months, ever since Pirie started his campaign to destroy my Agricultural Research Council financing. In fact, protecting the rest of the team from this concern has been paramount. Should I change that approach now? Is there anything they can do to help the cause? They've got nothing to lose but their peace of mind, and perhaps we've all got something to gain. I decide to leap into the fray.

Squaring my shoulders, I glance at Don—who's sitting across from me—and then each of the other men in turn. "There's something I need to talk to you about. Something I've been trying to fix for months, so that I did *not* have to tell you." The smiles disappear as I ask, "Remember the article I wrote for *Nature*?"

"Which? You've written half a dozen since I've been working with you," Don says.

"The one demonstrating how TMV rods are all the same length? The one Pirie hated?"

"Of course," Aaron says. "We've become a virus-growing factory as a result."

"Well, Pirie's rancor has extended beyond withholding virus samples from us. He's trying to tank the Agricultural Research Council grant. The money is up next year, and Pirie is trying to poison Slater against us. Against me, actually, not you all." I take a deep breath. "Bernal has tried to help, but Slater's not a fan. Jim Watson has stepped in to advocate for us through a friend of Pirie and Slater's, along with a slew of other scientists. But I'm not certain it will be enough, even though we're publishing more papers than any unit and the invitations to speak at conferences are more than we can accept. I mean, Sir Lawrence Bragg asked for our models to display in the International Science Hall of the Brussels World's Fair. What more could the Agricultural Research Council want from a grant?"

"Jesus," Ken says, pushing back in his chair. John does the same and stares at the floor. We all know that they can move on to doctoral programs and that Don will be here for only a year anyway. The parties most at risk are me and Aaron.

"It doesn't help, of course, that I'm a woman. And that my fourteen years in scientific research entitles me to the title of principal scientific investigator, which the Agricultural Research Council does not want to give me." I don't articulate the obvious. For so long, I've been operating outside the usual system for scientists—where they typically fill lockstep roles at universities or institutions—that no one wants to give me a title and salary commensurate with my experience now that I'm finally seeking it.

"Narrow-minded bastards," Don says under his breath, and I'm both shocked at his language and thrilled at his protective instincts. I'd always secretly hoped he'd turn his affable charm on me but knew I should wish otherwise. I can't have anyone or anything disrupt the balance I've achieved with my group. At the *labo*, I learned the hard way what havoc a romantic entanglement can wreak.

"There have got to be other options," Aaron says, his bushy eyebrows furrowed. He has more to lose even than I do. He, his wife, and their young son live on his salary, smaller than mine, on the fifth floor of a rickety Victorian house in a decidedly unfashionable neighborhood. While I'm certain he could procure another position with ease, his family depends on him, and an interruption in paychecks could cause significant problems. "We are on the cusp of major breakthroughs—together. Any interruption in financing could cause a disruption in our research and our ability to stay together as a group."

My worries exactly, I think. I give Aaron an apologetic gaze.

Don suddenly sits up in his chair, and his expression changes from apprehension to excitement. "What about America? I bet you could get money from the U.S. National Institutes of Health; they've been known to fund important projects outside the country. And what's more important than your work answering fundamental questions about the mechanism of living processes? How could they say no to a beautiful British scientist who's about to unlock the secrets of RNA along with the hidden workings of viruses?"

CHAPTER FORTY-SEVEN

August 30 and 31, 1956
London, England

How delightful you could make the symphony, dear, although you look a little bloated. From the travel, I'm guessing? How I wish you could work and travel less than you do," Mama says as I settle into the scarlet velvet chair next to her, spreading out the full skirt of my crimson evening dress and thinking how fortunate it is that the two reds do not clash. How I wish she hadn't mentioned the bloating; it is a sensitive subject. I'd been struggling with it, particularly around my midsection, for months, long before my trip to America, and no amount of dietary restriction makes it diminish. I suppose I should simply be thankful that Mama doesn't notice that I've combed my hair in an unusual style so as to cover the small balding patch I discovered on the crown.

She strokes my hand as if I'm a small poodle. "Anyway, we're so glad you could be here. It will mean the world to Jenifer."

My sister is the fundraising chair of the Goldsbrough Orchestra, founded in 1948 by Lawrence Leonard and Arnold Goldsbrough, the noted conductor and harpsichordist, and even if I had been inclined toward my parents' sort of philanthropy, this would not have been my first choice of venerable institutions to serve. The orchestra focuses on early music, particularly from the baroque period, and quite honestly, I've always had a complicated relationship with music, enjoying my wireless nearly as much as a live symphony. Tonight's performance opens the season for the orchestra with a concert at Wigmore Hall, which will be followed by a celebratory benefit dinner. It seems the perfect, upstanding, philanthropic role and event for the younger daughter of Ellis Franklin, and my parents are extremely proud of her. *If only she'd find a suitable boy to marry*, I've heard them say often enough to realize this is their remaining lamentation about Jenifer, as they've long given up on the idea of me marrying. They certainly don't share Adrienne's view.

"When did you land? We weren't certain you'd arrive before the curtain call, with all the postponements to your flights home," Papa asks from the chair on the other side of Mama. The lovely Edwardian backdrop of Wigmore Hall frames him, the light marble and alabaster walls making him seem dark in his black suit and hooded eyes. I spot Colin, Charlotte, and Roland down the aisle and wave to them.

"About three o'clock this morning."

"Aren't you exhausted, Rosalind? You certainly look peaked." Mama fusses.

I feel absolutely done in, but I cannot say that to Mama. "No, in fact, I came here directly from the office." I'd specifically planned my return from America to maximize my time there while still ensuring a day in the office this week and this event. Sponsored by the Rockefeller Foundation, this second trip to America was even better than the first. Giving speeches and touring through laboratories in New England, where I spent some lovely time with the Sayres, the Midwest, and finally California felt like a homecoming and a revelation, particularly with the scientific connections and reconnections I made. But it also served another, urgent purpose—it gave me inroads to obtain the necessary U.S. National Institutes of Health funds. It heartens me to think I might be able to keep my band of scientists together after all, and I plan on starting the application process immediately.

"You mean to tell me that you went to Birkbeck after three flights, one of them transatlantic, and an arrival in the middle of the night? And then you came here after a full workday?" Papa's eyebrows arch in surprise.

Staring ahead at the sumptuous painting in the cupola over the stage—the central figure serves as the embodiment of the soul of music, staring up at fiery rays representing the genius of harmony against a vivid blue sky—I whisper so as not to disturb the other patrons. "I always keep my obligations, Papa. No matter how I feel and no matter what is happening in the world around me. Isn't that what you taught me?"

The jet lag doesn't hit me until the next morning. As I sit in the waiting room of Dr. Linken's office for my regularly scheduled checkup, required for all scientists working with radiation everywhere in England including Birkbeck, I fall asleep. When the nurse calls me in, I awaken from the middle of an unpleasant dream, in which my flight home is continuously cancelled and I can never reach my destination.

Bleary-eyed, I head into the doctor's office and disrobe for the examination. As I lie on the table for the poking and prodding, we engage in the usual pleasantries, part of pretending that we aren't engaged in this unpleasant intimacy. It's an old doctor's trick.

"I'm just back from America," I say to his question about recent travel.

He pauses, asking, "Where?" and then resumes his uncomfortable investigation.

I list the places I visited and then say, "The Rockies were, of course, spectacular, but it was southern California that stole my heart."

Smiling, I think about the unexpected adventure I took with Caltech colleague Renato Dulbecco and a guide, in which we set out at six o'clock in the morning. By eleven o'clock, we'd reached the base of Mount Whitney, the highest point in the United States at eighty-five hundred feet. Carrying sleeping bags and food for twenty-four hours, we hiked up that mountain, passing trees, foliage, lakes, and even snow that became more spectacular the higher we ascended. After awakening with a breathtaking view from the mountaintop, we climbed down, changed our clothes, and were in the laboratory by afternoon. It was glorious and even managed to distract me from the growing pain in my abdomen.

"Is that right? What about it did you particularly like?"

"The climate, the landscape, the science. If my family wasn't so ensconced in England, I might consider a move."

"Any trouble while you were there?" he asks.

"Not at all. The people were delightful and welcoming."

"I mean, did you have any physical trouble while you were there? Of a medical sort?"

I chortle. "Apologies, I thought we were still talking about the travel. I did have some sharp pains in my abdomen about ten days ago, not that long after my trip to the Rockies, but I visited an American doctor who gave me some painkillers and advised me to see a doctor on my return. Fortunately, I already had this appointment scheduled, so I thought I'd simply raise it with you."

"I see," he says distractedly while continuing the somewhat painful internal examination. "Anything else?"

"I had some trouble zipping my skirts and buttoning my trousers during my trip, but I guess I shouldn't be surprised by a little weight gain. America is the land of abundance, and I did indulge. You should see how much food they serve at meals—and no rationing."

"You may get dressed. I'll meet you in my office."

Yawning, I push myself up, put back on my white blouse, short-sleeved for the warmer weather, and pull on my dark-gray skirt. I still have every intention of returning to the lab after my doctor's appointment, but I realize that I'll need several cups of coffee to stay awake at my desk while starting the U.S. National Institutes of Health paperwork. Wandering into Dr. Linken's office, I settle into the taupe fabric and oak chair facing his desk.

He lights up a cigarette and offers me one, which I decline. "Miss Franklin, I've got to ask you an awkward question."

"Dr. Linken, I'm a scientist. There really isn't anything you could ask me that would make me feel awkward."

He exhales, and a cloud of smoke hovers between us. "All right. Is there any chance you could be pregnant?"

Pregnant? I almost laugh, because of course there is no chance of that. But an unexpected longing surges through me, and I wonder. Is that something that I would like? After all these years of telling myself and everyone else that I would never consider it, am I really thinking about the possibility of motherhood, at the age of thirty-six? Without a candidate for a husband in sight? *Silly*, I tell myself.

"No, Dr. Linken. There is no chance of pregnancy."

"Well then, Miss Franklin, there is no easy way to say this." He takes another big drag from his cigarette and says, "I think you need to see a specialist."

"Whatever for?" I ask, catching a glimpse of my file on his desk. He has written "Urgent" across the top in red ink.

"You have a mass in your abdomen."

CHAPTER FORTY-EIGHT

September 4, 1956
London, England

WHERE AM I?

It is so bright that I must keep my eyes closed, and yet I can still sense the piercing illumination behind my shut lids. Am I back in sunny California? I don't hear the cry of seagulls or feel the heat of warm sand underfoot, however, so perhaps I am wrong. But where else could I be that would have such radiance? Perhaps I am back in southern Spain with the surprisingly kind and lovely Odile and Francis Crick, touring through Toledo and Córdoba after the Madrid conference?

The sound of a familiar voice rouses me from the light sleep into which I have drifted. Is that Mama I hear? What would she be doing in Spain or California? With Aunt Mamie and Papa, whose voices are also echoing around me? The strain of processing this conundrum is making my head pound, and I allow the waves of exhaustion to take me over.

Pain surges through my arm and then my abdomen, waking me suddenly. I brave the light to open my eyes. Staring down at me is an unfamiliar face. A fair-haired, young woman with a stiff white cap and a white dress. She regards me for a minute and then switches out a bag hanging from a metal pole next to me. What on earth is happening?

A cold liquid pulses through my arm, and oblivion arrives along with it. My eyes become unbearably heavy, and as if from a long distance off, I hear the woman ask "How are you feeling, Miss Franklin?" before everything goes black.

When I wake from the darkness, the brilliant light is gone, replaced by uniform gray shadow. I dare to open my eyes, and I realize—for the first time in who knows how long—that I am in the hospital. All the pieces come together, and I remember that I've just had surgery for the mass Dr. Linken found in my abdomen. And along with the mass, the surgeon removed any fleeting glimpse of pregnancy I might have seen in the far, uncertain distance.

I hear voices again, possibly from the corridor outside my room. Male, female, soft, and loud, all jumbled such that I cannot make out a single word. Then, a single voice emerges from the morass, and it is one I don't recognize. Could it be the surgeon?

"Two masses. One on the right ovary, the size of a croquet ball. The other on the left ovary, the size of a tennis ball."

Is that the surgeon, talking about me? About what he found inside *me*?

Someone asks a question I cannot quite make out, but I do hear the surgeon's reply.

"We don't know what caused them, but of course there have

been quite a number of tumors recorded in scientists and employees who work with radiation, and we cannot rule out a connection, even though the evidence is mostly anecdotal at this stage. That's why the requirement to have annual physical examinations was instituted."

I cannot make out what he says next over the sound of Mama sobbing. That alone would not upset me—she regularly cries—but then I hear stoic Aunt Mamie join her. Tears of self-pity and fear well up in my own eyes until I hear Papa bark, "Stop! We need to listen."

I know his words aren't directed at me; my family doesn't know that I can hear them behind the closed door to my hospital room. They don't even know I'm awake, I'm guessing, or someone would be in here with me. But they have the same effect as an order, and the tears immediately stop. And I listen.

"I hate to see this in a lovely woman, so young, but it's why we have regular checkups for the scientists. Mr. and Mrs. Franklin, I'm sorry to have to tell you this, but your daughter has cancer."

CHAPTER FORTY-NINE

October 24, 1956
The Fenlands, England

"You're like a guardian angel who swooped in just before the catastrophe to save me," I tell Anne with a chortle as we enter the picturesque little cottage loaned to us for the weekend by the Cricks, which Francis had offered only if my "first-class mind could withstand some second-class lodgings." But then I cannot help adding a caveat to my compliment. "Even though I don't believe in angels, of course."

"Of course," she says with a laugh. "But you overstate my help, Rosalind. It's honestly my pleasure to come away with you for a few days in this bucolic setting. After all, I've missed you, and I'll be returning to America in a week. And if a long restful weekend helps you regain your strength, well, then that's simply a bonus."

Anne's words sound bullish and carefree, but I can see that they're a careful construct, meant to make me feel less like the invalid I am—survivor of not one but two surgeries—and more like the Rosalind of old. The scientist who worked around the clock to procure the most exacting results. The mountain climber who pushed others along to reach legendary peaks all across Europe. The hostess who always ensures her guests have their favorite treats while visiting me at my flat, whether that means buying Gentleman's Relish, Italian coffee, or particular biscuits. The Rosalind I *will* be again.

Even though I see right through Anne's depiction of this brief getaway as a sojourn of two friends rather than a convalescent's respite, I appreciate it, and I have every intention of playing along. It's a relief to act normal after the endless weeks of being fussed over by my mother and my aunts after my two surgeries. By the time Anne came to fetch me, I felt as though I couldn't breathe at my parents' house. Her offer to take me away was like a life raft.

"Oh, I'm not thanking you for helping with any sort of rest I might need—" I wave my hand as if I'm batting away a pesky fly as I lower myself gingerly onto the rich, brown leather sofa that sits before the fire. "That's not what I mean at all. I actually want to express my gratitude for rescuing me from my family."

Anne cackles at my little joke, and I giggle along with her, even though it makes my incision and abdomen ache. For the first time in nearly two months, I feel emotionally light and hopeful, even if my body hasn't quite caught up yet. The fussing and hand-wringing of my mother over those long, long days at my parents' house has been oppressive, not conducive to healing. And I *know* I will heal, despite rather than because of my mother, however well-intentioned she might be.

"Your parents mean well," Anne says, defending them out of habit and deference.

"Too well, I think. There are only so many times a day one's pillows can be fluffed."

"Probably true. But you are a formidable patient, and she very likely doesn't know how to tend you without offending."

"A formidable patient?" I scoff.

"Are you actually denying it? You're a formidable person, so why would you think you're *not* a formidable patient?" she replies with her hands on her hips. One of the things I enjoy best about Anne is not only her sharp intellect but her fierce honesty. I need the truth spoken to me bluntly, especially now. It makes me feel like myself.

I chuckle and concede the point. "I suppose you're right."

"You know I am," she says as her hands lower and a smile appears on her angular face. "Now I hope you won't be too prickly toward me if I make you beef tea?"

I sigh at the satisfying thought of beef tea in front of the fire in a cottage ringed by the fens—that beautifully marshy coastal plain in the east with such a wonderful diversity of creatures—and my dear friend at my side. The setting is nearly perfect. But for the cancer, of course. The diagnosis that everyone thinks about but never speaks of because of some dated superstitions. Not even blunt, truth-telling Anne.

But I'm a scientist, and why should I avoid a frank conversation about an invasive cellular growth, a biological anomaly? With Anne anyway, who I believe won't treat me differently when she hears how severe my condition *was*.

"The cancer is gone, you know," I say.

She freezes at "cancer." Why is everyone so scared of the word? It's not as if saying it aloud will make it contagious.

Launching into a dispassionate recitation of my condition, I say,

"The surgeon found tumors in my ovaries when I had the first surgery, so he removed the right ovary and part of the left. After some further tests and symptoms on my part, he went back in for a second surgery and took out the remainder of the left ovary and performed a hysterectomy. He told me afterward that the tumors had been completely contained, and when he removed those organs, he removed the cancer." I take a deep breath, suddenly exhausted. I don't think I've spoken this extensively about my medical situation with anyone except the surgeon, and while I believe it's necessary to say it aloud to *someone*, I'm surprised at how much it actually takes out of me. "So you see, Anne, I'm fine. I just need to heal from the surgeries."

Anne doesn't reply immediately. Instead, she slowly lowers herself next to me on the weathered leather sofa. I wince a little as my position is shifted, but I try to hide it. Showing weakness might undercut the bullish proclamation I just made about my status.

"You're sure?"

"Absolutely. I estimate I'll be fully healed and back to work before year's end."

Anne's body visibly relaxes. Only now do I realize how rigidly she'd been holding herself. What *has* my family told her?

She reaches for my hand and gives it a tight squeeze. "Oh, Rosalind, I'm so relieved. When I hadn't heard from you after I'd been in England for nearly two weeks—despite phone calls and letters—I reached out to your family. Your mother could barely talk through the sobs on the telephone. I thought the worst."

I squeeze her hand back and then release it. "You needn't think that any longer. I'm on the mend, as you can see, and in no time, we'll be gallivanting in New York again after my next conference. Science has taken care of me. As it always has."

CHAPTER FIFTY

January 7 and April 25, 1957
London, England

Work beckons. My parents beg me not to return, plead with me to stay recuperating at their home for a fourth month. To no avail. Everyone else knows better than to try. The deadline is nearing on the Agricultural Research Council decision, and I must urge along the U.S. National Institutes of Health funding as an alternative. I will not abandon my little family.

No one at Birkbeck knows the nature of my illness, of course. Cancer is not spoken of, not even in the company of typically blunt-talking scientists and not even cancer that has been addressed. When I pant my way up the steep five flights of stairs to my office on my first day back, I bat away the offers of help from Aaron, Ken, John, and Don. I don't want them fussing, and I don't want them to see me any differently. And anyway, the doctor told me that he thinks he got all the cancer.

Aaron and I stare at each other across my desk, and I wonder if I look different. Certainly I've lost weight. I look gaunt when I stare in the mirror, but does the extra cardigan I'm wearing to ward off the winter chill that bites now more than ever hide the thinness of my frame? I hope so.

"It's good to have you back, Rosalind. We were worried," he says.

I pretend not to hear his kind words; I cannot risk getting upset in the face of Aaron's sympathy. "Shall we run through the various projects?" I ask. "Check on their status?"

"What? You don't trust that I oversaw them properly while you were out?" He reverts to teasing, seeing that I'd rather not discuss my illness.

"Of course not," I joke back. "You've undoubtedly made minestrone soup out of the various vegetable viruses we are studying."

He laughs, but he's got the research charted and organized for my review. We launch into a comparison of the experiments and results the team has gotten from the potato, tomato, pea, and turnip viruses under review—our "minestrone." It exceeds my expectations and proves that the small RNA viruses like polio and the spherical plant viruses have similarities. Should we be expanding our scope to include deadly viruses? What impact might our RNA virus research have on humankind's suffering?

"Good grief, the data is so plentiful we might write a dozen papers on it. And we've already got seven lined up for journals this year alone," I note, and then, in the only nod to my illness and absence I can allow myself, I add, "You've handled things admirably while I was gone, Aaron."

"I've had an admirable leader to model myself after," he says.

We each glance away, and I suspect he's blinking away tears. Just as I am.

How could spring have arrived already? I think. The past three and a half months have passed in a blur of preparing specimens, taking crystallographic images, comparing the pictures from different types of vegetable viruses, and writing papers, not to mention administration and fundraising. I've worked hard to hide my ongoing exhaustion and regular medical appointments, and when I overhear Ken saying to John that I suffer from "female problems," I believe that's a good sign of my success at subterfuge. I do not want them to think me incapable of our work.

After we return from a particularly jolly lunch at a local Indian restaurant, I discover two intriguing letters on my desk, one of which I've been waiting for for weeks. Which to open first? The thin envelope from the Agricultural Research Council? Or the unexpected missive from the Medical Research Council?

My silver letter opener hovers in the air over the two envelopes. Decision made, I grab the Agricultural Research Council letter first, before I perseverate further or change my mind. Slicing the envelope open, I am astonished and thrilled at the first line: "We have decided to renew your grant."

I nearly jump up and call for Aaron, but then I read the next sentence. The money, it seems, is for one year only—not three, as had been given previously—and I must procure alternate funding. As I allow this to sink in, still relieved at the decision, I scan the next paragraph. The Agricultural Research Council has rejected my request for the title of principal scientific investigator.

It deems a university or research institution position to be more fitting for a scientist at my senior level.

A mix of relief and anger rushes through me. My group has enough funds for at least one more year, but the insult to me is deep. My scientists and I are publishing more papers—important papers at that—than any other unit receiving grants from the Agricultural Research Council. I know the resistance to funding my group stems from the sour grapes of one scientist, Pirie, over a woman besting him in virus research. And I cannot believe the insensitive remark about employment at a university or research institution—how easy do they think it is for women to secure those posts? And anyway, why must everyone follow the same path, male or female?

Even though I know I should be grateful for the grant, I nearly kick over my wastebasket in frustration when the second letter catches my eye. Why would the Medical Research Council be writing me? It funded Randall's unit at King's, but to my knowledge, it has nothing to do with Bernal's group at Birkbeck.

I stare down at the letter from the secretary of the Medical Research Council in disbelief. It states that Sir Lawrence Bragg drew his attention to my brilliance and the importance of my research, and consequently, the Medical Research Council would like to fund my assistants' salaries when and if my Agricultural Research Council grant runs out, even though I have never applied for funding. Is it possible that Bragg suffers from the same sort of guilt as Crick and Watson because he broke the gentleman's agreement with Randall—which compromised me and my research—and wants to assuage his conscience? I tell myself it doesn't matter why; what matters is that we got the money.

Leaping from my seat, I call for Aaron. When he doesn't come, I yell out, "Aaron, Ken, John, Don! We got the funding!"

No one races to my office at this monumental news, and I remember that Ken and John left to acquire supplies, Don headed to Cambridge, and Aaron went down to the basement, checking on experiments. How relieved they'll all be, I think. And shocked that we received unsolicited funds.

Suddenly, pain stabs my abdomen. I clutch at my midsection and fall to the floor in agony. A pool of blood forms under me, but all I can think is that my team cannot see me like this. I push myself to standing, grab a long coat to hide the blood, and practically crawl down the five flights of stairs to a cab on the street—and straight to University College Hospital.

CHAPTER FIFTY-ONE

August 12, 1957
Geneva and Zermatt, Switzerland

Does the pristine beauty of Geneva impress Don as much as it does me? Untouched by the war, this city gleams. The elegant older buildings abut the newer construction seamlessly, and the backdrop of white-capped Mont Blanc soars above the skyline. Presiding at the city center is the deep, vast Lake Geneva, dotted with sailboats and connected to the Rhône River, which meanders through the city streets. No wonder this shining place was chosen for the Geneva Summit, the conference for the leaders of Britain, America, the Soviet Union, and France to discuss peace. The city veritably pulsates with order and hope.

Don and I stand side by side, leaning up against the railing that borders this section of the azure Lake Geneva. Somehow, I find the sociable, even-keeled American even more attractive here than in London, and I'm delighted that he, among all the chaps, wanted to join me for this conference on viruses. I hope the fact that Dr. Jonas Salk, discoverer of the polio vaccine, is the keynote speaker isn't the only reason he leaped at the chance.

"Don, I am so grateful that you suggested I apply to the U.S. National Institutes of Health for funding, and my thanks is long overdue. I would have never considered it as a viable option except for you. And now look at us."

I'd long given up hope that the U.S. National Institutes of Health would even answer my application when a fat packet arrived in the mail last month, offering us $10,000 a year. Now, with the American money alongside the Agricultural Research Council and Medical Research Council funds, my group is flush with financing. The knowledge that Aaron, Ken, and John have settled positions for the foreseeable future and will be able to continue our work gives me peace. Especially now. Especially with what I know.

"Are you kidding?" he answers in that endearing American twang of his. "It's the least I could do for you and the guys. You've welcomed me into your lab with open arms, and I've had the most rewarding experience of my career. Look at the papers you and I have published!"

"Our skills and knowledge complement each other, don't they?"

Don nods and then smiles over at me. "This view is glorious. Thank you for encouraging us to skip the first lecture to tour the city. I knew you could be bold—but naughty? No, I didn't know that."

"Don Caspar, you have no idea what I'm capable of," I say with a flip of my hair. Strange how the nearness of death liberates one from prevailing social rules. I cannot think of a single time I've flirted overtly in my life.

Don has no idea the truth in my words. No one, in fact, comprehends the lengths I'll go to for science and life. After two weeks in University College Hospital after my hemorrhage in April, my surgeon informed me that a new cancerous mass had formed on the left side of my pelvis and that there was nothing for it but to seek the comforts of religion. After my fury abated over his patronizing tone and presumptuousness, for the first time since my cancer diagnosis, I fell into despair. Less at the thought of the incurability of my illness and more at the thought of science abandoning me when I needed it most. Science—my stalwart companion, the lens through which I see the world, my faith—was not coming through for me.

Even though science was letting me down, I couldn't quite let science go. Undertaking my own research, I advocated for the relatively new cobalt radiotherapy, which uses radiotherapy machines to produce a beam of gamma rays directed into the tumor to destroy the tissue. My doctors resisted, arguing that the side effects of the therapy—possible acute radiation sickness—outweighed the slim benefit it could bring, the short extension of my life. *Terminal* was the word the doctors used over and over with me and my parents, until Mama started screaming for a second opinion. I've never seen her so unhinged, and even Papa was so upset that he didn't attempt to stop her tirade. But neither the doctors nor my parents prevented me from going forward with the cobalt radiotherapy, and I finished my last treatment right before I left for Switzerland, a trip that no fewer than three doctors advised against and my parents begged me not to take. I chose instead to listen to Anne's advice that I should seize these days and do precisely what I wanted, especially since, should my health decline rapidly—she wept a little when she said this—the Swiss hospitals were every bit as good as the English ones. Listening to her words and her tears, I knew exactly what course to take. I needed to see the continent one last time.

I have no illusions about what my future holds. For the first time, I am using science for myself—to buy a little more time, yes, for my beloved science.

"Oh, Rosalind, I wish you could have joined us on the hike," Don calls over to me as he and his American friend Richard exit the trail and clomp over to me. I'm sitting on blanket in a field, enjoying myself thoroughly with a book and the stunning view of the pyramidical Matterhorn, that famous Alpine peak outside Zermatt where we travelled for a long weekend after the conference. "I've heard you're a phenomenal climber. Didn't you do a sixteen-hour hike along the Péclet-Polset ridges in the Haute-Savoie, starting out before dawn?" he asks about the famous range, running his hand through his hair, damp with sweat.

"I did," I answer, resisting the impulse to describe it further. I have no desire to draw more attention to the fact that I had to sit out the hike today.

Cancer has robbed me of many things, and one of the worst is the energy and stamina to climb. Amid the peaks and valleys of a mountain range, I could always lose myself in the immediacy of the quest for the right foothold and the safest handhold and in the inspiring views appearing around every rock and hill. Only there could I allow my busy, seeking mind to surrender and, for a fleeting second, quiet. It is—or rather was—my only form of prayer, not unlike my scientific quests.

"We still have time for another short hike if you like, Rosalind. I've scouted out one fairly close by," Richard says.

"Maybe another time. Why don't you join me for the picnic I've laid out?"

They take a seat on the blanket and loosen the ties of their boots. Soaking in the sun, we share cheese, bread, sausages, fruit, and sweet wine. The men talk over each other as they compete to share the most compelling and dangerous aspects of the climb. Laughter overtakes us all, and I think it's the most exquisite afternoon I've had in recent memory. Quite worth the pain it took me to get here.

Richard pushes to standing. "Should we try that short hike before we leave, Don?"

"You go ahead. I'll stay behind with Rosalind." Don gives me a smile.

"Don't miss out on a Matterhorn hike on my account, Don. Join your friend," I insist, not wanting his pity.

"Rosalind, I would rather stay here with you." His tone is sincere.

With Richard gone and the sense that we should talk about topics other than science gone along with him, Don and I chat easily about the conference, the inspirational words of Jonas Salk, and the dozens of interesting turns our research on viruses could take. I could talk to Don all day. As we finish the bottle of wine, he turns to me and says, "There's something I've been thinking about for a while, Rosalind."

"What's that?" I ask, assuming he has some views on a new avenue of research we might try or a wild new theory he thinks we should pursue through crystallography.

He leans forward to kiss me. I allow his soft lips to land gently on mine, and I enjoy the soft caress of his hand on my back and arm. I surrender to the sensations coursing through my battered body and permit myself to feel alive. To feel hope and dream about a life with Don. Even though I know it is illusory and fleeting.

"I've been wanting to do that since the first day I met you at Birkbeck."

"You have?" I'm astonished. He never once flirted with me, never even gave me a secret stare to my knowledge. But of course, I had thought about him too, quite differently than I thought about the other scientists in my group, even though he's thirty to my thirty-seven and age isn't the only factor keeping us apart.

"Absolutely. I feel about you like I've felt about no other woman before. Watson painted a picture of this brilliant, upper-class British scientist who was hard as nails and a genius to boot. When I arrived at the Birkbeck town house, you were sitting outside with Aaron, Ken, and John, with the sun shining down on your hair and a bright smile on your lips. You were beautiful, kind, *and* every bit as intelligent as Watson had described. But how could I even get past your loyal guards? Aaron, Ken, and John are like sentries around you."

"If only you knew my history with Watson, you would have discounted every detail he gave you about me."

"What I discovered was far more marvelous than *anyone* could have described," he says, scooting even closer to me.

I want to kiss him again. More than anything. But I cannot, and I know, with incalculable sadness, that my momentary fantasy must end.

"Don, you know I haven't been well, don't you?"

"Yes, of course. We were all terribly worried about you. But you returned to Birkbeck, a little more tired perhaps, but no less brilliant. Or lovely." He says this so tenderly, with a gentle caress of my arm, that I nearly cry.

"Don, I need you to understand something that's very hard for me to admit even to myself, let alone say aloud to another person." I take a deep breath, not entirely certain I can proceed, not entirely sure how to say the unfathomable. Then, suddenly, the words come to me. In a quivering voice, I say, "I can't begin something with you, because I cannot begin anything at all."

"What do you mean?" The furrow between his eyebrows deepens in confusion, and I can see I'll have to be blunt.

"Exactly how it sounds."

"You don't mean that you're dy—" He cannot finish the word.

"I am," I say and then realize, from the devastated expression of his face, how immediate that sounds. In my rush to reassure him, my own sadness lessens, and my voice strengthens. "Not right this minute, of course. But within months, a year at most."

He shakes his head and begins to cry. This is much harder for him to hear than I'd anticipated. "That can't be right, Rosalind. You look so well."

An unexpected calmness descends on me. "Appearances can be deceiving, and I will be able to deceive for only a little longer."

"No, no. Surely you, with all your scientific insights and the scientists you know, must be able to access some experimental treatment." Tears are streaming down his face.

"I've already done all those treatments." I reach for his hand. "They gave me time for more science and the gift of today."

CHAPTER FIFTY-TWO

April 16, 1958
London, England

Why are my scientists crying? I open my eyes to see Aaron and Ken and John and Don, whose hand I squeeze, sitting in chairs around my bed, their cheeks dripping with tears. Is that Ray I see standing behind Aaron? Goodness, only Vittorio would make this reunion complete. And then I remember this is not a homecoming; I recall where I am and why they're weeping.

"There's no need for tears, fellows," I say, but my throat is dry and the words come out as a croak. I hope they can understand me.

"You always were so damn foolish and so damn brave," Aaron half sputters and half cries. If I could get a sip of water to moisten my throat, I'd laugh at my kind but forthright friend.

I smile at these good, brave, brilliant men who stood by my side when I was my most demanding and difficult. They stood with me when the rest of the scientific community ostracized me, and they pushed me to discoveries and epiphanies I couldn't have had alone. Some of them even carried me up the final, steep staircase to my attic office at Birkbeck when I could no longer crawl that distance. I want to tell them all these things, but my Royal Marsden Hospital nurse pushes aside the privacy curtain surrounding me and the scientists, their signal to leave. Don will not let go of my hand, so Aaron has to peel his fingers off mine one by one. Don kisses me on the forehead and follows him out, sobbing uncontrollably.

Is it the pain medication, or does my family arrive on the heels of the men? My sense of time has changed, dilating in some ways and compressing in others. While I'm thinking about the relativity of time, the privacy curtain slides around me again, and the space is suddenly crammed with Mama, Papa, Colin and Charlotte, David, Roland, Aunts Mamie and Alice, as well as Jenifer and Ursula; even Anne is there in spirit as Ursula reads aloud a letter from her. The sight of Jenifer and Ursula reminds me of the tail end of my European trip this past summer, my very last. After an emotional parting from Don, Jenifer, Ursula, and I toured around Italy in Jenifer's Morris Minor, and I can almost feel the wind flying through my hair from the car's open windows. For a brief second, I could be anywhere in time, anywhere in the world.

Papa rouses me from this reverie. "Rosalind, my dear. Can you hear me?"

I nod, or think I do. Either way, he continues. "Your Mama and I want you to know how much we love you. How proud we are of the life you've led. We didn't understand your work, how important it was, and all that you'd accomplished, until Dr. Bernal walked us through your laboratory and told us. And then we saw your model at the Royal Society's *conversazione*, and Sir Lawrence Bragg sang your praises."

Oh good. I'm well pleased to please them. "Thank you," I say, though it comes out a faint whisper.

A procession of hands and cheeks and tears and kisses passes over me, with Ursula lingering the longest. I have the sensation of being carried by and through my family until I've reached the other side of them, as if they are the bases on the spiral steps of DNA and I am carrying on their genetic legacies into the future. And then they are gone, and I'm alone.

Or am I?

The climb is getting steeper. I am nearing the peak in this mountain range; can I muster the strength for the final ascent? I don't think I've ever hiked this far and this high by myself. Not that I'm entirely solo, mind. I've passed groups of climbers and walkers, and I console myself that—should I judge a pitch wrong or assess a foothold incorrectly—someone will find me. I allow myself to surrender to the immediacy of the quest for each right next step. Only then can I set myself free and soar.

I am almost there—until I'm not. Suddenly, I am back in my hospital room in the company of someone else. It is my dear Adrienne, who must have travelled from Paris to see me. We do not speak; there is no need. I feel her fingers stroking my hair and hear her whisper in ear, "*ma chère*," when another figure settles in the chair next to her. It is Jacques Mering.

"Rosalind," he says. I always loved the way he said my name. "Rosalind," he repeats, until I can hear and see and feel his regret at squandering our love and his pain at losing me.

But I am not gone yet.

I am only footsteps away from the summit. But what I thought were the markings of the pathway to the peak are the scattered dots of an X-ray crystallographic image, the unmistakable double helix of DNA. I realize that the patterns are one and the same, materializing before me like the perfect footholds in the sheer rocky face of a mountain, each one steady and leading the way to safety and epiphany. I have climbed this pattern before—uncovered it and shared it with the world, in fact—and I understand now that even though I have not passed on my genes, I will live on, as knowledge of my discovery replicates over and over, throughout time.

AUTHOR'S NOTE

The story of Rosalind Franklin is, in part, the story of how an unknown scientist became an icon, in some circles anyway (her name is emblazoned on medical centers, universities, laboratories, a Mars Rover, and even a Google doodle). Her narrative is many other things as well, of course, as I explore in this novel—the tale of a brilliant, exacting scientist who managed to coax the secrets of DNA out of the shadows, an account of how she had to combat stereotypes about women and female scientists to do her work and the toll that struggle took on her, a chronicle of the way her laborious contributions were misappropriated without her knowledge or permission, and an exploration of Rosalind's enormous, crucial legacy. Yet Rosalind's journey from anonymity to her later relative fame, made all the more poignant because of her untimely death, is both a consequence of her life's work and a tale unto itself, particularly because the manner in which it arose is so very unusual. And delving into the question of how her legacy grew wings after decades of being tethered to obscurity (as are many of the women I write about) is critical as we think about how both historical and modern women *should* have their legacies known and celebrated.

So, how does an ingenious but somewhat unknown scientist become a legend in her field? In Rosalind's case, it didn't happen during her lifetime, as readers undoubtedly know from *Her Hidden Genius*, and as such, I don't explore that in the novel itself. Nor did it occur in the years following her 1958 death, either before, during, or immediately after James Watson, Francis Crick, and Maurice Wilkins won the Nobel Prize in 1962 for papers and pronouncements based upon Rosalind's research. The seed for her renown began in a most unlikely place—in the memoir titled *The Double Helix* written by James Watson and published in 1968, which shares *his* account of the discovery of the double helix structure of DNA, that world-changing finding.

How on earth did a book by Rosalind's sometimes nemesis spark the flames of her fame? Particularly when that memoir casts Rosalind in a largely negative light, critiquing her for her perceived lack of femininity, lambasting her for refusing to act as though she were subordinate to Wilkins when she was hired as his peer, condemning her approach for being rigid and wedded to hard facts (usually a positive in science), and denigrating her by referring to her as the diminutive "Rosy," a nickname that she hated and no one used! And especially when the book was rejected for publication by Harvard University Press due to Crick and Wilkins's vehement objections. Well, it is precisely *because* Watson depicted Rosalind in such a loathsome "unrosy" light that Rosalind's journey to icon began.

Her dear friend Anne Sayre, who makes a few fleeting appearances in *Her Hidden Genius*, was outraged by Watson's portrayal of Rosalind in *The Double Helix* when it was finally published by Atheneum, as were her family and many scientists with whom she'd worked and played. The Rosalind in the pages of Watson's bestselling memoir simply did not reflect the Rosalind they knew; she instead resembled the stereotype of the hostile, unattractive, obstinate, and narrow-minded female scientist. And Anne was determined to get to the bottom of this unfair depiction as well as Watson's marginalization of Rosalind's contributions, especially because the person best suited to defend herself and claim her work—Rosalind—could no longer do so.

Thus began Anne's multiyear project to independently research the discovery of DNA's structure and Rosalind's role in it, an enormous undertaking in which Anne saw through Watson's machinations and ultimately wrote a book of her own in 1975, *Rosalind Franklin and DNA*. Anne's book, as well as the documents and letters that formed the basis of her research for it, reveals a very different Rosalind than the one created by Watson. In Anne's recounting and research, the reader sees a genius hard at work painstakingly unraveling some of life's biggest mysteries alongside colleagues who collaborate and admire her, all except Wilkins, Watson, and, to a lesser extent, Crick. And as the reader is drawn into Anne's fact-based narrative, we begin to wonder whether Watson made Rosalind into a caricature and devalued her efforts for a reason of his own—perhaps to deflect from his own use of her images and data? Or is Watson offering a rationale for using it, suggesting that since Rosalind herself was so unpleasant, he should be entitled to use the fruit of her labors? But, if the small-minded, unappealing "Rosy" didn't know what she was doing, why on earth would Watson have used her work? As Anne's book gained steam in the 1970s and beyond, Watson's portrayal began to be questioned, and Rosalind's legacy took flight.

It was Anne's depiction that inspired *my* Rosalind Franklin. I hope, in my small way, to have continued what Anne started in *Rosalind Franklin and DNA*, albeit in a fictional format that allows me to fill in the gaps in our understanding using imagination blended with research and logical extrapolation. If *Her Hidden Genius* can help nurture the seed that Anne planted, then one of my objectives in writing this novel—all my novels, really—will be achieved. While I wish Rosalind could be with us to present her truths in response to Watson and affirm her own legacy, I hope my fictional Rosalind helps readers appreciate Rosalind Franklin the scientist, the daughter, the sister, the friend, the colleague, the lover, and the icon. In all her hidden genius.

READING GROUP GUIDE

1. Before reading *Her Hidden Genius*, had you heard of Rosalind Franklin? What, if anything, did you know about the history of DNA, and how did the book affect your understanding of that history?

2. Compare Rosalind's experiences in France to her experiences in England. What was the biggest difference you noticed between each culture's expectations for scientists and women?

3. Rosalind asserts early on that marriage and science are not meant to coexist for working women. Do you think that idea is a product of her time period, or her personality? Does she reevaluate it throughout the book, and if so, how?

4. How does Rosalind's Jewish identity shape her behavior and priorities throughout the book? How are she and her family still contending with the events of World War II?

5. What did you think of Rosalind's approach to lab safety? How do you think things have changed for modern scientists?

6. Jacques pushes Rosalind to be honest with their colleagues about the nature of their relationship. Why does she resist? How would you feel in her position?

7. Watson and Crick are not the first colleagues to use Rosalind's work without her permission. Compare Wilkins's use of Rosalind's preliminary data at the Cavendish conference to Watson and Crick's acceptance of credit for discovering the structure of DNA. How much do you think Rosalind knew or understood about the data and images that Watson and Crick used without her knowledge or permission? How does this affect her?

8. Collaboration in science is crucial for the most robust discoveries, so how should collaborative projects proceed in a fair fashion, and how should credit be assigned for those discoveries? Do you think the so-called gentleman's agreements between heads of institutions that were meant to govern areas of focus in Rosalind's time still exist today, or have they been replaced by more definitive guidance and contracts? Are there still people like Rosalind whose contributions are ignored or attributed to others?

9. What do you think is Rosalind Franklin's greatest legacy? Does the author's note make you think more expansively—or differently—about Rosalind's legacy? Any other takeaways?

A CONVERSATION WITH THE AUTHOR

How did you first hear of Rosalind Franklin and decide to tell her story?

After I started writing historical fiction about the often unknown but key women of the past, my friends and family became very attuned to noticing these women when they come across them in the course of their own lives. In the case of Rosalind Franklin, while I'd had a very high level awareness of her story and incredible discoveries for some time, it was only when a dear physician friend of mine read about her contributions and sacrifices in a medical book and really advocated that I do a deep dive into research on Rosalind that I took a close look. I am so grateful to my friend, because the life and legacy of Rosalind Franklin is crucial and captivating on so many levels, some of which I didn't appreciate until I was already writing the novel.

Did your research process differ for Rosalind's scientific and home lives? How do you develop a full understanding of someone like Rosalind, whose life was so dominated by

work? And how does historical research compare to scientific research?

In some ways, the research process for *Her Hidden Genius* was similar to the one I undertake for all the women I write about. I gather as much original source material about the woman as I can and then supplement it with whatever robust, credible secondary material I find, then assemble an understanding of the macro and micro historical aspects and timelines of the woman's world, from political, social, and cultural developments to details such as fashion and food in order to create a realistic world for her to inhabit. Researching Rosalind's story did differ in that, in addition to the research I detailed above, I had to spend an enormous amount of time not only understanding DNA itself but also comprehending the developments in genetics from a historical perspective. As I was reading about the origins of genetic understanding and its progress up until Rosalind's era, I encountered many brilliant scientists whose lives were devoted to the solving of these critical questions, and their struggles and passion for the work helped me understand the professional Rosalind in part, as did accounts by people who knew her well, like Anne Sayre, who knew her both professionally and personally. The insights I had about the personal Rosalind came from family memoirs like Jenifer Glynn's *My Sister Rosalind Franklin*, the terrific biography *Rosalind Franklin: The Dark Lady of DNA* by Brenda Maddox, Anne Sayre's wonderful book *Rosalind Franklin and DNA*, and the astonishing collection of Sayre's research that she deposited in the American Society for Microbiology's archives, which included original letters from and to Rosalind, interviews with most of the people involved in her scientific career, and letters with Rosalind's family members after her death. These latter, original source materials were invaluable in bringing Rosalind alive for me, and the experience of working with letters written in her own hand was unbelievably moving.

The scientific communities in France and England are starkly different. Where do you think these differences came from?

While I cannot speak for all French and English scientific communities, certainly the institutions with which Rosalind was familiar were quite distinct, primarily in terms of the social interactions and tone of the laboratories. Rosalind found the French *labo* a marvelous mix of camaraderie, support, and intellectual stimulation—both about science and the world—regardless of her gender. Whether this was a function of a unique atmosphere created by its heads Jacques Mering and Marcel Mathieu or simply the sort of intellectual environment fostered in Paris at that time, as Brenda Maddox suggests in her book, it suited Rosalind perfectly. When Rosalind returned to England, she didn't find either the scientists (for the most part) or the institutes themselves to be particularly welcoming to women or especially cerebral, outside of the specific scientific investigations upon which they were working. In particular, she found this to be the case in her unit at King's College, much to her disappointment, and she struggled to find a place to belong.

What was the most surprising thing you learned about Rosalind Franklin?

While Rosalind was fully engaged in her scientific research and musings, it didn't encompass the whole of her life by any means—no matter the amount of time she actually spent working or the vast breadth of her contributions. In addition to being a wonderful, thoughtful friend who invested in her relationships, she was a dedicated, skilled mountain climber. She would plan elaborate travels for her holidays, jaunts that typically encompassed significant hiking and strenuous climbs. Once I learned this fact about Rosalind, it opened up another level of understanding about her, and I came to view her time immersed in the mountains and their challenges as another facet of her appreciation for the natural, scientific world. Almost like a sort of personal spirituality.

When writing historical fiction, many of the choices you'd normally make for your characters are already decided. How do you approach character growth and narrative arcs without changing the historical facts?

Although I absolutely write fiction and the women at the center of my novels are my versions of real-life women, I do try to stay as close to the historical facts as we know them in crafting my stories. I usually find room to shape their characters and narratives when we *don't* know the definitive facts, in the shadows of history—and there are *always* gray areas where we don't know exactly what transpired or how the women felt about the events. There, I use a mix of the women's characters as I've come to know them through my research and the sort of logical extrapolation I developed from my years as a lawyer. For example, in *Her Hidden Genius*, we don't know precisely what Rosalind understood about the nature of Watson and Crick's use of her research and data in their ultimately famous model building of DNA, and there, I used my own sense of Rosalind and the arc of her story to fill in the gaps with fiction.

Much of *Her Hidden Genius* centers on institutional competition. How do you think scientific inquiry is impacted by a competitive spirit? Do you consider yourself competitive?

In reviewing the scientific developments around genetics, I came to understand how critical it can be for scientists to be apprised of the work that's been undertaken before them (so often if work isn't shared, it can be overlooked, only to be rediscovered and its importance understood decades later, or even longer) and the ongoing investigations that relate to their subject. Only by comparing and studying all these projects can science advance. That said, as vying for institutional funding comes into play and recognition for being "first" grows in importance, scientists and their establishments may well be inclined to be secretive around their discoveries as competition grows—an unfortunate fact in a field that really relies on sharing of information. In terms of my own competitiveness, I have very high expectations of myself, although I wouldn't consider myself drawn to a traditionally understood desire to "win," and in this way, I could identify with Rosalind, who was always her own harshest critic and held herself to sometimes impossibly high standards.

These days, many textbooks discuss Franklin's contributions alongside those of Watson and Crick, though during their lifetimes, she was not given the credit she deserved. What benefit do we gain from rediscovering and giving credit to figures like her, even if they will never see that recognition?

With all my novels, I aspire to offer a lens through which readers can look at the past and see the women and the scope of their legacy. It is my hope that they will then take the lens and see not only our past differently but also our present and our future—to identify and celebrate the historical women where they've been hiding in plain sight and then to ensure that we do the same for the women of today and tomorrow. While it would have been wonderful to honor Rosalind Franklin and give her the accolades she deserved (like the Nobel Prize) in her lifetime, it is critical that we excavate the important women of the past so we can free ourselves and our society from any lingering preconceptions about women, their abilities, and their capacity for contributions.

ACKNOWLEDGMENTS

The list of people to whom I am indebted for this novel seems as long and interconnected as the chains that form the double helix of DNA. Every single one of them is an integral link in the process that allowed the story of this brilliant, determined scientist and her momentous legacy to come to light after so many decades lost in the dark recesses of history. And to each, I am immensely grateful.

As always, I must begin with my wonderful agent, Laura Dail, upon whose wise and crucial guidance I depend utterly and without whom this book would not be possible. How fortunate I am in the marvelous team at Sourcebooks, who helped ensure that my humble manuscript would become the best book imaginable and that Rosalind Franklin's story would reach an abundance of readers, especially my insightful and brilliant editor, Shana Drehs; Sourcebooks's inspirational leader, Dominique Raccah; as well as the following wonderful, talented folks—Molly Waxman, Cristina Arreola, Todd Stocke, Valerie Pierce, Lizzie Lewandowski, Margaret Coffee, Tiffany Schultz, Ashlyn Keil,

Findlay McCarthy, Heather Hall, Ashley Holstrom, Kelly Lawler, Sarah Cardillo, Dawn Adams, and Heather VenHuizen. And, of course, *Her Hidden Genius* needs enthusiastic booksellers and librarians and readers to enjoy and recommend the book, and to them, to you, I am incredibly thankful.

For this unique historical woman, I have a few unique thanks. I am grateful to Rosalind's dear friend Anne Sayre, who dedicated years of her life to the research and defense of Rosalind's work, personality, memory, and legacy, during which Anne laid the groundwork of Rosalind's elevation to iconic status with her brilliant biography *Rosalind Franklin & DNA* and galvanized my work in the process. How lucky we are that, when Ann completed her book, she gave all the letters and interviews and research upon which she based the biography to the library at the American Society for Microbiology, which created a special collection for the priceless papers and to which its wonderful librarian Jeff Karr assisted me with access. More than anyone, I am beholden to Rosalind Franklin herself—for inspiring this novel and for the world-changing, invaluable contributions she gave to humanity.

Last but by no means least are my three boys—Jim, Jack, and Ben. You three are the reason and inspiration for it all.

ABOUT THE AUTHOR

Marie Benedict is a lawyer with more than ten years' experience as a litigator at two of the country's premier law firms and Fortune 500 companies. She is a magna cum laude graduate of Boston College with a focus on history and a cum laude graduate of the Boston University School of Law. She is also the author of the *New York Times* bestsellers *The Mystery of Mrs. Christie* and *The Only Woman in the Room*, as well as *Carnegie's Maid*, *The Other Einstein*, and *Lady Clementine*. Her books have been translated into multiple languages. She lives in Pittsburgh with her family.

CARNEGIE'S MAID

SHE INSPIRED AN AMERICAN DYNASTY

The mesmerizing tale of the woman who could have inspired an American dynasty

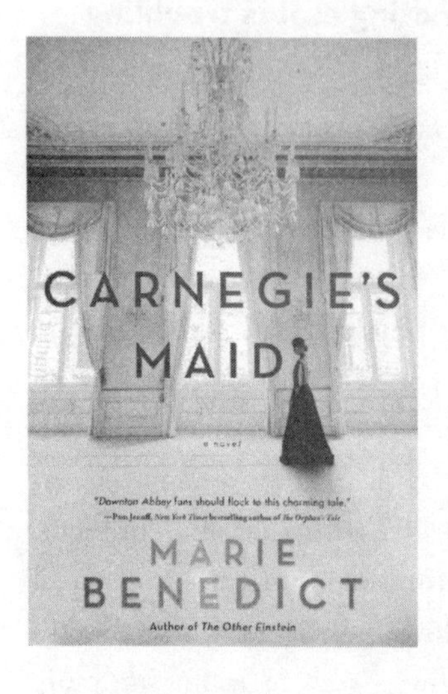

Clara Kelley is not who they think she is. She's not the experienced Irish maid who was hired to work in one of Pittsburgh's grandest houses. She's a poor farmer's daughter with nowhere to go. But the other Clara has vanished, and pretending to be her might be her best option. If she can keep up the ruse, that is. Serving as a lady's maid in the household of Andrew Carnegie requires skills she doesn't have, answering to an icy mistress who rules her sons and her domain with an iron fist. What Clara does have is a resolve as strong as the steel Pittsburgh is becoming famous for, coupled with an uncanny understanding of business, and Andrew begins to rely on her. But Clara can't let her guard down, even when Andrew becomes something more than an employer. Revealing her past might her ruin her future—and her family's.

Carnegie's Maid tells the story of the brilliant woman who may have spurred Andrew Carnegie's transformation from ruthless industrialist to the world's first true philanthropist.

"*Downton Abbey* fans should flock to this charming tale."

—Pam Jenoff, *New York Times* bestselling author of *The Orphan's Tale*

For more Marie Benedict, visit:
sourcebooks.com

LADY CLEMENTINE

SHE WAS A HERO OF WORLD WARS I AND II

An incredible novel of the brilliant woman whose unsung influence helped shape two World Wars: Clementine Churchill

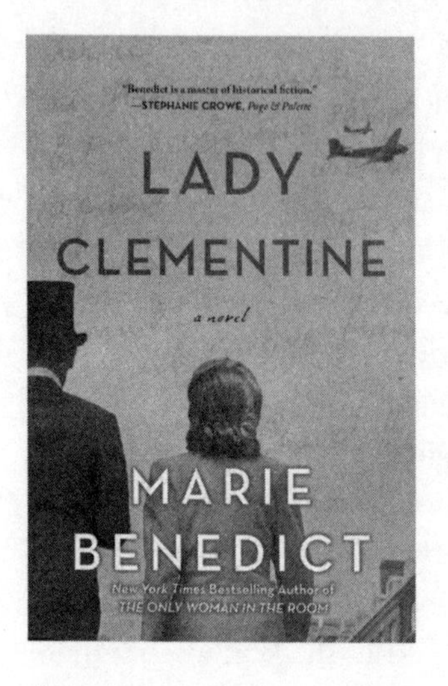

In 1909, Clementine steps off a train with her new husband, Winston. An angry woman emerges from the crowd to attack, shoving him in the direction of an oncoming train. Just before he stumbles, Clementine grabs him by his suit jacket. This will not be the last time Clementine Churchill will save her husband.

Lady Clementine is the ferocious story of the ambitious woman beside Winston Churchill, the story of a partner who did not flinch through the sweeping darkness of war, and who would not surrender either to expectations or to enemies.

"Fans should be tantalized by the possibilities of Benedict's as-yet-unexplored heroines."

—Pittsburgh Post-Gazette

For more Marie Benedict, visit:
sourcebooks.com